A WITCH WORTH Praline FOR

BEWITCHED BY CHOCOLATE
MYSTERIES

BOOK EIGHT

H.Y. HANNA

Contents

Chapter One

"It's a waxing gibbous moon tonight... the witch's new year is upon us."

Caitlyn Le Fey looked up, startled, to find a tall woman watching her intently. Clad in a flowing black velvet dress accessorised with satin trim, black lace, and an enormous silver pendant in the shape of a crescent moon, the woman looked as if she'd strayed from the backstage of a theatre. She was attractive, with perfectly arched eyebrows that looked more drawn-on than natural, and deep-set, heavily lashed eyes, expertly highlighted by strong make-up. But the thing that drew Caitlyn's gaze the most was the mane of red hair that cascaded around the woman's shoulders, so vibrant that it looked almost like a halo of fire—and so similar in colour to the red hair on Caitlyn's own head.

Her pulse quickening, Caitlyn searched the woman's features for any sign of similarity to her own reflection in the mirror. *Her eyes... are they a bit like mine? And her mouth... do my lips also dip at the top like that?* She knew that she was probably being silly—after disappearing for over twenty-two years, her mother was hardly going to just saunter up and say hello! And yet her heart still pounded with desperate hope. *Maybe my search is over at last... maybe I'll find out why I was abandoned as a baby... maybe I'll finally learn the truth about—*

"Are you all right?"

Caitlyn jumped and came out of her

thoughts to find the strange woman looking at her in concern. She realised that she had been standing, frozen in place, staring avidly.

"Oh… er… yes, fine," Caitlyn mumbled, flushing. "Sorry… my… um… mind wandered." She hesitated, unable to stop herself giving the woman another covert look. She knew that her mother, Tara, was here in England, maybe even right here in this village in the Cotswolds. There had been proof—that video footage the police had found showed Tara operating incognito at the recent Mabon ball—so Caitlyn knew that it wasn't just her wistful imagination. "We… we haven't met before, have we?" she blurted.

"I don't believe so," said the woman, looking amused for a moment. Then she smoothed her features into a polite smile and added: "I'm Leandra Lockwood. I just moved to Tillyhenge recently." She held out a hand, her expression bland, her eyes empty of anything but a perfunctory courtesy.

Caitlyn shook her hand, trying to ignore the sense of disappointment. "I'm Caitlyn—Caitlyn Le Fey."

Leandra gestured to the basket of orange pumpkins that Caitlyn was holding: "You do realise that Samhain is the witch's new year, don't you? I hope you're not just using that as a commercial prop without understanding the significance of such an important pagan festival."

"Oh… no… I mean, yes, I do," stammered Caitlyn, still trying to recover her composure. She took a deep breath, banishing her wayward thoughts, and reminded herself that while this woman might not be her long-lost mother, she could still be a valuable customer.

Plastering a bright smile on her face, Caitlyn indicated the chocolate shop housed in the cottage behind her. "We have a special collection of chocolate treats this month that's been created in honour of Samhain, and they all feature flavours and herbs associated with the ancient traditions. Would you like to come in and sample some? The dark chocolate truffles with pumpkin liqueur are really delicious... or there's Belgian chocolate Florentines with autumn nuts and berries... oh, and you must try some of the chocolate fudge with apple-and-cinnamon spice—they're absolutely heavenly! My grandmother the Widow Mags just made those this morning."

"The Widow Mags..." A fleeting expression crossed Leandra's face, then it was gone and she said, smoothly: "She's the owner of this shop, isn't she? I've heard people talking about her in the village pub."

Caitlyn winced, wondering what was being said about her grandmother. As a cranky old woman with an unfortunate resemblance to a "storybook witch", the Widow Mags had long been feared by the other residents of the village. In fact, Caitlyn could remember her own arrival in Tillyhenge nearly six months ago. When she had come to this tiny Cotswolds village seeking answers about her past, she had met several locals who warned her to stay away from the chocolate shop nestled at the edge of the forest.

Of course, when she had finally ventured into *Bewitched by Chocolate* and sampled the decadent confectionery, it had been easy to see why everyone thought the Widow Mags's chocolates must have been enchanted— they really did taste too good to be true! And it had been a shock to discover that the Widow Mags really *was* a witch (although her delicious creations owed more to her skills as a chocolatier than to any spell!)—and an even greater shock to discover that the old woman was, in fact, her grandmother.

Talk about skeletons in the family closet, Caitlyn thought wryly. *Or a whole collection of ghouls and goblins, or vampires and witches in this case!* When she had set out to find answers about her real family, the last thing she had imagined was discovering that she was actually descended from a long line of witches. As someone who had always been sceptical about the existence of magic, she was still struggling with the revelations of the past few months— and, most of all, with the fact that she herself had the ability to conjure spells and enchantments.

"...carving Jack-o'-lanterns?"

Caitlyn started. "Sorry?"

Leandra looked at her impatiently. "Your mind really is wandering today, isn't it? I said, I assume you're taking those to carve Jack-o-lanterns?" She pointed to the pumpkins in the basket

Caitlyn was holding.

"Oh no, these are actually for making pumpkin soup," said Caitlyn. "I've already carved some Jack-o-lanterns, but I used turnips for those."

"Ah." The woman's face eased into a look of approval. "So you are aware of the proper Samhain tradition. Good. Not many people realise that the original Jack-o-lanterns were carved from turnips and other root vegetables."

"Yes, well, pumpkins didn't grow in the old Celtic lands," Caitlyn said, with a smile. "It was only when the Irish and Scottish went to America that they started using pumpkins."

Leandra nodded, like a teacher pleased with a pupil. "I see you *have* done your homework. I'm glad someone is paying proper respect to the old traditions and is honouring Samhain authentically, rather than just milking it with cheesy Hallowe'en clichés." Her dark eyes flashed as she warmed to her subject. "It's disgusting how such an ancient sabbat has been hijacked by capitalist greed and trivialised by modern gimmicks which bear no relation to the original purpose of the festival! Samhain is a time to celebrate the final harvest before the long, dark winter, and a time to honour the dead. It's the start of a new Wheel of the Year, and a time when the connection with the Otherworld is particularly strong—"

"You seem to know an awful lot about Samhain," Caitlyn blurted, taken aback by the woman's vehemence. Most of the customers who wandered into the chocolate shop were perfectly happy to just enjoy the "Hallowe'en clichés", but this woman seemed to take them as a personal affront.

Leandra gave her a lofty look. "I ought to. I'm a witch."

Caitlyn blinked, her heart skipping a beat. "I... I'm sorry?"

"Well, not a 'witch' in the usual sense. I don't dabble in the usual crude witchcraft methods—bubbling cauldrons and herbal potions and all that stuff," Leandra said, contemptuously. "I use more refined and elevated magical practices, tied to a deep understanding of ancient knowledge and wisdom that was gained from years of diligent study."

"Oh. Er... right..." said Caitlyn, slightly taken aback.

Leandra noted her expression and said sourly: "I suppose you don't believe in witches and magic, do you?"

"Well, I..." Caitlyn fought a sudden hysterical urge to laugh. *If you only knew...*

For a moment, she was tempted to tell the other woman the truth, and maybe even *show* her by transforming one of the pumpkins in her basket into solid chocolate. Or perhaps she could enchant some of the toffee brittle offered on the shelf outside the shop, to fly through the air like miniature broomsticks. It would have been so nice to own her witch identity for once, to dispense with the evasion and lies.

Then she quashed the urge. If there was one thing that had been drummed into her, it was that no witch—no *true* witch—ever broadcast their abilities. It was a carefully guarded secret, one which had in centuries past—and, in some countries, still today—brought hostility and persecution. Caitlyn felt that stab of disappointment again: the fact that Leandra Lockwood could stand there and blithely announce that she was a "witch" probably meant that she had no real affinity for magic.

She gave the other woman a polite smile, "I'm sure there are some things that can't easily be explained by science."

"Hmm..." Leandra regarded her for a moment and Caitlyn caught a glint of approval in her eyes. Then to her surprise, the other woman changed the subject entirely and said: "I heard that you're the Widow Mags's long-lost granddaughter who came from the United States? Though I must say, you don't sound very American."

Caitlyn gave an embarrassed laugh. "You've been listening to village gossip."

"Best way to get to know a place," Leandra declared. "But in this case, it was actually Manor staff gossip. Yes, I've leased the newly converted barn at the rear of the Huntingdon Manor estate, and I've been chatting to some of the staff." She gave Caitlyn a sly look. "Seems that you're very friendly with our handsome young 'lord of the manor'?"

Caitlyn felt an involuntary blush rise to her cheeks and silently cursed herself. Why did she have to react like a bashful schoolgirl whenever James Fitzroy was mentioned?

Lifting her chin, she tried to keep her voice cool as she replied: "Yes, Lord Fitzroy and I are friends. He's very welcoming to all the tenants on his estate." Hurriedly, she tried to turn the conversation back to the woman herself. "And are you moving to Tillyhenge permanently? I thought the outbuilding conversions on the estate were mainly for holiday rentals."

"I've taken early retirement," said Leandra, her mouth tightening for a moment. "And I've always fancied living in the Cotswolds, so I thought I'd rent somewhere temporarily and have a look around before I decide where to buy. A converted barn at the Manor was being advertised as a short-term let, and it seemed ideal: comfortable and modern, on a beautiful estate, and close to the village. Perfect for walks."

"Yes, it's lovely here, although it might take a bit of getting used to if you've been living in a big city." Caitlyn looked at the other woman curiously. Was she imagining it, or did Leandra seem reticent to give any information about herself? "Er... were you living in London?"

"Yes, but I'm tired of life in the Big Smoke. I think village life will suit me fine. There seems to be ample shopping in the local area, and I hear that there's even a fine dining restaurant on the Manor grounds, now?"

"Oh yes, James—I mean, Lord Fitzroy had the great idea of converting the old coach house into a gastropub. He's done a really amazing job modernising the estate and creating jobs for the local residents," said Caitlyn, trying not to sound too gushing.

"Mmm, yes... I've heard that Lord Fitzroy is an exemplary landlord. And very liberal-minded too, it seems. I was gratified to see that the estate is organising an event in honour of Samhain," Leandra said, her face brightening. "It will help to educate people and keep the ancient traditions alive. I believe there will be a Samhain bonfire. And opportunities to try out 'apple-ducking' and divination workshops, maybe even a 'dumb supper' that visitors can take part in!"

Caitlyn smiled to herself. She had a feeling that the planned activities were less a genuine homage to the pagan festival and more a clever ploy of the Manor marketing department to attract visitors to the estate. There was a healthy competition for tourists amongst the many equally picturesque villages dotted around the Cotswolds, so they were always searching for new ways to help Tillyhenge stand out. Making the most of the village's historical associations with the paranormal had been an obvious choice. People already came from far and wide to view the ancient stone circle that sat atop the hill beside the village, so it was a logical step to capitalise on that interest by staging festivals that tapped into local folklore and legends.

It's certainly helped business in the chocolate shop, Caitlyn thought. Once a sad, empty place avoided by the locals and barely selling enough to stay in business, *Bewitched by Chocolate* was now a bustling tourist hotspot, brimming with customers and filled with the sounds of talk and laughter. In fact, the vicious rumours painting the Widow Mags as the "local witch" had only piqued tourist curiosity and brought even more customers to their door.

Caitlyn felt a sense of pride as she turned to look through the cottage's open doorway and caught sight of the Widow Mags standing behind the counter. Although the old witch still cut an intimidating figure with her flashing dark eyes, hooked nose, and wild grey hair escaping the bun at the nape of her neck, she had learned to soften her manner. Even now, she was waiting with long-suffering patience as a couple pondered a tray of truffles, trying to select their favourite flavours. Compared to Caitlyn's own first experience in the shop, when the Widow Mags had thrust some truffles at her and snarled: "*Hurry up and choose your chocolates!*"—her grandmother's customer service skills had come a long way!

Caitlyn glanced back at Leandra, who was also looking through the cottage doorway. "Would you like to come in?" she invited. "I can show you that special Samhain chocolate collection I was telling you about."

The woman hesitated for a moment, and once again, Caitlyn got the impression that there were undercurrents she was missing. Then, as Leandra inclined her head and said, with a tight smile: "Well, I never say no to chocolate!"—she wondered if perhaps it had been her over-active imagination after all.

They entered *Bewitched by Chocolate*. They had barely stepped through the shop doorway when a ball of black fur shot out from behind some boxes and attacked Leandra's ankles.

"Nibs... no!" Caitlyn cried as the other woman gasped in surprise and nearly tripped and fell over. Hastily, Caitlyn bent and scooped up the ball of fluff.

"Oh... it's a kitten," said Leandra, clutching a hand to her chest and looking at the baby black cat in Caitlyn's arms.

"Yes, this is Nibs. I'm sorry—this seems to be his new thing: ambushing people and attacking their ankles," Caitlyn said, apologetically. "I think it's just a phase he's going through, though, and he'll grow out of it soon."

"*Mew!*" said Nibs, squirming in her arms.

Leandra eyed the kitten askance.

"Nibs... unusual name."

"As in cocoa nibs," Caitlyn explained with a smile. "You know, those little nuggets of crushed cocoa beans, which are small, dark, and full of intense flavour. Sort of like this little monkey. He's tiny but always getting into trouble and causing chaos."

"*Mew!*" cried Nibs, indignantly, trying to wriggle free.

"How old is he?"

"I'm not really sure. I found him in the woods when I arrived in Tillyhenge about six months ago—"

"Six months?" Leandra raised startled eyes to her. "But... he looks barely six weeks old!"

"Yes... er... he doesn't seem to have grown much," Caitlyn admitted, the other woman's words an unwelcome reminder of Nibs's strange condition.

The kitten had undergone a battery of

veterinary tests and examinations, and none had produced an explanation for his lack of growth. Caitlyn had told herself that as long as Nibs was happy and healthy, that was all that mattered, but the truth was that the mystery had remained like a thorn in her side.

"Has he been to see a vet?"

"Oh yes, he's had all the tests." Caitlyn gave a frustrated sigh. "They just can't seem to figure out why he doesn't seem to be growing."

Leandra leaned forwards and fixed her with an intent gaze. "You know, when science can't give you answers, you have to turn to magic."

Chapter Two

Caitlyn blinked at the other woman. "I... I'm sorry?"

Leandra nodded, her voice dropping into a dramatic whisper. "Your kitten could be the victim of a time warp spell. It's a common phenomenon that happens to those who have been trapped in a liminal space."

"Trapped in a what?"

"A liminal space. Haven't you heard of them?" asked Leandra, looking scandalised by her ignorance. "They're well known in folklore and mythology, even in literature—like C.S. Lewis's land of Narnia, for example. That's a liminal space, where time moves differently compared to the real world."

Caitlyn wracked her childhood memories of that famous book series. "Um... you mean how the children spent years in Narnia, even growing up into adults, but when they returned to our world through the wardrobe, barely a day had passed?"

Leandra nodded. "That's right. Lewis probably borrowed the concept from Celtic folklore... or the Greek myths, perhaps... or maybe the Norse legends. Really, though, almost every culture has similar stories: Japanese, Jewish, Hindu, Native American... They all have this concept of a liminal space—an in-between realm where time doesn't function as it does in the human world. And if you get caught there, you may find that time speeds up or stands still." She nodded at Nibs. "That could explain why your kitten won't grow."

"But Nibs isn't trapped somewhere any more," Caitlyn said, sceptically. "Surely, now that he's back in the so-called 'real world', he shouldn't still be frozen in time?"

Leandra shrugged. "Who knows how these places affect you?"

Before Caitlyn could reply, they were interrupted by a middle-aged woman with a mane of carroty-red hair walking in through the door of the chocolate shop behind them. Despite the grey skies and chilly weather, the newcomer was dressed in a voluminous purple kaftan, with only a grey shawl around her shoulders to stave off the autumn chill. Still, Caitlyn wasn't too surprised. She smiled to herself—she hadn't ever seen her aunt Bertha wear anything other than purple kaftans, whatever the weather.

Her smile widened as she turned to greet the older woman. When Caitlyn had discovered that in addition to a grandmother, she also had an aunt, she had been extremely relieved to find that Bertha—her mother's older sister—had a warm, maternal manner and soothing presence that was nothing like the prickly Widow Mags. Her aunt didn't seem her usual calm self at the moment, though. In fact, Bertha looked decidedly frazzled as she came bustling up to them:

"Where is your grandmother, dear?"

Caitlyn looked around, surprised to see that the Widow Mags was nowhere in sight. "I don't know... she was behind the counter just a few minutes ago. Perhaps she's gone into the kitchen? Evie is in there, helping to finish the latest batch of Florentines, but perhaps Grandma needed to add a few finishing touches herself."

Bertha nodded distractedly, pushing back a tendril of frizzy red hair. "Fine, I'll pop out the back to find her. I need to take her into town, and while I'm there,

I'll also need to pick up some supplies for the marketing team up at the Manor. They've asked me to help with last-minute preparations for the Samhain Festival, including building the bonfires..." She shook her head, making a tutting sound. "Just collecting the wood for that will take me a good couple of hours, and Goddess knows when I'm going to find the time—"

"Are you in charge of the Samhain bonfires?" Leandra interrupted.

Bertha turned. "Yes, that's right. The Festival is planned for this weekend, on Samhain Eve, and as part of the events, the Huntingdon Manor marketing team are resurrecting some of the old pagan traditions that used to be followed at the time." She paused, looking properly at Leandra for the first time. "Have we met before? You seem slightly familiar..." She snapped her fingers. "Oh, I remember now: you came into my herbal shop yesterday and purchased some comfrey tea. It's... Miss Lockwood, isn't it?"

Bertha turned to Caitlyn. "Miss Lockwood used to live in London and teach at one of the universities. Professor of Mythology and Folklore, wasn't it?" She glanced back at Leandra for confirmation.

"I was a Professor of Comparative Religion and Esoteric Philosophy, with a special interest in mythological traditions, folklore, and magical practices across different societies," Leandra said, loftily.

So that's how she seems to know so much about different mythological systems and beliefs, Caitlyn thought. She got the sense that Leandra was uncomfortable with the interest focused on her, though, as the other woman quickly turned the subject back to the Samhain Festival.

"You're collecting the wood for the Samhain bonfire, did you say?" she said, to Bertha. "I hope you are seeking the correct wood to build it. The bonfire flames are crucial for cleansing, purifying, and protecting against malevolent forces during Samhain."

"Yes, I know," said Bertha. "And I'll be collecting the appropriate type, don't you worry about that."

"Don't you mean *types*?" said Leandra, sharply. "Wood from one tree isn't enough, you know. It's essential to use tri-layer symbolism when building a Samhain bonfire. Ash on the bottom layer, hawthorn in the centre, and rowan on top. All three trees are steeped in magic and folklore, but the rowan is especially important in Celtic mythology because it is considered a gateway tree, a mediator between the living and the dead."

Leandra's voice rang out so loudly that the other customers in the shop looked across at them. Bertha looked slightly irritated by the other woman's patronising tone.

"The woods on the Fitzroy estate are filled with hawthorn and ash trees, so it shouldn't be hard to collect wood from those," she said. "As for rowan, there are several of those too. In fact, I believe there's large tree growing right by the main drive leading up to the Manor house, so—"

"Is it a single-trunk tree?" Leandra demanded.

"Er... yes, I believe so," said Bertha, taken aback.

"Oh no! That won't do! You *must* source the rowan wood from a dual-trunked tree, to highlight the meeting of the two realms during Samhain!" Leandra insisted.

Bertha made an impatient noise. "Really, I don't think that's essential—"

"You must! It is the only way to lend the bonfire the necessary protective properties." Leandra's voice rose even more. "Samhain is a time of great danger! It's the time when the veil between the living and the dead is at its thinnest, and evil and malevolent spirits will be walking the earth, searching for unwary victims... You need to protect yourselves! You need to do the utmost to ward off the harmful influence of the Otherworld and guard your families from witchcraft and black magic!"

By now, all eyes in the shop were riveted on Leandra. Caitlyn could see villagers whispering to each other, several tourists beginning to look uneasy, and the young children accompanying them staring with wide, fearful eyes. Bertha noticed as well, and she gave Leandra a severe look.

"There's no need for all this fearmongering," she said, tartly. "While it's true that many of these ancient traditions were supposed to have a protective element, you have to remember that they were mainly superstitious rituals. There is no real danger. At the heart of it, Samhain is a harvest festival, a time to mark the coming of winter."

"But you cannot deny that it is also a time when the veil between the worlds is at its thinnest, and when evil spirits and demons can cross over easily into our world," Leandra shot back.

"Yes, it *is* believed that the boundaries between the worlds are thinner at this time," Bertha conceded. "But that means that all spirits can cross over: good as well as evil. Samhain is when deceased loved ones can come back to visit; a time when you can reach out to family and friends who have passed away, and speak to them—and maybe even hear them speak back."

The tense atmosphere in the chocolate shop had eased with Bertha's soothing words, and Caitlyn could even see several customers smile wistfully. Leandra scowled, obviously not liking the wind being taken out of her sails.

"Well... you should still be following the best practices for building the bonfire, to maximise its protective potential," she insisted.

Bertha sighed. "Yes, don't worry, Miss Lockwood. I will make sure to collect all three types of wood and stack them with the necessary ceremonial layering."

"I can help, if you like," said Leandra, quickly. "I'm well versed in the magical symbolism associated with various British trees, and I can help you search the estate grounds for the right rowan tree, for example, and then consecrate the wood and bring it for your bonfire stack."

"Thank you, that's very kind, but I think I'll manage," Bertha said, in a firm voice.

Leandra's mouth tightened. She gave a loud sniff. "Suit yourself." She shot a sidelong glance at the other customers, who were still watching and listening, and added in a loud, carrying voice: "I do hope you know what you're doing. A mistake during the Samhain festivities could have disastrous consequences, and the people of Tillyhenge deserve to be safeguarded with the highest vigilance."

With that parting shot, she turned and strode out of the chocolate shop with a whirl of black velvet skirts.

Chapter Three

"What a pompous cow!" Bertha said, under her breath, as she watched Leandra disappear through the shop doorway. Then she sighed and added, more charitably, "Although... I suppose she *was* just trying to help. Maybe it was silly of me to refuse her offer. One shouldn't really look a gift horse in the mouth, and Goddess knows I could do with the help—I have so many things to get done before Samhain Eve that I don't know if I'm coming or going!"

"Is there anything I can do?" asked Caitlyn.

Bertha gave her a distracted smile. "Well, if you and Evie could make a start on supper, that would be wonderful. I see you've got the pumpkins—good. The recipe for the soup is in one of the books on the shelf above the kitchen counter. Evie will know which one. And if you girls get hungry, just start eating first. Don't wait for us. I hope we won't be too late, though—I was lucky to get the last appointment at the dentist." She sighed again and shook her head in exasperation. "I can't believe Mother has been nursing that sore tooth for three weeks now and hasn't said anything! Really, sometimes your grandmother drives me around the bend. I know she's very proud and hates admitting any weakness, but clove oil can only do so much. At some point, you need to get professional help."

As if conjured by the mention of her name, the Widow Mags appeared suddenly in the doorway at the rear of the cottage. She had thrown a dark woollen shawl around her shoulders and was brandishing a gnarled wooden walking stick. The scowl on her face was so fearsome that several customers took a step back as she hobbled across the shop to join Caitlyn and Bertha.

"Caitlyn, I need you to mind the shop for me while I go out into the woods," she said, without preamble. "That fool girl Evie has completely ruined the latest batch of Florentines I made for the special Samhain collection. I told her to just drizzle chocolate on them the old-fashioned way, but she had to try to use some silly spell—and now they're nothing but a sticky mess. I'm going to have to redo the entire batch!"

"Evie means well," said Caitlyn, feeling sorry for her young cousin.

Although Evie had had the benefit of being born and raised in a witch family, with Bertha as mother and the Widow Mags as grandmother to guide her, somehow the young girl had always struggled to master magic. Her spells constantly went awry, often with hilariously disastrous consequences, and her frantic attempts to fix them just made things worse. Caitlyn could still vividly remember the first time she met Evie—when her cousin's well-meaning attempt to ease her headache through magical means had resulted in leafy vegetables growing out of Caitlyn's ears!

"Humph!" said the Widow Mags, looking slightly mollified. "Well, she should stop meddling with spells she can't control and just do things the way I've shown her. There's no need to use magic at all to create amazing chocolates—all you need is some skill and patience." She glanced out the shop window. "Anyway, if I pop out now, I should still be able to gather enough berries for a new batch—"

"Mother, you can't go into the woods now," protested Bertha. "For one thing, it'll be dark soon, and you might pick the wrong berries—"

"I may be old, but I'm not blind," snapped the Widow Mags. "In any case, I know all the bramble patches and elder clusters in this area like the back of my hand. I never pick the wrong berries."

"Well, you still can't go because I need to take you into town. I've managed to get an appointment with the dentist to take a look at your sore tooth—"

"I don't need to see a dentist," growled the old witch. "I told you, I'm fine. A bit of toothache never killed anyone."

"Mother, you could have an abscess or something!" Bertha said, in exasperated tones. "And if you get an infection at your age, it could spread to your bloodstream and cause serious illness—"

"I'm not going and that's that," said the Widow Mags, her mouth set in an obstinate line.

"*Mo-other!*" Bertha had gone red and she looked as if she was about to burst a vessel.

Caitlyn spoke up hastily. "I can understand why you wouldn't want to go, Grandma," she said, with exaggerated sympathy. "I mean, it's well known that dentists are at the top of the list of things that people are most terrified of—"

"Terrified? Who said I was terrified?" demanded the Widow Mags.

Caitlyn gave her an artless look. "Oh... well, I don't know why else you wouldn't go, then. I mean, it's no big deal, really—just a few minutes sitting in a chair. Why wouldn't you go, unless you're scared?"

The Widow Mags bristled. "Being scared has nothing to do with it! I just think it's a waste of time, but if you're suggesting that... Oh, fine. I'll go." She turned to Bertha, glowering. "But I warn you, I won't be kept waiting, hanging around for hours in the surgery waiting room!"

"Oh no, I'm sure you'll be seen promptly, Mother," said Bertha, throwing Caitlyn a grateful look from behind the old witch's back. "Now, are you warm enough in that shawl? And perhaps you should change your shoes—"

"I'm fine, child. Stop fussing!" said the Widow Mags, irritably brushing Bertha's hands away. She turned to Caitlyn and nodded to the other side of the room. The couple from earlier were still bent over the glass counter, staring at the rows of chocolate truffles and bonbons on display. "Go and see if those two have made up their minds yet. Really, I've never known anyone to take so long to choose some chocolates!" she grumbled. "And tell Evie to stop faffing with the Florentines. Even if she manages to salvage them, they won't be fit for sale in the shop now. I'll make a fresh batch tomorrow."

With a few more barked instructions, the old witch finally allowed Bertha to hustle her out of the chocolate shop. Caitlyn saw them out, then quickly turned to serve the many customers still browsing. Thankfully, the couple by the counter had made their selections at last, and Caitlyn enjoyed chatting with them as she carefully wrapped their chocolate truffles in a box tied with a ribbon. Next were a pair of German tourists keen to buy some traditional English fudge, followed by a mother and daughter drooling over the chocolate-dipped strawberries, and finally a group of pensioners eagerly asking about the flavours of soft nougat on offer.

By the time she'd waved the last customer goodbye, the sun was low on the horizon. Caitlyn leaned against the counter with a happy sigh. It had been a busy, exhausting day, but it was lovely to see the emptied shelves, and how all the treats that the Widow Mags had lovingly created had been snapped up with such enthusiasm.

The ominous sound of smashing crockery broke into her thoughts. It had come from the back of the cottage, and Caitlyn recalled suddenly that Evie was still in the kitchen. *Yikes. I'd better go and see what she's up to*, thought Caitlyn. *I hope she hasn't decided to try another magic spell...*

But before she could head into the kitchen, the door to the chocolate shop swung open again and a young man stepped in. He was dressed in brown corduroy trousers and a tweed jacket with leather elbow patches, with a pair of round-framed spectacles perched on his nose. The whole outfit should have made him look prematurely middle-aged, but instead it had the effect of making him look absurdly young.

"Er… dreadfully sorry to bother you," he said, diffidently. "But I seem to have lost my way… er… Could you possibly direct me to Huntingdon Manor?'

"Do you have a car?" asked Caitlyn. "Are you driving?"

"I've got my Audi parked by the village green," said the young man. "I thought it was possible to walk from the village to the Manor, but I must have been mistaken."

"No, you can walk. The quickest way is actually up the hill behind this cottage," said Caitlyn, waving towards the rear of the chocolate shop. "The way up is quite steep, but once you get to the top of the hill, you'll see Huntingdon Manor in the distance, and the slope down the other side of the hill is quite gentle. The Manor sits in a dale that's slightly raised, so the descent is fairly easy. Still…" Caitlyn looked doubtfully down at the young man's expensive leather brogues. "I'm not sure you've got the right shoes for walking. It's been raining quite a lot lately and it's very slippery and muddy in places, especially going up the hill from this side. So I think you're best to drive, really. You'll have to head out of the village and take the motorway, which circles around. The official entrance to Huntingdon Manor is on the other side of the dale."

"Ah, I see. Well, cheers, much obliged." The young man smiled and started to turn away, then paused as his gaze fell on the display next to Caitlyn. It was a stand showcasing the four special treats that the Widow Mags had created for the Samhain collection: dark chocolate truffles with a pumpkin liqueur ganache, rich fudge laced with apple-and-cinnamon spice, milk chocolate bonbons filled with salted caramel-and-elderflower essence, and luxurious Florentines featuring wild forest berries and autumn nuts.

"I say, those Florentines look

smashing! They're a bit different from the ones you normally see—"

"These are part of our limited time collection which has been specially created to celebrate Samhain," Caitlyn explained. "The Florentines are made using wild forest berries, sourced from the local woods. The tart flavour is just wonderful against the sweetness of autumn nuts and the crispy caramel base. And of course, there's the smooth Belgian chocolate that's drizzled on top—"

"Say no more!" cried the young man, laughing. "I'll take two packets, please."

Caitlyn smiled, pleased. She had been practising her sales spiel all week, and she was delighted to see it working so well. She lifted a couple of the Florentine stacks from the display, each carefully wrapped in clear cellophane with a gold ribbon on top, and turned back to the young man. "Would you like anything else?"

"Ooh, what are those?" he asked, turning to the shelf next to them. "Are they coffee beans?"

"Yes, dipped in dark chocolate and dusted with cocoa powder. They're fantastic with a cup of coffee."

The young man smacked his lips, his eyes glowing as he went eagerly towards the shelf for a closer look. "Mmm, I can just imagine! I always—"

He broke off as he stumbled, knocking into a pyramid of boxed chocolates standing next to the shelf. He gave a cry of dismay and flung out a hand towards the collapsing pyramid, but instead of saving it, all he succeeded in doing was smacking the shelf above, sending bags of coffee beans flying everywhere. One bag burst and a shower of dark pellets rained on them, scattering across the floor.

"Oh cripes!" cried the young man in anguish. "I'm so sorry! I'm so terribly sorry! I... I'll pay for everything, I promise!"

Caitlyn suppressed a groan and crouched down to pick up the fallen boxes. "It's okay. It was an accident—"

"*Uurrghh!*" he cried as he bent to help her and lost his balance again, tumbling sideways and falling to the ground.

"Oh my goodness, are you all right?" asked Caitlyn.

"Yes, yes... never better..." mumbled the young man, his face red with embarrassment as he rolled back upright. As he climbed to his feet, Caitlyn caught sight of something glimmering on the floor beneath him. She reached for it and held it up curiously. It looked like a heavy chain necklace with a large pendant made of a dull gold metal, shaped like a cone, and etched with engravings.

"That's mine!" said the young man, snatching it out of Caitlyn's hands. "It...

it must have fallen out of my pocket," he added, hastily stuffing it back into the side of his tweed jacket.

"What is it?" asked Caitlyn, curiously, as they both rose to their feet.

"Uh... nothing, really... just... just an old family heirloom," he mumbled, making a great show of dusting himself off. Then he made to bend again to pick up the fallen boxes.

"Oh no... never mind... Look, just leave it. I'll clean it up later!" Caitlyn cried as she saw the young man inadvertently step on a bag of coffee beans, crushing them into a mess of chocolate and cocoa powder.

If I don't get him out of here, he's going to destroy the whole shop! she thought, grimly. A few minutes later, Caitlyn breathed a sigh of relief as the young man finally took his leave. She stood in the shop doorway and watched him stumble away in the fading light, still stammering apologies, until he was just a faint figure at the end of the cobbled lane. He had paid a generous additional amount as compensation for his clumsiness, so she couldn't really complain. Still, she grimaced as she went back in and surveyed the damage in the shop. *What a waste of chocolate*, she thought with a sigh. *It's a good thing the Widow Mags isn't here; she'd have had a fit!*

She reached for the broom and was about to start sweeping up the mess when a *BOOM!* erupted from the kitchen, rattling the windows and seeming to shake the very foundations of the cottage.

"Oh God... Evie!" Caitlyn muttered. In the kerfuffle with the young man, she had completely forgotten about her young cousin. Dropping the broom, she rushed through the doorway that connected the shop to the rear of the cottage.

Chapter Four

Caitlyn paused in the small hallway, her heart sinking as she saw the white smoke billowing from the kitchen doorway.

"Evie?" she called, stepping cautiously inside. Then she stopped short at the scene before her.

Flour and cocoa powder rose in great clouds, swirling towards the ceiling and making her cough. Smears of butter and chocolate coated the walls, and the large wooden table in the centre of the kitchen looked as if it had been hit by a meteorite of baking ingredients.

Sprawled on the floor next to it, her frizzy red hair streaked with flour and cocoa, was a lanky eighteen-year-old girl with a woebegone expression on her face.

"Evie! What on earth happened?" asked Caitlyn. Hazelnuts crunched underfoot as she rushed to her cousin's side.

The younger girl gulped. "I... I dunno. One minute I was mixing the ingredients and chanting the spell and everything seemed to be perfect and then..." She flushed with humiliation, her mouth wobbling and her eyes welling with tears. "It's me. I'm rubbish. I just can't work magic properly. I'm... I'm the most useless witch in England!"

"Oh, Evie—don't be silly!" cried Caitlyn, giving the other girl a quick hug. "I'm sure it was just a... uh... slight miscalculation. We all make mistakes sometimes."

"No, you don't," said Evie, in a small voice. "Even you, Caitlyn—you only started training as a witch a few month ago and you're already better than me."

"That's not true," said Caitlyn, staunchly, as she helped the younger girl to her feet. "It's only because I always play it safe and never attempt anything too creative or ambitious, whereas you're much braver."

"*Mew!*" cried Nibs, as if in agreement, as he jumped up on the wooden table and scampered across the surface, leaving a trail of tiny pawprints in the scattered flour.

"Nibs!" cried the two girls in unison, and Caitlyn lunged to grab the kitten. She picked his wriggling body off the table and deposited him back on the ground, then turned and smiled encouragingly at Evie.

"What were you trying to make, anyway?"

"Some Truth Nougat pralines," Evie said, sheepishly. "They're—"

"Holy guacamole, what happened in here?"

They whirled around to see a young woman standing in the kitchen doorway. She had hair of honey gold, eyes of cornflower blue, and she would have easily resembled a fairytale princess were it not for the hot-pink velour jumpsuit that hugged her ample curves, with the word "Booty" glittering in diamanté letters across her bum, and the oversized handbag she carried, which resembled a fluffy flamingo. She strode into the kitchen—somehow managing to avoid several puddles of chocolate sauce despite wearing white ankle boots with enormous platform heels—and stopped in the centre of the room, placing her hands dramatically on her hips as she surveyed the mess.

It was an entrance worthy of a supermodel, but then Caitlyn would have expected nothing less from Pomona, her flamboyant "American cousin". The daughter of a famous actress, Pomona had grown up in the whirl of Hollywood awards ceremonies and showbiz parties, and embraced glitz and glamour like a second skin. She was loud, bubbly, and confident—everything that Caitlyn was not and wished she could be—but despite the huge difference between their personalities, the two girls had been best friends since their first toddler steps together. As the niece of Caitlyn's late adoptive mother, Pomona might not have been her cousin in blood, but that didn't change the fact that she had always felt like family.

"Pomona!" Caitlyn cried, smiling in surprised delight. "I thought you left yesterday. Have you changed your mind about going back to LA?"

Pomona waved a dismissive hand. "Tell me what happened here first!"

Evie started her explanation again. "I

was trying to create some pralines filled with Truth Nougat. You know, like a truth serum, but in nougat form."

"That's so freakin' cool!" said Pomona, her eyes lighting up. "You're a genius, Evie! You could sell them to MI6 and the CIA and all those other intelligence agencies. They could get people to spill state secrets just by force-feeding them chocolates!"

Evie grinned. "Thanks. Actually, I was planning to submit the pralines as my entry for the Samhain Gourmet Glory competition. It's the biggest event in the Mystical Almanac," she explained. "Every year, witches from covens all over the world compete to win the title for the best magical chocolate, dessert, or pastry. It's got to be something completely original—not based on a recipe that was created before—and it's also got to be something that truly wows the judges with its extraordinary magical power. For example, last year's winning entry was a chocolate bar that made you lose weight!"

Evie glanced at the mess on the big wooden table and gave a wistful sigh. "I thought... well, nobody's ever created a Truth Nougat before, as far as I know. So if I could make a really delicious chocolate praline, filled with this magical nougat and decorated with buttery almond crunch on top, I might really impress the judges." She looked at the other girls. "If I could win the title of Samhain Gourmet Glory, it would be a *huge* honour and I... I really wanted to surprise Grandma and have her be proud of me for once."

"Evie, she *is* proud of you," said Caitlyn, gently. "I know the Widow Mags might not express it—she's always biting my head off too, you know, and telling me I could do better—but deep down, I'm sure she's proud of the witch you're becoming—"

"No, she isn't," said Evie, wretchedly.

"She thinks I'm a complete ninny. But if I were to win the competition, I could prove her wrong!"

Pomona glanced at the big wooden table where they could see a bowl of soft brown paste. "So how do you make this Truth Nougat? Wait—is that it? I thought nougat was that white chewy stuff?"

"You're thinking of the type you usually see in shops, which is made with egg whites and sugar or honey," said Evie. "This is Viennese nougat, which is a different type. It's made of roasted hazelnuts, cocoa, sugar, and butter. It's really delicious, and if I can just enchant it with the right spell, it should make you to tell the truth as well." She sighed. "But I just can't seem to make the spell work! I've tried reciting the spell backwards or holding my breath while casting the spell, but it just wouldn't infuse the nougat. And then I thought maybe I could try to force the magic in by repeating the spell quickly, three times in a row, while spinning *widdershins*—you know, in an anti-clockwise direction... That's when everything exploded," she added, darting a guilty look at the mess around the kitchen.

"Wait—why did you spin *widdershins?* Why not *deosil*?" asked Caityn. "Didn't the Widow Mags say that *widdershins* is the direction of undoing or breaking? You have to use *deosil*—clockwise—movements for constructive magic."

Evie groaned and smacked her forehead. "Oh Goddess! You're right! I mixed them up..."

"Okay, just, like, try again and spin the other way," urged Pomona.

"I don't think it's just that, though," said Evie, with a sigh. "I think... I just don't have what it takes."

"Aww, come on, Evie! Now you're just feeling sorry for yourself—"

"No, you see, truth-forcing is a form

of advanced magic because it requires you to bend others *against* their will. I think I just don't have enough witch skill to perform such a powerful spell."

Pomona shrugged. "Well, you just need to practise and—"

"No, no, you don't understand," said Evie, earnestly. "It's... it's a bit like artistic ability, you know? Like some people are born able to draw and paint amazing pictures with hardly any training, and other people can only draw stick figures. Even if they have art lessons and practise loads... well, they might get a bit better, but they'll still never be a great artist. They just don't have the natural gift. Working magic is the same. Some witches are born with great magical ability and others..." She trailed off, her thin shoulders slumping.

"I don't believe that," said Caitlyn, squeezing the younger girl's hand. "I'm sure you have the ability in you, Evie. You just need a bit more experience and... and maybe time to practise and get better."

"Yeah, you can't just give up!" agreed Pomona. "I mean, okay, so you're not some Magical Picasso—bummer—but isn't there something you can do to, like, boost your witchy powers? I mean, some people are born with short stubby lashes and flat chests, right? But they use mascara and push-up bras and look freakin' awesome! There must be something like that for magic as well— something to enhance your natural potential."

Caitlyn started to make a sarcastic remark, but she was interrupted by Evie who sat upright and cried: "Oh, wait— you're right—there *is* something! And in fact, it was Grandma who created it!"

"Huh?" Pomona looked at her quizzically.

"It was Grandma's Samhain Gourmet Glory entry when *she* was a young

59

witch," said Evie, excitedly. "I remember Mum telling me about it when I was a little girl. She said that Grandma had created a chocolate philtre that could boost the inherent magical abilities of witches, so that they can cast far more powerful spells or work magic at much higher levels than they could normally. In fact, the philtre was supposed to be so powerful that even if you didn't know you were a witch but had some hidden magical ability, it could act as a catalyst to awaken those abilities."

"You mean—it could turn normal people into witches?" said Pomona, in an awed voice.

"Well, not really. I mean, you have to have some dormant magical ability within you. Like, for example, if you're descended from witches but didn't realise it. So you have a connection to the magical world. Then the philtre could unlock the potential within you and give you the ability to do magic." Evie smiled, proudly. "No one had ever created something like that before and the judges were really impressed, so Grandma won the title that year."

"Well... that's perfect!" said Pomona, clapping her hands. "All you need to do is take some of this chocolate philtre, and then your witch powers should be boosted enough to tackle the Truth Nougat spell."

"Yes, but I don't know how to get hold of this chocolate philtre. Grandma doesn't keep a bottle of it anywhere. I know because I've searched for it before."

"Don't you have her recipe? You could just make some yourself."

Evie shook her head. "I've never seen it. It's not in any of the books in the kitchen here."

"Have you looked in her *grimoire*?" Pomona asked Evie. "I'll bet she's written it in there."

Evie turned wide eyes on her. "Look in Grandma's *grimoire*? Oh, no, I can't!"

"A *grimoire* is a book of spells, isn't it?" asked Caitlyn hesitantly.

Pomona gave a snort. "Honestly, Caitlyn, it's embarrassing that you don't know that, given that you're a witch!"

"Well, I never had your obsession with witchcraft and magic, Pomie. You're like a walking encyclopaedia on the occult. Besides, I only found out that I was a witch a few months ago," protested Caitlyn.

"Yeah, a *grimoire* is a book of spells. It's where a witch keeps all her favourite spells and incantations. I'll bet the Widow Mags records all her best magical chocolate recipes in hers."

"But it's also really private," said Evie, quickly. "You're *never* supposed to look at another witch's *grimoire* unless you've been invited. Mum's shown me hers only once. It was quite boring, though," she said, wrinkling her nose. "Full of Latin names of herbs and how to grow them and harvest them. But then, Mum's never really been into hexes and charms and all that stuff—she says she's more of a gardener than a witch." Evie giggled, then added: "Mum said it was always Tara who was more interested in 'pure' magic and who used to pester Grandma to see her *grimoire*—"

"Tara? My mother?" cried Caitlyn. "What else? What else did Bertha say about her?"

Evie shrugged. "That's it, really. She didn't say much else. Just that Tara was always obsessed with Grandma's *grimoire* and trying to have a peek at it, but Grandma kept it really well hidden."

"I'll bet I know where she keeps it," said Pomona. "It's obvious! In her bedroom. We've got to go and search in there."

Evie swallowed. "Go in Grandma's

bedroom?"

"Well, yeah! And now's the perfect time to search for it!" She glanced around. "She's out, isn't she, the Widow Mags? So this is the perfect opportunity to snoop in her room."

"Er... I don't think that's a good idea, Pomie," said Caitlyn, nervously. She had breached the sanctity of the Widow Mags's bedroom once, when she'd been desperately searching for information about her mother, and she could still remember the Widow Mags's cold anger when she had been caught, red-handed, looking at the old witch's photo album.

"Aww, come on!" said Pomona, impatiently. "What's the big deal? We'll be in and out of there before anyone even knows we were in there." Not waiting for the other girls to respond, she whirled and left the kitchen.

"Pomie, wait—" cried Caitlyn, rushing after her. She stumbled and tripped as a little black ball of fluff shot out suddenly from behind a chair and latched onto her ankles. "Ooh Nibs!" she said, in exasperation, reaching down to gently grab the baby cat by the scruff.

By the time Caitlyn managed to dislodge the mischievous kitten and hurry after Pomona, she found her cousin already hovering outside the door to the Widow Mags's bedroom.

"Pomie, wait!" she said, urgently. "Don't you think that we should—"

Too late. The American girl had opened the door and disappeared into the room, leaving Caitlyn standing in the hallway. She stood, flabbergasted, for a moment.

"Should... should we go in too?" asked Evie, timidly, coming up behind her.

Caitlyn hesitated. A part of her was infuriated by Pomona's bold, reckless attitude, but another part of her secretly admired it. She wished she could be like her cousin. *Well, you can start now*, she thought. Straightening her shoulders, she took a deep breath and stepped through the darkened doorway.

Chapter Five

Caitlyn paused, letting her eyes adjust to the dim light, and looked around the Widow Mags's chamber. It looked much the same as the last time she had been in there: an old oak bed dominated one side of the room, accompanied by a sagging couch, a couple of armchairs, and an ancient writing desk. On the opposite wall stood an old-fashioned wardrobe with an enormous chest of drawers and several boxes and trunks piled alongside it.

"There's too much stuff in here. We're never going to find it," she said, looking around uneasily.

"Aww, don't be such a Debbie Downer!" said Pomona, impatiently.

"We shouldn't be in here," agreed Evie in a nervous whisper as she tiptoed behind Caitlyn. "If Grandma catches us…"

"Relax! We'll be in and out in a second. No one will know," said Pomona, moving over to peer at the writing desk. "Hmm… I wonder if the *grimoire* might be in here," she mused, bending to pull the drawer under the desk open.

"Pomie, I don't think we should be doing this…" said Caitlyn, watching her uneasily. Aside from her fear of discovery, the thought of going through the Widow Mags's private belongings made her very uncomfortable.

Pomona obviously had no such qualms. She rummaged happily through the drawer as she said over her shoulder: "Quit being such a chicken,

Caitlyn! Besides, aren't you curious about the *grimoire*? Don't you want to see if it gives you any info about your mother?"

Caitlyn paused. "Oh. I hadn't thought..."

Pomona slammed the drawer shut and turned away from the writing desk. "C'mon—are you gonna just stand there or are you gonna help me search?"

She strode over to the chest of drawers on the other side of the room and began poking through the assortment of boxes and knick-knacks scattered on top. "Ooh, check this out... it looks like a moonstone amulet..." The sound of tinkling glass and metal broke the hushed silence in the room. "And wow—this looks like a silver witch's knot pendant! Look at that!" She held up something that glinted silver in the dim light.

"*Pomie!* You're supposed to be

searching for a book, not snooping through the Widow Mags's personal things!"

"Hey, I'm snooping with a purpose," said Pomona, indignantly.

She lifted another object from the tray. It was a diamond-shaped, pale-green stone attached to a long silver chain, but what really drew the eye were the strange markings on the stone's surface: a series of overlapping patterns that bore an uncanny resemblance to snakeskin.

"Oh! That's a dowsing pendulum," cried Evie, forgetting her nervousness. She pushed past Caitlyn and hurried over to join Pomona at the chest.

"A what?" said Caitlyn,

"It's a divination tool," Evie explained. "It gives you answers to questions or helps you find the location of things."

"Yeah, and this is a serpentine crystal," added Pomona, touching the green stone reverently. "I've seen a couple of these in an occult shop back in LA. They're, like, really powerful, with strong magical energy. They're used in Kundalini activation—that's a kind of divine energy," she explained to Caitlyn, who was watching them sceptically.

"Uh... okay..." said Caitlyn, feeling totally lost.

Not for the first time, she reflected that Pomona should have really been the one to discover that she was descended from witches. Her American cousin had believed passionately in magic all her life and had always been fascinated by the paranormal, spending the better part of her teens dabbling in tarot cards, crystal healing, and other occult practices. When they'd first discovered that witches and magic really *did* exist, Caitlyn had struggled to reconcile her feelings of bewilderment and disbelief, but Pomona had instantly taken it in stride, embracing it all with a gleeful "I told you so!"

Now Pomona held up the serpentine pendant triumphantly and said with a smug smile: "I bet this'll help us find the Widow Mags's *grimoire*."

She stretched her arm out in front of her, holding the end of the chain with a thumb and forefinger, letting the serpentine pendant swing freely. The green stone twirled through the air, catching the light as it swung first one way, then another.

"Show me where the *grimoire* is," Pomona intoned as she began walking slowly around the room. "Show me where it's hidden!"

The serpentine pendulum swung and twirled, winking in the dim light. In spite of herself, Caitlyn held her breath, her eyes following the green stone, expectantly. The whole thing seemed silly and ridiculous. But then again, she had been wrong to scoff at the existence of magic. *Perhaps I ought to keep an open mind for once*, she thought.

When a few minutes had elapsed, though, with Pomona doing nothing more than walking aimlessly around, Caitlyn spoke up impatiently: "Well? Is it telling you anything?"

"No," Pomona admitted, looking slightly crestfallen. Then she brightened. "Maybe it needs a spell! Yes, that's it. It probably needs a spell to activate it or something. Go on, do something to make it wake up."

"Me? I don't know what to do—" Caitlyn started to say, but Evie interrupted her.

"Oh, I do! I know just the spell," cried the younger girl, eagerly. "I learned it last week. Well, it's actually to activate the compost heap in Mum's garden—you know, to draw forth the natural energies and speed up decay—but I'm sure it'll work just as well."

73

"Er, Evie—are you sure?" asked Caitlyn, nervously. "Remember the last time we sneaked in here, your spell to find the photo album went wrong and monster roots started—"

"Yes, but that was different," said Evie, looking hurt. "You don't think I can do magic at all, do you?"

"No, it's not that," said Caitlyn, quickly. "I just..." She hesitated, seeing the wounded look in the younger girl's eyes, then she forced a weak smile. "Of course, I believe you. In fact, we're... we're lucky you know a spell."

"Yeah, go on, Evie—do your thing!" urged Pomona.

Evie flushed and looked pleased. "Hang on a minute—let me try to remember the words..." She raised a hand, hovering it over the serpentine pendant. "*Elicio luminae, invigorus vita emergere!*"

There was a puff of smoke, and

Pomona yelped and jerked back her hand as if she had been burnt. The pendulum dropped to the stone floor with a clatter, and Caitlyn cried out in dismay.

"Oh no—is it broken?" she gasped, peering through the smoke. "Can you see the stone? Is it still in one piece?"

Then the smoke cleared, and she saw what was by her feet: a slithering, rolling mass of green scales and sinuous muscle.

"*Aaaahh!*" she screamed, jerking back from the huge green python coiled on the floor. "Evie—what have you done?"

"Holy guacamole, you've really activated the... um... serpent in serpentine," said Pomona, laughing. "Wow, this thing must be, like, ten feet long. And look at those scales!" She leaned closer to the giant snake. "You know what... it's kinda cute. It's sort of cross-eyed and there's this adorable little notch in its mouth where its tongue comes out—"

"What are you doing, Pomie?" gasped Caitlyn. "Get back! It might bite you!"

"Pythons don't bite," Pomona scoffed. "They just wrap around you and squeeze you to death. But this one doesn't look aggressive."

She's right, Caitlyn admitted. If anything, the python looked slightly confused as it looped over itself, its tongue flickering out hesitantly to taste the air.

"Poor thing," said Pomona, reaching out a hand. "They say pythons make great pets, you know. They're, like, really docile and love to snuggle up around your neck—"

"Don't do that!" cried Caitlyn, grabbing her cousin's hand before Pomona could touch the python. "It's a live snake, for heaven's sake!"

"*Sss-sss!*" lisped the python, weaving

its head back and forth in a bewildered manner. "*Sss-ssssss!*"

"What are we going to do?" Caitlyn said, looking at it despairingly. "How do we explain to the Widow Mags why there's a giant green python in her bedroom?"

"It's okay, it's okay—I can fix it!" said Evie. "I'll change it back to the pendulum just by saying the incantation backwards." She inched closer to the python and held out her hand again. "*Emergere vita invigorus, luminae elicio!*"

There was another puff of smoke and Caitlyn coughed violently. Then she waved the haze away and peered down eagerly. To her dismay, the pile of green coils was still there... only now they seemed to be made of rubber.

"Um... Evie... I think you've turned the python into a garden hose," said Pomona, with a giggle.

"That's okay! That's good. At least a garden hose can't bite," said Caitlyn.

Pomona rolled her eyes. "I told you, pythons don't bite!"

Caitlyn ignored her, bending down to try and heave the coils up into her arms. They were heavier than they looked, and she only managed to drag one loop up. "If we can't change it back, we can at least hide this outside and—*aaahhh!*" She shrieked and jumped back as the garden hose suddenly writhed in her hands.

"*Sss-sss?*" lisped the garden hose as it looped around her arm, its brass connector "head" raising and looking blindly around. "*Sss-ssssss?*"

"Omigod—it's a garden hose that thinks it's a snake!" cried Pomona, squealing with laughter.

"It's not funny, Pomona!" said Caitlyn, in exasperation as she wrestled with the rubber hose, which was now trying to wind itself lovingly around her shoulders.

"Aww, I think it likes you," Pomona teased.

The garden hose nuzzled Caitlyn's cheek and water dribbled out of the brass connector "head". It was like being licked by a very wet, very cold tongue.

"Ugh!" said Caitlyn, wiping a knuckle over her cheek.

Pomona whooped with laughter, and even Evie started chortling before hastily stopping as she saw Caitlyn glaring at them.

"This isn't funny!"

Pomona wiped tears from her eyes, then put her hands up in the classic pose of surrender. "Okay... okay... why don't we get it out of here first?"

Between them, the three girls managed to heave the wriggling garden hose up and out of the room, with

Caitlyn at its brass connector "head", Evie lifting the sagging middle, and Pomona dragging its "tail". They shuffled out into the shop and paused for a breath.

"Where are we going to put it?" asked Caitlyn, panting. "We can't just set it loose outside. It'll probably slither off and cause mass panic in the village."

"What—by watering everyone's garden?" sniggered Pomona.

"I could try the spell again," Evie offered.

"No, no, that's okay," said Caitlyn, hastily. A slithering, lisping garden hose was bad enough—she didn't want to risk it turning into something even worse.

"I know! We can put it in the trunk of my car," said Pomona. "That way, it'll be safe and locked up until we decide what to do with it."

Caitlyn groaned, thinking of the winding cobbled lanes of the village.

"You want us to drag this thing through Tillyhenge?"

"We can put it in that," Evie said, pointing to where an enormous vintage-style wicker basket sat on the shop counter. "Mum brought that over earlier in case Grandma wanted to use it to make up a chocolate hamper. It's got a lid and it'll be easier to carry."

She hurried to bring the basket over, and together they lifted the wriggling garden hose and wrestled it into the basket. Somehow, they managed to stuff all the coils in, then slammed the twin flap-lids shut on top.

"Whew!" said Pomona, sagging against the side of the wooden table. "Man, who knew garden hoses could be so heavy—"

"What are you girls doing?"

Chapter Six

They whirled to see the Widow Mags and Bertha standing in the cottage doorway, looking at them quizzically. Caitlyn and Evie both sprang to stand in front of the basket, trying to block it from view, and began stammering:

"Oh! Er... nothing..."

"Grandma! Mum! We thought... I mean..."

Behind them, Pomona cut in with a dazzling smile: "You're back! Awesome! I came over tell you guys that there's gonna be a dinner party over at the Manor tonight—"

One of the flap lids on the basket popped open and the end of a green garden hose peeked out. "*Sss-sss?*"

Pomona hastily elbowed it shut. "—uh—yeah, so you're *all* invited!"

"Dinner party?" said Bertha, in surprise. "I didn't realise that Lord Fitzroy was giving a dinner party. That's very nice of him to invite us, but I'm afraid I can't make it. I have a large order of herbal supplies to prepare for delivery tomorrow. And Evie has some homework to finish, I believe," she added, giving her daughter a pointed look. "Just because you're in your last year of school doesn't mean that you can skive off." Then she paused, taking in Evie's guilty expression. "What is it, Evie?" She leaned to one side, trying to get a better view of what was behind the girls' backs. "Is there something in that basket? I thought I saw something move just now—"

"Oh, that's just Nibs," said Caitlyn,

quickly. "He's being his usual naughty self, you know, climbing into everything and—"

"*Mew?*" The little black kitten appeared in the doorway from the back of the cottage, obviously hearing his name—and very obviously *not* in the basket.

Caitlyn flushed. "Oh... er... how did you get there, Nibs?"

One of the basket lids fluttered again and they heard another inquisitive "*Sss-sss?*" Pomona lunged and threw her weight on the basket lid, then—as she saw Bertha and the Widow Mags staring at her—quickly said:

"So... um... yeah, about this dinner party... who's coming?"

The Widow Mags scowled. "I haven't got time for any dinner party nonsense. I still have to remake that batch of Florentines, not to mention all the other chocolates needed to restock the shelves." She paused and looked around the shop, taking in the mess of fallen boxes and crushed coffee beans on the floor. "What on earth happened here?" she demanded.

Caitlyn groaned silently. If her grandmother thought this was bad, she should see the state of the kitchen!

"Um... a young man—a customer— had a bit of an accident," she explained. "I was just about to clean it up. And we'll clean up the kitchen too—don't worry."

"The kitchen? What's happened in the kitchen?" asked the Widow Mags, sharply. "What have you girls been doing?"

Without waiting for a reply, she turned and hobbled through the doorway that led to the rear of the cottage, with Bertha at her heels.

"Yikes..." said Pomona, pulling a face. Then she brightened. "Actually, this is perfect. Evie—you go and keep them busy back there, and it'll give me and Caitlyn a chance to deal with this." She indicated the hamper.

"M-me?" said Evie, in dismay.

"Yeah, it's the perfect opportunity. Go on, before they come back!" urged Pomona.

Caitlyn started to protest. It seemed unfair to make Evie bear the brunt of the Widow Mags's annoyance with the mess in the kitchen. But on the other hand, Pomona was right: it would be infinitely worse if the old witch saw the enchanted garden hose and realised that they'd been snooping in her bedroom. This was their perfect chance to hide the "Garden-Hose-Python" whilst the older women were distracted.

"It's all right, Evie—we'll join you as soon as we can," she said, giving the younger girl an encouraging smile.

Evie gulped, and then, with the air of a brave martyr, she headed into the kitchen. Caitlyn turned back to the hamper basket and tried to lift it. She lurched sideways, staggering under the weight, and would have fallen over if Pomona hadn't caught her elbow. Together, the two of them tottered towards the door of the shop, but they had barely staggered out of the cottage before they had to drop the basket on the ground, gasping and panting with effort.

The lid flap opened and the garden hose poked its head out, lisping indignantly. "*Sss-sss! Ssss!*"

"Okay, sorry, but you weigh a tonne, you know that?" grumbled Pomona. Then she rolled her eyes. "I can't believe I'm talking to a garden hose."

Caitlyn sighed and looked worriedly at the village lane winding away from the cottage. "It's so heavy, Pomie. How are we going to get it to your car?"

"Can't you, like, magick some extra

muscles for me?" joked Pomona, making a show of flexing her biceps.

"Actually... you know what? I've got a better idea," said Caitlyn, snapping her fingers.

She laid a hand on the basket, closed her eyes, and concentrated. She didn't have a specific spell in mind, but she recalled the Widow Mags telling her that magic didn't really rely on words or incantations. The spell verses were simply there to help you focus, especially when you were inexperienced. The real power lay in the force of your will to effect a change—that's what magic really was.

Now, she focused on the basket and imagined it rolling smoothly along the ground, gliding over the cobblestones of the village lanes with ease... and she opened her eyes to see that four little wooden wheels had appeared on the corners of the wicker frame.

Pomona gave an exclamation of delight. "Awesome! You've turned it into a wheelie-basket." She grabbed the handle of the basket and began to wheel it down the lane, pushing it in front of her like a baby pram. "Okay, I can manage this on my own. You'd better get back in the kitchen to give Evie some moral support. I'll see you later at the Manor for dinner, yeah?"

"Is there really a dinner party?" asked Caitlyn in surprise. "I thought you were making that up."

"Well, maybe not a dinner party exactly," Pomona admitted. "But you know James's sister is arriving at the Manor tonight."

"Oh yes... James *had* mentioned to me that Vanessa was coming to visit," said Caitlyn, remembering. She had been so busy with the chocolate shop and preparations for Samhain that it had completely slipped her mind.

"I think she's here especially for the Samhain Festival this weekend. That sounds super fun, you know—there's gonna be loads of games and events and awesome food and stuff. That's why I changed my flight to LA. I thought: what the heck, I can delay my trip another week." Pomona wagged a finger at her. "Anyway, you'd better get dolled up when you come over later. Vanessa's arriving with a bunch of her Sloane friends, and they sound like they really know how to party!"

"Oh... I... I don't know if I'll come tonight," said Caitlyn, uneasily.

The thought of meeting James's socialite sister had been intimidating enough, but now that she knew that Vanessa's friends were part of the infamous "Sloane Ranger" set—the unofficial name given to the glamorous residents of the famously posh London neighbourhood of Chelsea—it made the whole thing even more nerve-wracking.

Even though Caitlyn herself had grown up with a wealthy celebrity mother who'd lavished material luxuries on her, she didn't have the easy confidence that many of those born to privilege seemed to exude so effortlessly. She'd always been a shy wallflower, struggling in parties and big crowds. She certainly didn't have the chic style, social prowess, and languid sophistication that the Sloane Rangers were famous for!

"Don't be silly," said Pomona, impatiently, obviously reading her mind. "You can't hide here in Tillyhenge forever, you know. You're gonna have to come to the Manor and meet James's sister at some point, so you might as well get it over with. Look, you've just gotta be yourself and everyone will love you."

"That's easy for *you* to say," muttered Caitlyn, looking sideways at Pomona's flamboyant outfit, gleaming hair, and make-up, and then glancing down at herself. Her sweater was soft and stretchy, but old and worn, and her jeans were faded and liberally covered in flour and cocoa powder—and probably did no favours for her pear-shaped figure. Even if she let her rich red hair down from its usual messy ponytail and tried to apply some make-up, Caitlyn knew that she could never match the glamorous poise of girls like Pomona and Vanessa and her friends.

"Hey." Pomona caught her gaze and gave her a stern look. "Remember, James chose *you*, okay? He's surrounded by gorgeous, high-society girls all the time, and he chose *you*. Even if you do dress like Mrs Potato Head half the time," she added with a grin, then ducked as Caitlyn gave her a mock punch. "No, but seriously, Caitlyn, how many times do I have to tell you: if you have big hips, you should own them!" She wiggled her own for emphasis. "Show off that booty! Be proud of your curves! Don't hide them under baggy sweaters and oversized jeans. You're a beautiful woman—if you can just let yourself believe it."

Caitlyn stood outside *Bewitched by Chocolate* and watched her cousin disappear down the lane, Pomona's words still echoing in her ears. Then she turned with a sigh and walked back into the chocolate shop. She found the Widow Mags standing by the counter, surveying the mess of crushed coffee beans and jumble of boxes on the floor.

"I'll have this cleaned up in no time," Caitlyn said, and she hastily crouched to pick up the spilled coffee beans.

But the Widow Mags put a hand on her elbow and held her back.

"You don't need magic to make good chocolates, but it doesn't hurt to use a House-Proud spell or two when cleaning up the mess they make," said the old witch, her lips twitching into a rare smile.

Then she waved a hand, and Caitlyn watched in delight and wonder as the coffee beans lifted off the floor of their own accord and clustered together, like a swarm of glossy brown bees, before flowing through the air and pouring into a container that the Widow Mags held out. Next, the old witch nodded her head at the pile of boxed chocolates that had been knocked over and said to Caitlyn: "Now, you try."

Caitlyn held out her hand, concentrating on making the boxes stand up and re-stack into their original pyramid shape. But although a few tilted upright and several others wobbled around, she couldn't get them to move more than an inch along the floor.

"Imagine a wind sweeping in through the front door, lifting the boxes up and carrying them into their correct places," the Widow Mags suggested.

Caitlyn took a deep breath and tried again. This time, she visualised a gust of wind blowing in through the narrow cottage doorway and sweeping underneath the boxes scattered on the floor. To her surprise, she saw the boxes surge up, as if blown by an invisible wind. They tumbled together into a messy pile, then—as she imagined the gust of wind spinning around them, forming a vortex—she saw the boxes cluster together and arrange themselves into a cone-shaped stack, assembling neatly one on top of the other, until the final box hovered at the very top, then settled at the apex of the pyramid.

"I did it!" breathed Caitlyn, her eyes wide with delight. "Did you see that? I did it!"

The Widow Mags nodded, approvingly. "You're coming along, child."

Caitlyn flushed with pleasure. Those words, coming from the old witch, were high praise. She turned to head to the rear of the cottage, keen to put her newly learned spell to use on the mess in there, but the Widow Mags stopped her.

"What were you girls doing in my bedroom?"

"Oh!" Caitlyn froze, unable to control the expression of dismay on her face. She had been lulled into a false sense of security by the Widow Mags's genial demeanour earlier, but she should have known that they couldn't easily fool the old witch.

"Um… we… er…" she stammered, groping for a good cover story. "We were just…"

"Yes?"

Caitlyn wished fervently that she had Pomona's easy insouciance and ready tongue. With the Widow Mags's penetrating gaze fixed on her, she found that she just couldn't lie. "We were searching for your *grimoire*," she said, in a small voice.

The Widow Mags stiffened. "You were *what?*"

"It was just to help Evie with her Samhain Gourmet Glory entry," she said, quickly, keen to show that they hadn't been snooping for no good reason. "She's trying to make a Truth Nougat and she was having trouble with the spell, you see. So Evie thought that if she could drink a bit of your chocolate philtre—you know, the one you created that can boost one's magical abilities— then it would enhance her witch powers and help her finish her entry. That's why we were in your bedroom. We were looking for your *grimoire* to find the recipe."

"You don't want anything to do with that philtre," growled the Widow Mags. "I was young and foolish when I created it. If I had known..." She shook her head bitterly. "I wish I had never concocted it."

Caitlyn stared at the old witch in astonishment. "But... but Evie said the philtre won you the title of the Samhain Gourmet Glory when you were a young witch—that's a huge honour, isn't it?"

For the briefest moment, Caitlyn saw a flash of remembered pride and joy in the Widow Mags's eyes, but it was almost instantly overshadowed by bitterness. "It was a hollow glory. A potion that bestows magical power on the drinker... that was a curse more than a gift."

Caitlyn wasn't sure how to respond. She had a feeling that the Widow Mags was talking about something much more than she could understand. Finally, she said: "Um... well, since Evie is already a witch, it can't really harm her to have a little sip of the philtre, can it? And if you could just let us peek at the recipe in your *grimoire*—"

"The *grimoire*'s gone," said the Widow Mags, harshly. "So don't waste your time looking for it."

"Gone? What d'you mean 'gone'?" Caitlyn stared at her. "How can it be gone? I thought a *grimoire* was the most valuable thing a witch owns. How could you possibly lose yours?"

"I didn't lose it. It was stolen from me," snapped the Widow Mags.

"Stolen? But who could possibly get through your..." Suddenly, the answer came to her. She drew a sharp breath. "It was my mother, Tara, who took it, wasn't it? Bertha mentioned that Tara was 'obsessed' with your *grimoire* and that she was always pestering you about it... *She* was the one who stole it from you!"

The Widow Mags didn't respond.

"Is that why Tara ran away and disappeared? Do you think she still has the *grimoire* with her?"

The Widow Mags remained stony-faced and silent.

"Why won't you tell me anything?" Caitlyn cried in frustration.

"I've told you before: I will teach you magic, but I will not answer your questions," said the Widow Mags.

Then, with a swirl of her dark skirt and shawl, she was gone, hobbling through the door that led to the rear of the cottage and leaving Caitlyn standing alone in the shop, fuming.

Chapter Seven

Huntingdon Manor was one of the last few remaining estates in England that still mimicked the old-fashioned "feudal" system, in the sense that the Fitzroy family really did own all the surrounding farms and properties, as well as the village of Tillyhenge itself. But James Fitzroy was certainly no feudal squire, hated and feared by his tenants—in fact, the farmers and residents of the village adored him, not only for his warmth, humility, and generosity as a landlord, but also for his willingness to roll up his sleeves and pitch in whenever there were problems on the estate.

The fact that James looks like a modern-day Mr Darcy doesn't hurt either, thought Caitlyn with a wry smile. Half the local female population, not to mention most of the aristocracy's eligible young ladies, were probably in love with James Fitzroy. And who could blame them—with that charming smile, those warm grey eyes, and that sexy baritone to boot?

Caitlyn crossed the sweeping driveway surrounded by formal landscaped gardens and approached the front door of the Georgian-style mansion. At the top of the front step, she set the cat carrier down by her feet. Nibs peered eagerly out from between the bars of the cage door and mewed excitedly. After she and James had rescued Nibs together, they had decided on a "kitten-share" arrangement, where Nibs spent part of his time at the chocolate shop and part of his time at the Manor. *And causes havoc in both places!* Thought Caitlyn as she glanced down at the little black kitten. Still, despite his naughtiness, Nibs had won over the hearts of everyone in both his homes, and she knew that staff at the Manor—not to mention James himself—would be looking forward to having the little rascal scampering around the estate again.

Before she could ring the bell, the front door was opened by Mosley, the Fitzroy's butler, and Caitlyn had to stifle the giggle that rose to her lips whenever she saw him. Whereas James was a thoroughly modern "lord of the manor", Mosley was the complete opposite. The man seemed almost to have been teleported from the Victorian era, with his devotion to etiquette and old-fashioned formality. In fact, Caitlyn sometimes wondered if Mosley was deliberately trying to act the stereotype of a pompous English butler!

Now, he hurried to take the cat carrier

and then ushered her into the front hall with great ceremony, saying sombrely: "Lord Fitzroy sends his apologies, Miss Le Fey, but he has been detained on one of the farms and may be late for dinner."

"Oh, that's okay," Caitlyn assured him. "Um..." She glanced over his shoulder, looking down the hall, and asked in a low voice: "Have the other guests arrived, Mosley?"

"Miss Vanessa and her friends have not graced us with their presence as yet. I'm afraid the traffic from London may be hindering any attempts at punctuality."

"Oh... right," said Caitlyn, struggling to keep a straight face. "Well, what about Pomona? Is she down yet?"

"Miss Sinclair is still dressing, I believe," said Mosley. "Would you like to go up to join her?"

Caitlyn hesitated. She could just imagine the state of Pomona's room, with discarded outfits strewn everywhere, shoes scattered across the floor and make-up spilling across tables, whilst her cousin danced around, trying on hair accessories and jewellery at random and singing along to the blaring music. It would be a scene of total mayhem and the last thing Caitlyn felt like joining at the moment. No, what she wanted was a quiet place and a moment of peace to collect herself, before the challenging evening ahead of her.

"Actually, I think I'll just wait in the Library," she said.

"Would madam like any refreshments while she is waiting?"

Caitlyn groaned inwardly. She'd tried dozens of times to dissuade Mosley from calling her "madam" but the butler insisted on following traditional etiquette to the letter. She started to protest again, then thought better of it and said simply: "No, I'm fine. Thank you, Mosley."

She reached towards the cat carrier and unlatched the door. "Shall I take Nibs with me? If I can keep him in the Library, he won't—" She broke off with a gasp as the kitten squirmed violently in her hands and wriggled out of her grasp. "Nibs!"

The kitten landed nimbly on the polished flagstones of the Manor's main hall and scampered off without a backwards glance.

"Nibs! Come back here!" shouted Caitlyn. She made an infuriated noise as she saw the kitten's furry body disappear around a corner. "Ooh! The little monkey!" She gave Mosley an apologetic look. "Sorry. He's probably going to get under everyone's feet now."

"Do not fret, madam. The staff are well versed in the kitten's antics and his presence will not affect our duties," Mosley assured her. "Now, I will show you to the Library—"

"Oh no, it's fine, I know the way. I'm sure you must be really busy with the preparations for the visitors coming to stay."

"It is no bother, madam. All the necessary preparations are well in hand," said the butler, stiffly.

"Oh, well, then why don't you sit down and have a cup of tea before they arrive?" Caitlyn suggested, ignoring the butler's horrified expression. "You're going to be run off your feet with all these guests staying for the next few days and the Samhain Festival going on as well. You should take the chance to catch your breath while you can."

Mosley's face softened and he gave her a prim smile. "It is very kind of you to think of my welfare, Miss Le Fey. And it is certainly true that you have been to the Manor so often, you are more than familiar with the surroundings. Indeed, you hardly merit the title of 'guest'." He hesitated, then cleared his throat and added: "In fact, if I may be so bold, madam, many of the staff and I are truly delighted to see you together with his Lordship, and we hope that you will be making Huntingdon Manor your permanent abode before long."

Caitlyn blushed bright red and hurried away, torn between feeling embarrassed and feeling incredibly touched. She knew that residents of both the village and the estate loved to gossip and speculate about her relationship with James. After all, she was a shy, frumpy interloper from overseas who had only arrived a few months ago and yet she had somehow managed to capture the heart of one of England's most eligible bachelors. Still, knowing how much James was loved and respected by his staff, it was heartwarming to hear that she was so welcomed.

Stepping into the Library at last, Caitlyn let out a sigh of pleasure. She'd always loved this place. Although it was not a "cosy" kind of book sanctuary but rather the formal type of bibliotheca found in grand stately homes, it was nevertheless an oasis of peace and calm for a bookworm like her. The walls were filled with floor-to-ceiling bookshelves, displaying rows upon rows of leather-bound volumes, and more bookcases were arranged in various configurations down the centre of the vast room. The air was permeated with that unique smell of old ink and paper, which all booklovers treasured, and Caitlyn smiled and inhaled deeply as she walked further into the room.

She had barely rounded the side of a bookcase, however, when she heard a grunt and a sigh, followed by what sounded like a bear shaking itself vigorously. The next moment, heavy, padding footsteps approached and then suddenly, a cold wet nose thrust itself into her back.

"Bran!" she gasped, laughing, as she

turned and clutched wildly at the head of an enormous English mastiff. The huge dog wagged his tail with vigorous delight and butted his head against her, nearly knocking her over. "Yes...yes... It's lovely to see you too," she said, staggering to keep her footing.

She grabbed his giant head and tried to hold it away from her. "Ugh... Bran, stop... you're drooling all over me," she protested, jerking sideways to try and avoid the dog's slobbery jowls. The movement caught her off balance and the next moment, she tripped and tumbled to the floor. Bran gave a woof of delight and climbed on top of her, obviously deciding that this was a great moment to prove that English mastiffs could be lapdogs too.

"*Ooph!*... Bran... get off me, you great oaf... *ughhh...*" Caitlyn gasped as she wrestled with the huge animal. After a bit of tussling, she managed to push the dog off at last, although not before the mastiff had given her an enthusiastic licking.

Great, thought Caitlyn, looking down at herself. She had taken Pomona's advice and made a huge effort for the evening, choosing a velvet tunic dress, which complemented her vivid red hair and hazel green eyes, paired with black leggings and smart black ankle boots. With carefully applied make-up and her hair brushed until it gleamed, she had been feeling glamorous, even "beautiful", when she'd arrived at the Manor. Now, she was dismayed to see that the tunic was covered in dog hairs, the black leggings showed several smears of canine slobber, and her backside had probably picked up grime and dust from sitting on the Library floor.

"Oh Bran!" she said, in exasperation.

The English mastiff sat back on his haunches and tilted his head to one side, looking at her anxiously. His baggy face looked so comically bewildered that Caitlyn felt her irritation evaporate.

She gave a rueful laugh and reached out to pat his massive head. "Never mind. The British aristocracy love dogs, don't they? So covered in dog slobber, I should fit right in with Vanessa's friends."

She started to rise from the floor and Bran sprang up again, coming forwards to snuffle in the folds of her tunic dress.

"What is it, Bran?" asked Caitlyn. "What are you looking for?"

The dog whined and sniffed earnestly again, then raised his head and looked at Caitlyn, a questioning expression in his dark eyes.

"Oh! You're looking for Nibs, aren't you?" Caitlyn guessed, laughing. She should have known. It had been love at first sight when Bran had met the kitten, and the mastiff was always excited to be reunited with his little friend. Now, he looked hopefully at her and whined again, softly.

"Yes, I've brought Nibs with me," Caitlyn assured him. "But he's run off in the Manor somewhere. He's not here in the Library."

She wasn't sure if the dog understood her, but the mastiff gave a gusty sigh and laid his enormous head down on Caitlyn's thigh, effectively pinning her in place. She laughed and gave up, letting herself relax, and eased her weight back against the wall behind her. It felt a bit silly, sitting here on the floor in the corner of the Library, but there was also something quite nice about it. They were tucked cosily away in a sort of alcove behind the bookcase—like somewhere hidden and safe to watch the world—and the weight of the dog's head on her lap was strangely soothing. *Almost like a furry weighted blanket*, she thought with a grin as she gently stroked the wrinkles on Bran's velvety brow.

After a several minutes, however, her legs started to go to sleep. Wriggling her numb toes, Caitlyn tried to shift Bran off so that she could get back to her feet. He was like a dead weight. She heard a deep rumbling sound fill the air. *He's snoring,* she realised, looking down at Bran in dismay. *Great. The stupid dog has fallen asleep.*

She poked him softly, trying to wake him up, but to no avail. She was just wondering if she could gently heave his head off her lap when a sound on the other side of the Library made her look up. Through a gap between the bookcases, she saw a slight figure enter the Library and begin moving down the room. It was a young man—probably one of Vanessa's friends who had arrived early. She was about to call out a greeting when something about the way the young man was walking made her pause. His movements were quick, almost furtive, and he kept casting nervous glances around, as if checking to see if anyone else was in the Library.

He approached the centre of the room and paused beside one of the old leather armchairs. His back was to Caitlyn, but there was something familiar about that tweed jacket with the leather elbow patches... The next moment, he turned so that his profile was illuminated by the lamp on the side table, and Caitlyn caught her breath as she recognised him: it was the clumsy young man who had come into *Bewitched by Chocolate* earlier that day and asked for directions to Huntingdon Manor.

She watched him curiously as he cast a furtive glance around once more, then slowly reached into his jacket pocket and withdrew something that glinted in the light from the lamp. *It's the metal necklace he'd dropped in the chocolate shop,* she realised. As she watched, the young man held the necklace up with the end of the chain pinched between his thumb and forefinger, so the heavy pendant dangled freely beneath. The action reminded Caitlyn of Pomona in the Widow Mag's bedroom earlier that day and then it hit her: *Of course!* This was a dowsing pendulum, similar to the serpentine one they had found in the old witch's bedroom.

The young man began walking in slow circles, his gaze fixed on the gold cone pendulum as he muttered something under his breath. Every so often, he would approach a bookcase and hold the pendulum up against the rows of books. The gold cone swung haphazardly, sometimes fast, sometimes slow, and the young man watched it avidly. Once or twice he seized a volume and pulled it off the shelf, only to return it with a sigh after he'd flipped through its pages.

What's he looking for? Wondered Caitlyn, thoroughly intrigued now. It was obviously a book, and she had a feeling, from the furtive way he was behaving, that it wasn't a book he wanted to be openly searching for.

The young man turned suddenly and approached the bookcase beside her. Instinctively, Caitlyn hunched down. It was silly—she should really have just spoken up and showed herself—but something made her shrink back instead. The darkened alcove, formed by the angle of the wall behind the bookcase and the lack of lamps in this corner of the Library, meant that most of the area was hidden in shadow. If she kept very still, he might not notice her...

In fact, the young man seemed so intent on the books in the bookcase that he barely even glanced in her direction. He stretched his arm out, holding the dowsing pendulum up and moving it slowly along the spines of the books. Then, just when Caitlyn thought he was about to give up and turn away, he froze. Eagerly, he reached up towards the top shelf. There was a moment of urgent rustling as he pulled out several volumes, then cast each aside with a frown... before he gave an exclamation of triumph.

Caitlyn craned her neck to see. The young man was staring down at a fat textbook in his hands. It was open, and Caitlyn saw with a jolt of surprise that a rectangular cavity had been cut out of the centre of the thick stack of pages, creating a hollowed-out "hiding place" within the textbook. In that hollow space lay another book. The young man lifted it out slowly and held it reverently up to the light. It was a slim volume, almost like a journal or a diary, with curling yellow pages and leather covers cracked and worn with age. There was some writing on the front cover, and Caitlyn caught her breath, her eyes widening.

It was too dark to read properly, but as the light from the lamps strayed over the young man's shoulder and played across the faded gold leaf of the embossed letters, Caitlyn caught one word: "*...Grimoire...*"

Chapter Eight

Caitlyn's twitch of surprise accomplished what she hadn't managed to do earlier—it awoke Bran. The English mastiff stirred, snorting and grunting, and pedalled his legs, trying to lever himself upright. The movement and noise startled the young man, who gave a yelp of fear as an enormous dog seemed to appear out of the shadows behind the bookcase.

"Aaahhh!" cried the young man, stumbling backwards as Bran yawned in his face, showing off an impressive set of fangs set in cavernous jaws.

Caitlyn sprang to her feet, wincing as her toes tingled unpleasantly to life, and hobbled over to him. "It's okay... it's just Bran... he won't harm you," she said—an assurance that was spoilt the next moment by Bran shaking himself vigorously. Slobber flew in all directions and the young man recoiled in horror as a slimy string of drool landed on his forehead. He dropped the book and scrabbled blindly at his face.

"It's just dog drool," said Caitlyn, trying to calm him down.

"Bloody hell... I thought it was Cerberus come to life, venomous drool and all," he said, his chest heaving. He eyed Bran warily. "Should that thing be allowed indoors?"

"He's Lord Fitzroy's dog," Caitlyn explained. "And Bran's a gentle giant. Really, he's incredibly sweet."

She bent to pick up the slim, leather-bound volume he had dropped, but the young man snatched it out of her hands before she could turn it over and look at the front cover.

"Ahh... thanks," he said, smiling awkwardly.

"What is it?" asked Caitlyn, resisting the urge to snatch the book back.

"Oh... just some old book I found," said the young man, dismissively. He turned away from her and made a show of scanning the bookshelves around them. "Um... it's an incredible library, isn't it? Really impressive for a private collection. So many priceless first editions and rare titles—"

"Is that what that book is?" asked Caitlyn, ignoring his attempt to change the subject. "I saw you take it out from where it was hidden in that textbook."

He flushed. "Were you spying on me?"

"No, of course not! I was playing with Bran earlier and just happened to be sitting in the alcove behind the bookcase. I saw you come into the Library... with your dowsing pendulum," she added pointedly.

The young man gave a shifty laugh. "Oh... er... yeah, that's just a little hobby of mine. You know, just a bit of fun..."

"What are you searching for?"

"I... er... well, I'm always on the lookout for rare and valuable books. I'm a book dealer, you see," he explained. He held a hand out to Caitlyn. "Percy Wynn. I own a bookshop in London, specialising in rare books."

She returned his limp handshake. "Caitlyn Le Fey. We met earlier, actually—you came into the chocolate shop in Tillyhenge and asked for directions."

"Oh, of course!" cried Percy, smiling. "I thought you looked a bit familiar. Sorry, didn't immediately recognise you in your glad rags. Those Florentines were smashing, by the way. I helped myself to some on the way here. Really, the best I've ever tasted."

"Thanks," said Caitlyn, refusing to be distracted. "So... what's this book you found?"

"Oh... it's nothing, really..." said Percy, with a shrug. "Just an old homemade recipe book, it looks like. Probably compiled by some local housewife... haha... I suppose it must have got mixed up with the more scholarly volumes through careless archiving." Quickly, he retrieved the hollowed-out textbook and slipped the leather-bound volume back into the cavity, then closed it firmly.

"But why is it hidden like that—"

"Oh, that was probably a mistake. I mean, hollow book safes were a fairly common gimmick for hiding things, especially in olden times. Modern safes didn't become easily available until the 1800s, you know." He indicated the textbook. "This old thing was probably modified to hide jewellery or personal knick-knacks or something and then got relegated to the Library... and the recipe book probably got shoved in there at random. Anyway, I'll just return everything to the way it was," he said, hurriedly, reaching up to slide the textbook back onto the top shelf of the bookcase and then rearranging the other books he had pulled out around it.

Caitlyn started to speak, then stopped as they heard a commotion in the hall outside: a babble of excited voices accompanied by thumps and laughter. It sounded like the other guests had arrived. Bran's ears pricked up and he padded eagerly out of the Library.

"Ah! Sounds like Vanessa's arrived with the rest of the crew," said Percy, brightly. "Come on, I'll introduce you to everyone—"

He put a hand under Caitlyn's elbow and urged her towards the Library door. Reluctantly, she let herself be led away, although she threw a lingering glance back at the bookcase. Was it too much of a coincidence that they should have been searching for a *grimoire* earlier... and then one turned up here in the Library? But what was it doing at the Manor? *I must come back later tonight and check it out*, Caitlyn promised herself. *At least I know where it's hidden now.*

Then her thoughts were completely distracted by the sight of the newly arrived guests in the front hall, with Mosley hovering around them and Bran wagging his tail excitedly beside the group. There were three young woman and a young man, all exuding style and sophistication. Their clothes were beautifully tailored, made with quietly luxurious fabrics and accessorised with classic pieces of jewellery and fine designer accessories. The girls all looked as if they had just stepped out of a salon, with immaculate hair and make-up, whilst the young man looked like he could have graced the cover of a men's magazine, with his muscled physique displayed to perfect effect in a cashmere polo neck and Neapolitan wool blazer. Instantly, Caitlyn felt like a "dowdy duckling" and her insides clenched anxiously, her steps slowing as she approached the group.

"Percy! You're here already!" squealed one of the girls, rushing forwards.

Percy faltered to a stop as the girl threw her arms around him and gave him an enthusiastic hug. Shifting uncomfortably, he patted her arm awkwardly and said. "Hi, Ness... er... great to see you."

The girl tossed back her long blonde hair and turned to Caitlyn. She had a heart-shaped face and big grey eyes—so like her brother's!—thickly fringed with dark lashes. Her delicate make-up highlighted her "English rose" complexion and rosebud mouth, making her look sweet and childlike, almost like a doll. The angelic effect was enhanced further by her outfit: a snowy white cashmere sweater embellished with gold sequins, paired with designer jeans.

Caitlyn realised that she was staring and hastily dropped her eyes, not wanting to seem rude. The other girl, however, seemed to have no such qualms. Vanessa Fitzroy continued looking curiously at her for several moments longer, until Caitlyn was practically squirming in her shoes.

"Ness, is that your brother's new girlfriend?" drawled one of the other girls at last.

Vanessa blinked and seemed to come to herself. She gave Caitlyn a bright smile and exclaimed: "Sorry, darling! I didn't mean to stare. It's just that you're nothing like my brother's usual girlfriends—" She clapped a hand over her mouth, looking like a little girl who had been caught saying a swear word. "Oh cripes, that sounded rude—I'm sorry! I didn't mean—"

"It's... it's okay," stammered Caitlyn. "And I'm not really your brother's... I mean, we're not..." She trailed off, not knowing what to say.

In truth, despite the constant gossip and speculation that surrounded them, Caitlyn didn't know what the official status of her relationship with James Fitzroy was. Their one attempt at a "date" had ended in total disaster, and they had both been so busy since— James with the new restaurant on the estate, and Caitlyn with the boom in business at the chocolate shop—that they hadn't had much of a chance to spend private time together. So she was shy about calling herself his "girlfriend", even though Caitlyn knew that there was something between them that went beyond the normal romantic clichés.

Still, it doesn't help things when

you're introducing yourself, she reflected dryly. Clearing her throat, she tried again, saying simply: "I'm Caitlyn Le Fey. I live in the village with my grandmother—she owns the chocolate boutique there."

"Yes, and her grandmother makes the most divine chocolates," Percy piped up. "I stopped in the shop to ask for directions and met Caitlyn earlier."

"I thought you two were looking very chummy when you walked in together," said the other young man, with a smirk. "You're a fast mover, Perce."

Percy flushed. "No... Caitlyn and I are just... We bumped into each other in the Library and... it wasn't... I mean..."

The other young man laughed at Percy's discomfort and came forwards to offer his hand to Caitlyn. "Hi, I'm Benedict. Vanessa's ex."

"Oh..." Caitlyn shook his hand, slightly taken aback. She glanced at Vanessa, who seemed completely unperturbed by this unorthodox introduction. In fact, the girl was grinning good-naturedly as Benedict dropped a lazy muscled arm around her shoulders. *Maybe that's the way the fashionable set lives?* Caitlyn wondered. *Everyone is best friends with their ex and carries on like it's totally normal.*

"And I'm the 'bestie'," said the girl, with the drawling voice, giving Caitlyn an ironic smile as she came forwards. She was a stocky girl with dark, shrewd eyes in a rather horsey face. "I'm Victoria Fanshawe-Drury—but you can call me Tori," she added, coolly giving Caitlyn a once-over. Then she turned and pointed to the last girl, who was standing slightly apart. "And that's Katya. Part-time model, Chelsea darling, fashion 'It' girl, and Daddy Novik's little princess... *and* Katya still finds time to meditate daily with healing crystals and journal her dreams for cosmic clarity. Is there anything this girl doesn't do?"

She spoke in a joking tone, but there was a sour edge to Tori's voice that made Caitlyn wonder about the group dynamics. Still, looking at Katya as the other girl sauntered over, she could see how anyone would be envious. Katya was strikingly beautiful, with high cheekbones, delicate features, and a long-legged, willowy figure that could have easily graced any catwalk. For all Tori's expensive clothes and carefully applied make-up, she was no match for Katya's exotic beauty, and it was obvious from her pinched mouth that she knew it.

"This is terrific!" exclaimed Vanessa, beaming and clapping her hands like a little girl—and seemingly oblivious to the undertones in her group. "We're going to have the most brilliant fun together! I've got the whole weekend planned. We're going to have early morning rides around the grounds and do clay pigeon shooting and—"

"Ness... you told us were coming up here to relax," groaned Tori.

"Riding and shooting *are* relaxing," said Vanessa, airily. "Besides, it's only you who's a lazy cow in the mornings, Tori. Katya's up at dawn every day, doing yoga and casting morning circles for her manifestation rituals, and even Benedict's up early doing his workouts."

Tori turned to Caitlyn with a smirk. "Benedict's one of those ponces who's always up at the crack of dawn, going to the gym to 'pump iron' and measure his biceps."

Benedict flushed. "That's bollocks! I just like to stay fit, and what's wrong with that? Better than turning into a fat cow." He shot Tori's stocky figure a pointed look.

The other girl scowled, but before she could retort, Mosley cleared his throat and said diffidently:

"Excuse me, sir, but may I ask where you have parked your car? It is just that with the Samhain Festival on this weekend, some of the usual places in the rear yard have been appropriated for various games and activities."

"I parked in one of those spaces by the coach house restaurant. You know, next to that old stone well. That do?"

"Ah yes, sir. That should be fine." Mosley turned to Vanessa and gave another diffident cough, then said apologetically, "Miss Vanessa, I am afraid I haven't been able to give you your old bedroom as there is an issue with the plumbing in the bathroom. Would it be all right to place your bags in one of the guest bedrooms, alongside your friends? I have taken the liberty of placing a basket of fruit with some seasonal selections in there," he added.

"Oh yes, of course, Mosley," said Vanessa, distractedly. "By the way, where's James—"

Her words were interrupted by the tall figure of the very man in question, coming in through the front door of the Manor. James Fitzroy paused in surprise, his gaze taking in the front hall filled with luggage and people, then his face lit up as Vanessa rushed towards him.

"Ness! It's great to see you. When you did you arrive?" he asked, sweeping his younger sister into a hug.

"Just ten minutes ago. Oh my God, James, the traffic was dreadful from London! I thought we were going to be stuck on the M40 all night... and Benedict kept losing his rag... and then Katya thought she was going to be carsick... then when we got near Tillyhenge, there was the most awful smell as we passed one of the farms—honestly, James, I thought I was going to throw up! You should tell them to stop putting whatever it is on the fields."

James smiled down at his sister, looking unperturbed by the

extraordinary torrent of nonstop chatter. Before he could say anything, though, she rushed on, gesturing to the others and saying:

"You know Tori, of course... and that's Katya, I don't think you've met her before, have you? Katya's father owns half the factories in Eastern Europe or something... and this is Benedict Danby. Benedict and I were going out for a while, but then we decided that shagging was a bore so we're just friends now. His father owns Danby Antiques and Fine Art. We have some pieces from them in the London house, don't we?"

James nodded a greeting to them all, then glanced across the room at Caitlyn and touched his sister's arm, saying: "And I hope you've met Caitlyn? She's—"

"Hey there, beautiful people! What did I miss?"

Everyone looked up at the sound of the loud American voice. The next moment, Caitlyn saw Pomona descending the grand staircase into the hall. Her cousin looked stunning, with her blonde hair swept into an asymmetrical side arrangement that matched the one-shouldered dress she wore, and her blue eyes highlighted by dark kohl liner. She swept down the last few steps to join them and beamed at everybody.

"Hello! You must be James's baby sister, right?" she said, grabbing Vanessa's hands. "You've got the same eyes and that famous Fitzroy charm." She grinned. "I'm Pomona. Caitlyn's cousin all the way from LA..." She spun towards Tori and looked admiringly at the other girl's feet. "Omigod, are those Louboutin boots? They're to-die for! I've gotta see if I can get a pair... Well, hel-looo," she purred as her gaze lit on Benedict and took in his handsome features and muscled physique. She gave him a wink. "This party just got a *lot* more interesting..."

Caitlyn watched enviously as Pomona moved through the group, making friends with carefree ease. She could see everyone instantly responding to her cousin's bubbly personality and she wished, for the hundredth time, that she could have a bit of that social confidence. Then she looked up and caught James gazing at her with a soft expression in his eyes. He gave her a little smile and she felt a rush of love and gratitude. It was as if she could hear his voice saying: *I don't mind you being shy and quiet; I don't need you to be a social butterfly*—and she felt her spirits lifting.

The hubbub of talk and laughter was suddenly interrupted by the sound of a gong, and they all turned in surprise to see Mosley proudly brandishing a mallet striker in one hand and holding a miniature brass gong in the other.

"Good God, Mosley, where did you unearth that from?" laughed James. "I've told you, there's really no need for such formality any more. I know my father favoured the old way of doing things, but I really prefer a more casual style."

"Sounding the dinner gong is a most respectable tradition, sir," said Mosley, looking hurt. "It has great merit in providing a clear announcement of the evening activities and ensuring timely attendance in the Dining Room—"

"Oh God, we're not going to sit down to a stuffy formal dinner, are we?" complained Vanessa, pouting. Then she snapped her fingers. "I know! I've just had the most brilliant idea: let's go and have a picnic in the Portrait Gallery instead!"

"A picnic?" James frowned at her.

Vanessa giggled. "Yes, we can take some food and have it sitting on a blanket in the middle of the Portrait Gallery." She turned to Katya. "That's the room I was telling you about, Katya! It's filled with all sorts of weird, spooky things that my father collected. It's positively creepy!" She gave a mock shiver as she giggled again and clapped her hands. "Ooh, it'll be the perfect start to a Samhain weekend!"

"But the Portrait Gallery is not a suitable venue for food consumption," said Mosley, looking aghast. "Not only are there priceless paintings of the Fitzroy ancestors, but the artefacts from the late Lord Fitzroy's occult collection are extremely valuable and delicate—"

"Aww, don't be such a cowpat, Mosley!" cried Vanessa impatiently. "It's not as if we're going to have a food fight and smear sauce all over the walls." She turned pleading eyes to her brother. "Can we, James? It'll be such brilliant fun!"

James hesitated. "Mosley's right. It's

not really appropriate—"

"Oh, come on, James! Don't be so square! You've got to break the rules sometimes. I promise we'll be on our best behaviour! Please, James... please?" Vanessa wheedled.

James wavered, seeming no match for his younger sister's cajoling. "Oh, all right," he said, giving her an exasperated but fond smile. "We'll have a 'picnic dinner' in the Portrait Gallery."

Chapter Nine

Caitlyn hung back as the group made their noisy, laughing way to the upper floor of the Manor and along the hallway that lead to the Portrait Gallery. She wished that James had vetoed his sister's suggestion. She couldn't think of a less inviting place to have dinner than in the Portrait Gallery: a long chamber that ran the length of the building and housed the collection of oil portraits depicting the Fitzroy ancestors.

As a room that was officially shut to the public, the Gallery had a musty, neglected air, which would have already made it an unappealing place to linger. But it was the presence of the old Lord Fitzroy's occult collection—an assortment of objects with mythical, magical, or supernatural connections—that really gave the place a creepy atmosphere.

Not that everyone shared her unease, Caitlyn reflected as she glanced ahead to see Pomona at the front of the group. Her cousin loved the Portrait Gallery and eagerly jumped at any excuse to visit and poke around the eerie collection. With her own passionate interest in magic and the paranormal, Pomona had been delighted to find a kindred spirit in James's late father. Now, she barely waited for James to unlock the heavy wooden door before reaching eagerly for the brass ring handle to open it.

The metal-studded door swung open with a soft swish, instead of dramatically creaking like the beloved horror movie cliché, and Caitlyn gave herself a mental shake. It was just an old, unused room, with stale air and dusty furniture, and she was silly for always feeling so edgy about it.

Still, as everyone filed slowly into the Gallery, it was obvious that she wasn't the only one feeling the "creepy vibe". The group had fallen silent, conversation dying and laughter drying up as people stared around them. On one side, a long wall hung with oil paintings stretched away from them, and on the other, a row of tall, arched windows, each with a view onto the Manor grounds. Moonlight streamed in through the curtains, sliding over the collection of ghostly white shapes occupying the centre of the room.

"Wh-what are those?" Katya whispered, pointing a finger at them.

"Relax! They're just cabinets covered with sheets," said Pomona, picking up the edge of one white shroud and flipping it over to reveal a glass display case filled with various items.

James had switched on the row of chandelier lights that hung down the midline of the room, but even so, the Gallery remained cloaked in shadows. Tori and Katya huddled closer to Vanessa, looking around with wide eyes.

Vanessa herself didn't seem too bothered, but perhaps that wasn't so surprising, given her familiarity with the room from childhood. She did survey the room with a thoughtful expression on her face, though, and Caitlyn hoped that she was having second thoughts about the "picnic".

She glanced at the men, wondering if they, too, were affected by the eerie atmosphere. Percy was shifting his weight, looking nervous and trying not to show it. Benedict, however, seemed completely at ease and hurried forwards to examine the cabinet that Pomona had uncovered, his eyes glowing appreciatively as he bent to peer through the glass pane.

"Blimey, that looks like a genuine ancient Greek astrolabe," he murmured, touching the glass reverently. "And that alchemy set with alembic and crucible must be from the Renaissance era. Look at those Latin inscriptions! And this..." He bent to get a closer look. "This looks like it could be an Ælfpoca, a magical elf pouch. I've only seen drawings of those in books. Never realised they actually existed. This must be worth a fortune—"

"Check out that Victorian skeleton clock," said Pomona, pointing to an item at the back. "It's a memento mori piece, isn't it? I'd love to own something like that."

Benedict smirked. "You'd be paying a pretty penny for it. I've seen similar memento mori pieces go for tens of thousands at auction." He suddenly moved to the other side of the case. "Bloody hell... this is one of the best preserved witch bottles I've seen! Sixteenth century, definitely, and it even has an intact clump of human hair. I can just imagine what that might fetch at auction."

"What's a witch bottle?" asked Tori, coming over to peer through the glass.

"Oh, it's just one of those things that were used to protect against witchcraft," said Benedict, rolling his eyes. "Load of superstitious nonsense, of course, but still, its value as an antique—"

"It's not superstitious nonsense," said Katya sharply. "Witch bottles can counteract spells and magical attacks. But they need to be made correctly; you need to fill them with iron nails or human hair or even urine—"

"What? Carry a bottle of pee around to protect against witchcraft?" said Tori with an incredulous laugh.

"It can also be heart-shaped pieces of fabric or other personal items," said

Katya. "The important thing is that they have to be objects that can trap evil."

"Oh, my pee will do that after a big night at the pub, no question," said Benedict, grinning.

Katya scowled at him. "It is not a joke! These items can have great power. Like that…" She pointed to a piece of cord lying on the glass shelf next to the witch bottle that had several knots tied along its length. "That is a witch knot. It is another kind of protective charm. The best ones are made with the hair of saints, the whispers of monks, and the blessings of priests—" She paused and glared at Benedict, who guffawed at her words. "—and when you tie a specific sequence of knots, while chanting a special incantation, you can bind a witch in place and drain her of her magical abilities, making her powerless."

Pomona looked at Katya with admiration. "Wow! You know a lot about witch stuff."

"Yes, Katya is amazing!" said Percy, gazing at her with adoration.

Katya gave an embarrassed shrug. "It is a subject that has always fascinated me, ever since I was a little girl."

"Me too!" said Pomona, beaming. "I was always, like, reading books and watching shows about witches and magic."

"Yes, me as well," said Katya, looking delighted to have found a kindred spirit. "I even wanted to study this at university, but of course, my parents said no." Her face clouded. "They do not approve of my interest in such things, and they forbid me from taking any classes about witchcraft and the occult." She paused, then said with a defiant smile, "But they cannot stop me. I always find ways to learn, without them knowing." She glanced at Vanessa. "I was so excited when Ness told me that her father has a whole room full of things to do with magic and witchcraft. I could not wait to see it."

Caitlyn also looked at James's younger sister, who didn't seem to be listening to the discussion. Instead, she was staring at the witch knot in the glass display case with an odd expression on her face: fear mingled with curiosity. She blinked and looked up, though, when she heard her name mentioned.

"Yes, I thought it would be just your cup of tea, darling," she said, smiling at Katya.

"I must say, Ness, I didn't think it would be *your* cup of tea," said James, giving his sister a slightly quizzical look. "I was surprised to hear you suggest a picnic in here. When you were younger, you were always terrified of this room and refused to come in the Gallery. So much so that I used to tease you about it all the time. In fact, I remember once, I even tricked you into coming in here late at night and you screamed the place down." He shook his head, laughing at the memory. "I was soundly punished by Father for it... don't you remember?"

Vanessa gave a weak smile. "Oh... oh yes, I remember now." She shifted her weight, looking embarrassed. "Well... um... people grow up and change, don't they?"

"Good thing too, otherwise I'd never have had the chance to see these beauties," said Benedict, turning back to the glass display case and eyeing the items inside with relish. "This place is like Aladdin's cave! I can't imagine what the lot would fetch at auction..."

He glanced over his shoulder at James. "Any thoughts of selling the collection, Fitzroy? I could get it valued immediately and streamline the whole process. My father has the best contacts in the country—hell, the world—and we could handle everything for you, for a small commission, of course."

James shook his head. "Thank you,

but I have no desire to sell. This collection was important to my father, and while I don't share his obsession, I feel that it should be preserved in his memory. I might consider donating it to a museum at some point."

Benedict pulled a face. "Donate it to a museum? Are you mad? This lot here is worth a bloody fortune! Seriously, you could make a tidy sum. Enough so that you don't need to worry about opening the Manor to the public and having to deal with plebs coming and gawking at your home all day."

James gave him a polite smile. "I don't have an issue opening Huntingdon Manor to the public. I think that in this day and age, it is actually our moral duty as large estate owners to share our properties with others, rather than just keeping them for our selfish enjoyment."

"What do you mean, 'selfish enjoyment'?" cried Benedict. "These are our homes, man, handed down through generations. Of course we have a right to enjoy them! No one wants to see their house overrun with tourists and turned into a bloody coach tour destination."

"I beg to differ," said James in an even tone. "There's a great satisfaction in seeing visitors from other countries experiencing the delights of an English stately home and knowing that ordinary couples can plan their weddings in the grounds and make use of the beautiful rooms. I've even been approached to use the Manor as a film location. I think adapting to new uses gives the estate a new sense of purpose and ensures that it remains of worthwhile value to the local community."

Benedict shook his head in contemptuous disbelief. "Well, let me know if you change your mind, Fitzroy. I know many private collectors who would give their eyeteeth for some of these items, and you'd be crazy to say no to all that dosh—"

"It's not always about the money, Benedict," Katya cut in suddenly. "You're just like my father! He can never understand that either. There are some things that have a value beyond what you can put in your pocket. I mean, that witch bottle—it's priceless for protecting against curses and evil spells. You cannot replicate the magical aura from such an ancient bottle easily. That is an authentic piece with real power—not a cheesy Hallowe'en toy made by companies who just want to exploit Samhain traditions for capitalist greed!"

Caitlyn turned to look at Katya, slightly surprised by her vehemence. Beside her, she heard Tori mutter under her breath: "Bit rich when your father is the biggest example of capitalist greed and you're benefiting from Daddy's purse strings."

Katya flushed slightly as she felt everyone's eyes on her, but her expression remained defiant.

"Whoa... no need to get your knickers in a twist, Katya," said Benedict, raising his hands in a gesture of surrender. "I was just trying to do Fitzroy a favour."

"No, you're not. You're just thinking of... of your 'main chance'—that's what it's called, isn't it?" snapped Katya. "You're just like a cheap car salesman, always looking for a way to make a fast buck!"

There was an awkward silence following this outburst, then Tori cleared her throat and said: "So... are we going to have this picnic or not? I'm famished!"

"We should not have dinner here," said Katya, looking uneasily around the room. "The butler was right. It is wrong and disrespectful to eat in here. This is a solemn place devoted to magic and should not be desecrated."

Everyone looked at Vanessa expectantly, and to Caitlyn's relief,

James's sister didn't argue this time. In fact, Vanessa seemed to have lost some of her previous enthusiasm for a "spooky picnic", and she followed her brother quietly as James led the way back out of the Gallery.

Chapter Ten

Mrs Pruett was delighted to hear that dinner was returning to the orthodox setting and that she could serve the lavish four-course meal she had prepared in the conventional way. However, despite the delicious food, everyone seemed to be slightly subdued. Vanessa had insisted on sitting at the opposite end of the long table to James, and the rest of the guests were spaced out in between them. The seating arrangement, coupled with the formal grandeur of the Dining Room, seemed to turn the meal into a stilted affair, and Caitlyn was relieved when the last course was brought out.

She had been seated too far away to speak to either James or Vanessa properly; instead, she had been placed between Katya and Tori, and had found it a strain trying to ignore the simmering tension between the two girls. She was also very aware of Vanessa's scrutiny; several times, she had looked up to find James's younger sister watching her intently and had squirmed in her seat, wondering what the other girl was thinking. Was Vanessa puzzling over what James had seen in her? Did she think Caitlyn wasn't good enough for her brother?

As the last dessert plates were removed and tea and coffee were served, a tray of chocolate truffles was brought out and offered around the table with great flourish by Mosley. The luxurious confectionery seemed to work wonders, with the mood turning mellow and everyone becoming more chatty and relaxed as they enjoyed the rich, decadent flavours.

"Mmm... these are scrumptious," said Tori with her mouth full. "Don't think I've ever tasted such incredible chocolates."

James smiled. "These are from *Bewitched by Chocolate*. That's a chocolate shop in the village that belongs to Caitlyn's grandmother. We're incredibly lucky to have such a skilled chocolatier in Tillyhenge," he added proudly, catching Caitlyn's eye across the table.

She flushed with pleasure and smiled back.

"Is that the shop you were talking about earlier, Perce?" asked Benedict, making a show of tossing a truffle into the air and catching it with his mouth.

"Yes, the one in Tillyhenge. It's got all sorts of amazing chocolates and sweets." Percy looked at Katya across the table from him and added shyly,

"Er... actually, I thought of you, Katya. I remembered you saying that you love Florentines and I bought an extra packet. I... I can bring it over to your room later, if you like?"

"Aw, that's sweet, Percy," said Katya, not even looking up as she fiddled with a truffle on her plate. "Don't worry—you can just give it to me at breakfast tomorrow morning."

As Percy tried to conceal his disappointment, Caitlyn saw Vanessa watching them with a slight frown on her face. It was the same expression that Caitlyn had seen several times on Vanessa's face during dinner, whenever Percy had tried to flirt with Katya or get the latter's attention. Caitlyn began to wonder just how much James's sister liked the young book dealer.

Katya stood up suddenly and covered her mouth as she yawned. "You'll have to excuse me. I am really tired. I think I'm going to go to bed early tonight."

Everyone began making similar noises and moves to get up from the table. Caitlyn hurried over to Pomona as they followed the others out of the Dining Room.

"Oh, Pomie... I'm so glad to get a chance to talk to you at last," said Caitlyn, grabbing her cousin's arm so that they fell back from the others. "I've been bursting to tell you about this all through dinner."

Pomona looked at her expectantly. "Tell me what?"

"It's something I found in the Manor Library. Well, actually, it was Percy who found it. I arrived early and went to wait in the Library, and I saw him come in— this was before everyone else had arrived—and he was walking around with a dowsing pendulum—"

"A dowsing pendulum!"

Caitlyn nodded eagerly. "Yes, I recognised it! Just like the one we found in the Widow Mags's bedroom. Well, except that his had a gold cone pendulum instead of a serpentine stone. Anyway, he used it to find a book hidden inside another one, up on one of the shelves." She lowered her voice. "It was a really old, leather-bound notebook that looked a bit like a diary or journal or something and—listen to this, Pomie—I saw the word '*grimoire*' written on the cover!"

Pomona stared at her. "No way! Are you sure? It said '*grimoire*'?"

"Shh! Keep your voice down!" Caitlyn hissed. "Yes, I'm sure that's what it said."

"Did you see what was inside?"

Caitlyn shook her head regretfully. "Percy snatched it out of my hands before I could open the book to have a look. He put it back where he found it and then everyone else arrived, so we left the Library. But it's still there! And we can go back—"

She broke off as she suddenly became aware that Vanessa, who had been walking ahead of them, had slowed down and was very close in front. She saw James's sister cocking her head slightly, as if listening. Had the other girl overheard their conversation?

Hastily, she said, in a louder voice: "Er... yes, so I think you'd love this book I found in the Library on... on cosmetics in the Middle Ages! It's full of really fascinating information—"

"Didn't women do crazy things at that time?" asked Benedict, turning around from in front of them. "Putting all sorts of poisonous things on themselves, like lead paste on their faces to make their skin white."

"Yeah, and arsenic," said Pomona with a grimace. "I saw a show on TV last year that was all about this. They used freakin' arsenic for hair removal—can you believe it?"

"And belladonna juice to make their pupils dilate so that their eyes looked bigger," said Tori with scornful amusement. "You always read about that one in magazines and books."

"That's how the deadly nightshade plant got its popular name," said Percy, eager to add his contribution. "It means 'beautiful woman' in Italian—*bella donna*—see?"

Tori gave a sarcastic laugh. "It should have been called '*donna stupida*', if you ask me. I mean, how daft can you get? Squeezing juice from deadly nightshade berries straight into your eyes!"

"Well, to be fair, people didn't have the benefit of scientific knowledge then, so they didn't really understand the toxic effects of deadly nightshade," said James.

"They knew enough to know that it was dodgy," argued Tori. "Belladonna—

deadly nightshade—was associated with witches, wasn't it?"

"Yes, belladonna is a witch's plant," said Katya softly. "It was used in witches' flying ointments and for visions and divinations. The juice of the berries can give you great power if you know how to unlock them..."

Tori rolled her eyes. "Yeah, power to kill people! Isn't belladonna one of the most powerful poisons out there?"

"Yes, but only in high doses. Atropine—the active ingredient in the berry juice—is actually still used today for medicinal purposes. Ophthalmologists use it, for example, in eyedrops so they can dilate their patients' pupils and examine their eyes properly," said James.

Tori gave Vanessa a wry look. "Your brother is like a walking encyclopaedia."

Vanessa giggled. "I know! He was worse when he was working for the BBC as a foreign correspondent: he always knew every detail of every political situation and world disaster and economic crisis that was happening at the time."

"Yeah, but James can even make a Wikipedia entry sound sexy with that gorgeous British accent of his," said Pomona, with a wink at Caitlyn.

James looked embarrassed and hastily changed the subject, turning to Caitlyn and saying: "You're not planning to go back to Tillyhenge tonight, are you?"

"Well, yes, I was..." Caitlyn trailed off as she glanced at the time on the grandfather clock in the front hall. She was surprised to see that it was later than she'd thought.

"You shouldn't drive back in the dark," said James. "Why don't you stay the night?"

"It's only a few minutes' drive back to

Tillyhenge," protested Caitlyn.

"I can ask Mosley to have a guest room prepared in no time," James insisted. He gave her a tender look. "Stay. Please."

Caitlyn blushed, aware that the others were watching them. She was touched by James's obvious desire to have her around a bit longer. "Well... thank you, that would be lovely... Oh, but I haven't brought any things for an overnight stay—"

"You can borrow some of my stuff," offered Pomona.

"It's settled, then," said James quickly, smiling. "You'll stay the night. I'll go and see Mosley about it right away."

He left them, and Caitlyn followed the others to the foot of the sweeping staircase in the front hall. Tori, Benedict, and Vanessa were busily discussing their plans for the next day, but Katya had turned away and was starting up the stairs. Percy hurried after her, saying breathlessly:

"Er... Katya? Fancy... fancy a nightcap in the Library? I... er... there's something I want to show you in there, something that I think you'd really—"

"Sorry, I told you: I'm tired and I want to go to bed," said Katya impatiently, brushing Percy's hand off her arm. Without another word, she turned and ran up the staircase, disappearing beyond the top landing.

"Now there's a brush-off if I ever saw one," said Benedict with a chuckle as he came up behind the other young man. He gave Percy a mock punch in the shoulder. "Bad luck, mate. But don't worry—*I'll* keep you company for that nightcap, eh? Won't be quite as romantic, but I promise you I'll help you drown your sorrows."

Percy flushed, looking both chagrined

and mortified. He winced as Benedict slung a proprietary arm over his shoulder, but he made no protest as the other young man steered him away from the staircase and back down the hallway towards the Library.

"Kinda an odd couple, huh?" said Pomona, watching them.

Caitlyn nodded. She wouldn't have expected the cocky, self-assured Benedict to have been overly friendly with a bookish type like Percy. "Maybe they've got interests in common that we don't know about. I mean, the group seems to have been friends for a while, so they must enjoy each other's company."

"You wouldn't know it from listening to Tori," muttered Pomona. "Talk about a bitter, jealous cow."

"Shh—she'll hear you, Pomie!" Caitlyn admonished, looking worriedly up the staircase, where Tori and Vanessa had started ascending to the upper floor. Luckily, they still seemed to be deep in conversation and barely glanced backwards as they reached the top landing and made their way to Tori's room.

Pomona shrugged, but she refrained from saying anything else until they were in her own room and out of earshot. As soon as they'd shut the door, she flopped onto the bed and curled up against the pillows, obviously settling down for a good gossip.

"Did you see Tori at dinner?" she said. "It's obvious that she can't bear Katya being prettier than her and being so popular back in Chelsea, even though Katya's not 'old money' like she is. I heard her actually trying to put Katya down as a 'nouveau riche' wannabe, and I'll bet she would have said more, except that she knows Vanessa likes Katya, so she can't get *too* nasty. But you can tell that she's just dying to scratch Katya's eyes out!" She giggled.

"Well, Katya *is* gorgeous," said Caitlyn with a wistful sigh. "You can see how anyone would feel envious when they're around her—"

"It's not just about looking like a model," scoffed Pomona. "You gotta have personality. Take it from me. Gorgeous girls are, like, a dime a dozen in Hollywood. The ones who get the attention are the ones with more than just a pretty face and a perfect body."

"Well, Katya seems to be getting plenty of attention, especially from the boys," said Caitlyn, thinking of Percy.

Pomona chuckled, putting her hand over her heart in a theatrical manner. "Oh yeah, especially Percy, right? Man, that guy's got it *ba-aad* for her. I kinda feel sorry for him 'cos he's *so* not in her league!"

Caitlyn shifted uncomfortably. Pomona's words reminded her of her own insecurities.

"What?" asked Pomona, instantly noticing.

"Nothing... it's just... well, I'm sort of not in James's league either," said Caitlyn in a small voice.

"Honey, that's totally different! Katya barely notices Percy, whereas you know James loves you—"

"He's never actually said that," said Caitlyn quickly. "I mean... okay, maybe he likes me and enjoys my company, but that doesn't mean he really... Maybe it's just like a... a... 'pleasant diversion' for him, you know? Like he's a nice guy and he's just being gallant—"

"That's bull," said Pomona rudely. "Anyone can see that James has been smitten with you from the day he met you. Seriously, Caitlyn, what else does the poor guy have to do to convince you that he's into you?" She gave Caitlyn an impatient look. "You know what the problem is? It's *you,* not James. *You've* got this hang-up about not being good enough for him or whatever, and it's *your* insecurities that are the problem." She leaned forwards. "Honey, if *you* don't believe that you're good enough for him, then you really never will be."

Caitlyn swallowed, not wanting to admit that Pomona's words had hit a bit too close to home. Hastily, she changed the subject: "Anyway, enough talk about me. What about you?"

"What d'you mean—what about me?" said Pomona, looking puzzled.

"Well, you know... with what happened to you recently, with Thane Blackmort..." Caitlyn faltered. Her cousin had seemed to bounce back so quickly from her traumatic experience that it seemed almost abnormal. "You went through a lot, you know. You were practically kidnapped and held hostage and brainwashed, for heaven's sake! Most people would need therapy after that."

"I guess all that therapy in my teens must have topped me up," Pomona quipped.

"But maybe it *would* be good for you to talk to someone about it—someone professional, I mean," persisted Caitlyn.

"Only if he's cute."

"I'm serious, Pomie! It's... it's not normal to be so blasé about things!"

"Hey, take it easy," said Pomona, giving her a reassuring pat on the arm. "I'm dealing with things my own way, okay? I mean, I kind of went through this weird phase right after everything happened when I was seeing Blackmort everywhere." She made a face. "You know, like you're out shopping and you look up and think you see him in a crowd across the street... or you're trying on clothes and you suddenly see him standing behind you in the mirror, looking at you with those icy blue eyes..."

She gave a shudder. "And I knew it was stupid 'cos I'd heard that Blackmort had gone to develop some new business interests in Outer Mongolia or Siberia or somewhere like that. So I knew that he was out of the country and was gonna be, like, gone for a long while. But still, I couldn't help—" she broke off as she saw Caitlyn's look of increasing concern and added hurriedly: "Anyway, it's a lot better now, Honestly. I've stopped doing that. I know it's just my mind playing tricks on me."

"Well... if you need to talk... or if there's anything I can do..." said Caitlyn hesitantly.

Pomona gave her hand a quick squeeze. "You betcha! Now, c'mon—let's see if I have a spare toothbrush..."

She bounced off the bed and disappeared into the ensuite. Caitlyn sighed and followed Pomona into the bathroom, deciding to let the subject drop.

Chapter Eleven

They washed their faces, cleaned their teeth, and got ready for bed, falling into the old familiar routines of giggling and teasing each other. As she watched Pomona rummage through her wardrobe for something that could double as makeshift pyjamas, Caitlyn was taken back to the many years of sleepovers that they'd had together.

"Don't you have anything that's not made of neon satin or see-through lace or covered in diamanté?" she asked in exasperation as she rejected yet another of Pomona's offerings. "Like an old T-shirt that you wear to the gym or something?"

"The gym? What's that? I get all my exercise going up and down escalators in shopping malls," said Pomona with a grin. She turned back to the drawer and rummaged again, then drew out a stretchy top in hot pink. "How about this?"

Caitlyn blanched. "Don't you have something in a more... er... *neutral* colour?"

"What about this? Orange is kinda neutral, isn't it?" said Pomona, holding up a bright tangerine T-shirt.

Caitlyn sighed and took the T-shirt. It seemed to be the best of a bad lot. At least it was fairly loose and long enough to cover her bum, although the colour clashed horrifically with her red hair.

"Here, you can wear them with these," said Pomona, tossing her a pair of (thankfully) plain black leggings.

"Quick, put them on, and then we can go down to the Library to check out that book you were telling me about."

"What?" Caitlyn paused in the act of pulling on the leggings. "I'm not going downstairs dressed like this!"

"Why not?" Pomona looked at her in surprise.

"Because... because I look a fright!" hissed Caitlyn. "What if we bump into someone? What if James sees me?"

"James would think you looked great if you were wearing a black garbage bag," scoffed Pomona, waving a hand. "Anyway, he sleeps in the other wing so we're probably not gonna bump into him."

"What if he's still downstairs?"

Pomona grabbed a bathrobe that was hanging on the back of the bathroom door. "Here, this is a spare one. Put this over your T-shirt and leggings."

Caitlyn took the fluffy robe gratefully, relieved that it was in a muted mink colour, and drew the soft, fleecy fabric around herself. "I still think we should wait a bit before going down."

Pomona gave a long-suffering sigh. "Fine! We'll hang around for a while and make sure that everyone's asleep."

"Benedict and Percy might still be in the Library, anyway, having their nightcap," Caitlyn reminded her. "We can't search for the *grimoire* if they're still there."

"Nah, I think I heard them go past in the hall a while ago," said Pomona. "Didn't you hear their voices? But it's all quiet now."

It was true. The corridor outside did seem very quiet. Still, Caitlyn insisted on waiting at least half an hour, and Pomona grudgingly agreed. She fidgeted and paced, though, watching the hands of the clock like a hawk, and tried to argue that they should "get going" every five minutes. To try and distract her, Caitlyn told Pomona about her frustrating attempt to ask the Widow Mags about her *grimoire*.

"Her *grimoire* is gone?" Pomona stared at her disbelievingly. "No witch loses her *grimoire*!"

"She said it was *stolen* from her. And Pomie, I think I know who took it: I think it was my mother!" said Caitlyn excitedly. "As the Widow Mags's daughter, Tara would have known her habits and routines, and she'd be in the best position to steal it."

"Plus she was supposed to be this witch prodigy, wasn't she, your mom?" added Pomona. "Like, much more powerful than usual for her age and experience?"

"Yes, she was probably one of the few people who could have broken through the Widow Mags's protective spells guarding the *grimoire*," Caitlyn agreed.

"Maybe it's why the Widow Mags won't ever talk about her!" said Pomona eagerly. "Stealing another witch's *grimoire* is, like, the ultimate betrayal. And in this case, it was done by her own daughter! That must really sting—"

She broke off as she caught sight of the clock. "Hey, it's been thirty minutes. C'mon!" She rushed over to the bedroom door and opened it a crack. "The coast looks clear."

Caitlyn came up behind her and peered doubtfully over her shoulder. "Maybe we should wait a bit longer, just to be sure—"

"Aww, c'mon, Caitlyn! At this rate, it'll be morning," said Pomona impatiently. Without waiting for a response, she slipped out of the bedroom and disappeared down the corridor.

"Pomie, wait—!"

Caitlyn sighed and hurried after her

cousin. She caught up with the American girl at the bottom of the main staircase, and together they tiptoed through the downstairs rooms, making for the Library. She was relieved to see that Pomona seemed to right: it *did* look like everyone had retired for the night. There were some distant noises coming from the rear wing, which housed the kitchen and old servants' areas, but everything was quiet on this side of the house. The main lights had been switched off, with only a few lamps left on to provide some lighting in the darkened rooms and hallways.

The Library itself was also dimly lit, the soft glow from the tall lamps in the corners barely penetrated the gloom. Caitlyn shivered slightly as she made her way between the bookcases. She didn't normally think of the Library as a creepy place, but tonight it seemed to have an ominous air. Shadows leaped and stretched across the walls, seeming to move at random.

"What's that?" she asked suddenly, stopping and jerking around.

"What?" asked Pomona, pausing a few steps behind her.

"I thought..." Caitlyn looked around her. "Did you see someone just now?"

"Uh-uh." Pomona shook her head.

"It felt like someone brushed past me," said Caitlyn, touching her right shoulder.

"Maybe you just felt a draught or something."

Caitlyn cast another uneasy look around, then turned back to lead the way to the bookcase in the far corner. She hadn't gone more than a few steps, though, when a small black shape shot out of the shadows and attacked her ankles. She gave a gasp and jerked back, colliding with Pomona.

"Ow! That was my toe you stepped

on!" cried Pomona indignantly.

"Sorry! It's just something jumped out at me—" Caitlyn made an exasperated noise as she looked down and realised what the dark shape was. "Nibs!"

The kitten ignored her, scampering away across the floor of the Library after some imaginary prey. He pounced and rolled over, knocking against a narrow side table, which wobbled alarmingly.

"Nooo... Nibs!" Caitlyn groaned as she rushed to catch the table. She managed to steady it just in time to prevent the vase on top of it from tumbling off and smashing on the floor.

"That kitten is gonna break something and bring everyone running in here," grumbled Pomona.

Nibs came bouncing past again, and Caitlyn hastily bent and scooped up the kitten.

"*Mew!*" cried Nibs, squirming and

looking up at her indignantly.

"Sorry, Nibs, but we can't have you making noise in here," said Caitlyn in a whisper. "Go on... go and play somewhere else," she urged, carrying him to the door of the Library and giving the kitten a gentle shove out of the room. Then she hurried back to Pomona, who was peering at the bookshelves ahead of them.

"Which one is the *grimoire* in?" her cousin asked.

"That one," said Caitlyn, pointing to a bookcase in the far corner. She led the way, circling around a set of armchairs that blocked their path. "It's up on the top shelf, hidden inside a textbook that had the middle hollowed out—"

She broke off, her eyes wide with shock as she came around the side of an armchair and saw the crumpled body lying at the base of the bookcase. It was Percy. His body was bent at an odd angle, with one hand seeming to clutch his chest, but it was the unnatural stillness about him that made Caitlyn's heart lurch uncomfortably.

"Omigod... is he dead?" gasped Pomona, seeing the body as well.

Caitlyn rushed over and dropped to her knees beside the young bookdealer. She reached out hesitantly with one hand to feel for a pulse in his neck. His skin felt cool and clammy. There was no pulse.

"Y-yes, I think so," she said, her voice trembling.

"What do you think happened?" asked Pomona in a hushed voice. She peered at the body. "I don't see any blood or any injuries. Do you think the poor guy had a heart attack?"

"I don't know... It looks like it but—"

Caitlyn broke off as she glanced up and saw the gap on the top shelf of the bookcase where a thick volume had been pulled out. Quickly, she dropped her gaze to the floor again and almost instantly saw a familiar thick textbook lying face down a few feet away. Leaning over, she snatched it up and flipped it over. The hollowed-out cavity was empty.

"It's gone!" she said, showing the empty cavity to Pomona. "The *grimoire* I was telling you about—it was in here!"

"Holy guacamole... Percy must have caught someone trying to steal it, and when he tried to stop them, they killed him!"

Turning back to Percy's prone form, Pomona bent and peered at the dead man's body. "Look... his other hand is sort of twisted under his body," she said, pointing. She reached out and began trying to roll Percy over.

"Pomie! What are you doing?" cried Caitlyn, aghast. "You shouldn't be moving him—"

She broke off as Pomona suddenly heaved the body over and Percy's trapped arm splayed out freely, showing what had been clutched in his hand and hidden under his body: a piece of parchment paper with ragged edges, like a page that had been torn from a book.

Caitlyn watched, transfixed, as Pomona carefully wriggled the paper out from Percy's grasp and smoothed it flat, holding it up to the light for both of them to see. It was a faded yellow page, with dark, spidery handwriting covering one side.

"...*whisk together one cup of enchanted caster sugar and 5 fluid ounces of spellbound cream, then fold into the melted dark chocolate...*" read Pomona, tilting her head. "Looks like some kind of recipe—"

"That's the Widow Mags's handwriting," said Caitlyn suddenly, staring at the dark scrawl on the page.

"Really?" Pomona looked at her, her eyes shining with excitement. "You know what? I'll bet this came from that hidden book Percy found—and I'll bet that was the Widow Mags's stolen *grimoire*!"

Chapter Twelve

Caitlyn shut the door of her bedroom behind her and made her way softly down the corridor, her feet making no sound on the plush carpet. The Manor was unusually quiet the next morning, and she wondered if any of the other guests were up yet. She knew that Pomona was likely to still be asleep—her cousin was definitely more an owl than a lark!—but after the disturbed night, she wouldn't have been surprised if everyone else was lying in too. By the time the ambulance and police left, and the staff had finally been sent home, the early hours of the morning arrived before any of them had gone to bed.

She herself had only had a fitful rest, but she had woken up soon after sunrise and been unable to go back to sleep. Instead, she had lain wide-eyed in bed, replaying the events of the night before in her mind—and, in particular, that awful moment when she had come across Percy's body. Sighing, she quickened her steps, heading for the top of the staircase that led down into the front hall. She had barely turned the corner of the corridor, however, when she was startled by a bloodcurdling shriek. The next moment, a door on her right was flung open and Katya came running out. From her flushed face, tangled hair, and the rumpled state of her pyjamas, she had obviously just got out of bed.

"There's... there's... there's a man... hanging from my ceiling!" she gabbled, grabbing Caitlyn's shoulders and pointing a shaking finger back at her room.

"What?" Caitlyn's heart lurched as she instantly imagined a lifeless body swinging from a noose.

Before she could ask more, however, doors were flung open further down the corridor and they were joined by Tori and Benedict. They were both bleary-eyed and dishevelled too, and had obviously rushed straight out of bed after hearing the commotion.

"What is it? What's happened?" asked Benedict, stifling a yawn.

"Yes, I heard a scream—was that you?" demanded Tori, looking at Katya accusingly.

"You would have screamed too if you woke up and saw a strange old man hanging upside down from your ceiling!" retorted Katya.

Caitlyn caught her arm. "Wait a minute—did you say, 'old man hanging upside down'?'"

Katya nodded and pointed to her bedroom doorway again. "Yes! You go and see for yourself!"

Caitlyn had a sinking feeling that she knew exactly who was in the girl's bedroom. Her worst suspicions were confirmed when she went into the room and saw the old man who was hanging upside down, seemingly attached to the ceiling by only his feet. He was wearing an ancient black suit, with coattails that were now flopped over and hanging past his ears, and he had a few wispy grey hairs carefully combed over his balding head. His sunken mouth looked like it was missing more than a few teeth, but his rheumy eyes were bright and keen as he peered down at Caitlyn.

"Ah... Caitlyn, my dear! How nice to see you."

"Viktor!" hissed Caitlyn, glaring up at him. "What are you doing up there?"

"Having a good night's kip—what does

it look like? I normally prefer the east corner of the Library, but there were so many people in there last night making an infernal noise! Police and paramedics and whatnot... I decided to find a quieter spot upstairs." He glanced approvingly at the ornate plaster moulding on the ceiling. "Very comfy cornices here. I might start sleeping upstairs more often—"

"Viktor, you can't just randomly wander into guests' bedrooms like this!" said Caitlyn in exasperation. "Come down now! Quick, before the others come in!"

"All right, all right... no need to get your fangs in a twist," muttered the old man.

He bent his knees and seemed to push off from the ceiling, turning a somersault in midair before landing nimbly next to Caitlyn. She glanced hastily over her shoulder and was relieved to see that the others were only just stepping into the room and hadn't seen Viktor's strange acrobatics.

Tori and Benedict came slowly forwards, eyeing the old man with some surprise. Given the strength of Katya's hysterics, this was not what they were expecting to see. The girl herself approached Viktor warily, stopping just behind Caitlyn and asking in a quavering voice:

"Who... who are you? Where did you come from?"

Viktor swept her a gallant bow. "Allow me to introduce myself: I am Count Viktor Dracul of the Megachiroptera Order of Vampi—"

"Er... just Viktor will be fine," cut in Caitlyn hastily. "And now, shall we all get dressed and go downstairs for breakfa—"

"How were you hanging like that?" asked Katya suspiciously. "I saw you: there was no rope or anything. Your feet were just stuck to the ceiling, as if... as if by magic!"

"Oh, Viktor's a... um... ex-circus performer," Caitlyn babbled. "He's very... er... athletic still and can hang from all sorts of—"

"Eh? What are you talking about?" said Viktor, looking at Caitlyn irritably. "I've never been to the circus in my life! Dreadful places, full of bendy people..." He turned to Katya and gave a modest cough. "Suspending from any structure is a fortunate facet of my shapeshifting abilities, due to my other form being a—"

"Shapeshifting!" cried Katya, her eyes bulging. "Are you a Púca? Or... or a spriggan? I know the veil between the worlds is thinnest at Samhain and malevolent spirits are everywhere!"

The old man bristled. "A Púca? How dare you! Do I look like a grubby gnome? And while I have occasionally shifted into creatures different to my native fruit bat form, I draw the line at goats, thank you very much. Mangy, flea-bitten beasts..." Viktor drew himself up to his full height. "I am a vampire, an Ancient Guardian Protector of the Other Realms, and as a member of that noble race, I always conduct myself with dignity and decorum—"

"You're a *what?*" said Benedict with a laugh.

"Er... what Viktor meant to say is that he's my... my uncle!" said Caitlyn quickly, trying to give everyone a breezy smile. "He's... um... got a very vivid imagination."

"Your *uncle?*"

"What is your uncle doing in my room?" demanded Katya, starting to sound hysterical again. "How did he get in? I'm sure I locked my door last night—"

"Pff!" said Viktor, with a dismissive

wave of his hand. "What are locks to a master infiltrator like me? I can enter any room I wish—"

Katya gave a squeal of horror. "Are you saying you broke into my room while I was sleeping?"

"You dirty old man!" exclaimed Benedict. "Are you some kind of peeping Tom?"

"Eh? Who's Tom?" said Viktor, looking confused. "No, I was merely explaining that my powers of penetration are impressive, especially when you consider my age. But, of course, that's only to be expected after the extensive training I've gained from comprehensive intercourse with various creatures of the Otherworld..."

Stop... Don't say anything else! Caitlyn groaned silently as she saw the others staring at Viktor with horrified disbelief and disgust.

The old vampire continued, oblivious

to the expressions on the faces around him. "Of course, it is easier to enter places when I am aided by my vampire powers of invisibility." He threw out his arms to either side and bent his knees, looking like a geriatric skateboarder. "I can glide unseen through shadows, drift as ephemeral mist, meld into the night... In fact, I can demonstrate if you like—"

"Uhh—no, no! That's fine, Viktor, I'm sure everyone gets the idea!" cried Caitlyn, grabbing his arm and dragging him out of the room. "Look, why don't you go down and see what Mrs Pruett has prepared for breakfast today? We'll leave everybody else to wash and dress."

With the others still watching in befuddlement, Caitlyn hustled Viktor out of Katya's room and down the corridor. It wasn't until they were on the landing at the top of the staircase that she paused and breathed a sigh of relief.

"Viktor! You can't do that!" she

chided, giving the old vampire a severe look.

"Do what?"

"You can't just barge into people's bedrooms and sleep on their ceilings! Especially when James has guests at the Manor—"

She broke off as she realised that Viktor was no longer listening. Instead, he had stuck his head out on his scrawny neck and was sniffing the air in an exaggerated manner.

"What? What is it?" asked Caitlyn.

"That scent..." Viktor frowned, turning his head back and forth like an animal scenting the air. "It is familiar and yet... I cannot quite place it..."

"What scent?" asked Caitlyn, looking around in confusion.

There was no one about; the landing was empty. On one side was the corridor they had just come from, leading to the guest bedrooms, whilst on the other side of the landing, a short corridor led to the wing where the Manor's master bedroom and other family rooms were situated. A hall table stood in the middle of the landing, showcasing an enormous arrangement of flowers: a mixture of dahlias, anemones, and faded hydrangea blooms, with sprigs of fragrant rosemary interspersed among the flowers.

"Is it the flowers?" she asked Viktor, pointing to the arrangement. "There's rosemary in there—"

"No, no, not the flowers... It is a scent from another time..." muttered Viktor. "I know it... it is most familiar and yet..." He made an irritable noise, tapping the side of his head. "Confounded garlic! This memory is not what it used to be."

Then he froze, turning his head towards steps sweeping down to the front hall. "Wait—!"

"Is the scent coming from downstairs?" asked Caitlyn.

"No, no, I can smell stewed prunes for breakfast!" said Viktor excitedly. He sniffed the air again. "Mmm... yes... and a spiced autumn fruit compote as well. Cox's apples, raisins, pears—Williams, I believe... Mmm, that Pruett woman might be an old windbag but she certainly knows how to cook." He rubbed his hands with glee. "This is too good to miss!"

Without a backward look, Viktor trotted down the sweeping staircase and disappeared from sight. Caitlyn sighed, feeling a mixture of exasperation and affection for the old vampire. Among the many surprises she had received since arriving in Tillyhenge, one of the biggest had been the revelation that not only did witches exist but that vampires did too. And they weren't the creepy, bloodthirsty womanisers usually portrayed in film and literature either.

No, they were more likely to be grumpy old men with an addiction to fruit salad and an ability to turn into a fuzzy brown fruit bat. It turned out that vampires were a misunderstood ancient race, with each individual following the diet of the type of bat they shifted into. In Viktor's case, this meant that he was an avid fruitarian who spent most of his waking hours searching for a juicy plum.

When he isn't searching for his lost fangs, thought Caitlyn with a wry smile. Still, she knew that she had to thank Viktor for coming to her rescue more than once in the past. The old vampire took his role as her "guardian uncle" very seriously, and despite often finding him exasperating, Caitlyn felt warmed by the thought that there was someone out there, always waiting to protect her.

The sound of her name jolted her out of her reverie, and she turned to see Vanessa coming from the other corridor to join her on the landing.

"Morning!" she said, giving Caitlyn a bright smile. "Am I the last one up?"

"Er... no, I think my cousin Pomona is still sleeping," said Caitlyn, fidgeting self-consciously.

As always, Vanessa looked effortlessly chic in a soft, pastel-blue cashmere sweater paired with high-waisted corduroy jeggings and calfskin boots— the perfect blend of contemporary fashion and countryside casual. Next to her, Caitlyn felt gauche and gawky, in spite of wearing a jersey dress borrowed from Pomona that was far more trendy than anything she normally possessed.

"Um... I hope you slept well?" she said awkwardly.

"Like a log! Which sounds awful, I know," said Vanessa, pulling a face. "Poor Percy. I did wake up and think of him first thing. What a terrible thing to happen... who would have thought you could have a heart attack at twenty-six!"

Caitlyn eyed Vanessa curiously. Last night, she had somehow got the impression that Vanessa had liked Percy much more than "just a friend"—and yet this morning, the girl didn't seem to be acting like a grief-stricken lover either. Some of Caitlyn's thoughts must have shown on her face, because Vanessa added hurriedly:

"You're wondering how come I don't seem more upset, since Percy was my friend. But people die sometimes, you know. It's very sad, but it happens. It's just your time to go and there's nothing you can do about it," she said philosophically. "The best thing everyone else can do is go on living and be happy. That's what my mum told me when she was dying of cancer."

"Oh!" Caitlyn stammered. "Oh, I'm sorry... I didn't realise that your mother... James never said... I'm very sorry—"

"Don't be sorry! She died ages ago. Not that I don't miss her, of course, but

I try to do what Mum told me and be happy now. I'm sure Percy would have felt the same way. His parents died when he was fairly young too, you know, and he always used to say that the best way of honouring their memory was to enjoy life. And it's not like he died a horrible death, is it? The paramedics last night said that he probably had a heart attack, and that happens very quickly," said Vanessa ingenuously. "At least Percy wasn't murdered or something, was he?"

"Er... well..."

Vanessa's eyes widened. "Do you think something happened to him?"

Caitlyn hesitated. She didn't feel like she knew James's sister well enough to feel comfortable voicing her suspicions. "I don't know. I suppose we should wait for the coroner to confirm things before jumping to conclusions," she said at last, trying to compromise between being diplomatic and being honest.

Thankfully, Vanessa seemed to have lost interest already. Instead, she glanced down the corridor leading to the guest wing and asked: "Where are the others? Are they up yet?"

"They're up, but I think they're going to need a bit of time to wash and dress," said Caitlyn. She indicated the stairs. "I'm just heading down first."

"You're not leaving already, are you?" asked Vanessa, falling into step beside her as they began to descend the staircase.

"Well, I *was* planning to head back to Tillyhenge after breakfast—"

"Oh no, you have to stay for the weekend!" Vanessa pouted. "I want everyone here so we can have a big house party for Samhain!" She looked at Caitlyn earnestly. "It'll be a great chance for us to get to know each other."

Caitlyn felt pleased that James's sister wanted to get to know her. "I'd love to stay," she said, smiling shyly. "But I'll still need to go back to Tillyhenge to get some things. I didn't bring an overnight bag last night, so I've been borrowing Pomona's stuff—"

"Oh, make sure you bring back some riding gear! We might go for a hack around the estate this afternoon."

"Er... actually, I'm not much of a rider," said Caitlyn, feeling embarrassed.

"Oh, don't worry. The horses here are great. That's one of the best things about coming up to Huntingdon. James always says that I practically live in the stables whenever I come up here." Vanessa giggled.

A soft, alluring fragrance wafted over Caitlyn and she paused. "Your perfume—"

"Oh, d'you like it?" Vanessa beamed at her.

"It's gorgeous. Did you have it on

when you arrived yesterday?"

"No, I only put it on before dinner. Why?"

"Oh..." Caitlyn frowned. "I just thought I might have smelled it when you first arrived. It seems vaguely familiar." She shook her head. "It's probably just similar to a perfume I've smelled before—"

"Oh no, it can't be. It's a custom fragrance made up by a *parfumerie* in Paris. I mean, Givenchy and Dior and all that are nice, but who wants to be one of the millions of women wearing Chanel N°5 I wanted something nobody else would have except me." Vanessa smiled. "It was James's gift to me for my last birthday. Wasn't that sweet of him?"

Chapter Thirteen

Vanessa was keen to visit the stables before breakfast, but Caitlyn declined the invitation to join her. She wanted to grab some food quickly so that she could pop back to Tillyhenge as soon as possible. As she was making her way to the Morning Room, however, she was stopped by Mosley, who directed her to James's study instead.

"Inspector Walsh is with his Lordship, madam, and he has asked to see you as soon as you were down. Would you like me to bring you a cup of tea or coffee in the study?" asked Mosley.

"Oh, don't worry, Mosley. I'll just get something in the Morning Room afterwards, thank you," said Caitlyn.

She hurried to the study, pleased at the prospect of being able to speak to the CID detective. There had only been uniformed constables in attendance last night, and she had felt uncertain about voicing her vague suspicions to them. She knocked on the study door and opened it to find James behind the big mahogany desk, with a grizzled middle-aged man in a sombre grey suit sitting in a chair facing him.

"Caitlyn... good morning!" James's face lit up as he saw her and he made to rise, with Inspector Walsh following suit.

"No, please, don't stand up," said Caitlyn, waving them back into their seats as she walked over to join them.

"Good morning, Miss Le Fey," said Inspector Walsh. "I trust you slept well?"

Caitlyn gave him a polite smile. "Yes,

thanks. Er... Mosley said you wanted to see me?"

The inspector inclined his head. "Just tying up some loose ends." He indicated a slim folder on the desk in front of him. "I read your statement, which was all neat and tidy, but my constable mentioned that you didn't seem entirely happy with the paramedics' assessment that the young man died of natural causes?"

Caitlyn shifted uncomfortably. "Well, I'm not a medical professional but..."

"Yes?"

"It's just... well, Percy was only in his mid-twenties and seemed fit and healthy. Surely people don't have heart attacks at that age?"

Inspector Walsh raised his eyebrows. "You might be surprised, Miss Le Fey. It's true that heart problems tend to be more prevalent in the elderly, but that does not mean that it is unknown in younger age groups. Statistics show that in the UK, around twelve per cent of all heart attacks occur in people under the age of fifty, and some are as young as their twenties."

"Really?" said Caitlyn sceptically. "You mean, because they are overweight?"

"Not necessarily. It could be due to a congenital heart defect or an underlying health condition."

"Actually, even extreme stress can lead to heart problems in young people," James spoke up. "In my days as a journalist, I did a piece once on young athletes who developed cardiac issues from overly intense physical training. It can lead to things like irregular heart rhythms."

"But did Percy have a heart condition?" persisted Caitlyn.

"Well, not according to his medical records," Inspector Walsh admitted. "But it may be an undiagnosed one. We will know for sure once we have the results of the autopsy. That's being performed today, so if I'm lucky, I may get a preliminary report this evening. But I would say that all early signs point to a natural death."

Caitlyn thought of Percy's limp body, crumpled at the base of the bookcase. There had been nothing "natural" about the way he had looked. "But... what about the missing book?"

Inspector Walsh opened the folder and leafed through the written statements, coming at last to hers. "Is this the so-called 'secret book' that was hidden inside the textbook on the floor next to Mr Wynn's body?"

Caitlyn frowned, not liking his tone. "Yes, it was inside a hollowed-out compartment that had been cut out of the pages of the textbook."

Inspector Walsh raised his eyebrows. "And you are *sure* about this?"

Caitlyn nodded. "I saw it myself."

"The thing is... I have been speaking to Lord Fitzroy and he can find no trace of this hidden book," said the inspector.

James gave Caitlyn apologetic look. "Er... yes, I checked the official Library catalogue and there doesn't seem to be a book that matches your description."

"Well, of course it wouldn't be in the official catalogue. It was hidden! It was a secret book that nobody knew about," said Caitlyn impatiently.

"A book 'that nobody knew about' is hardly likely to be the target of a burglar, Miss Le Fey," pointed out the inspector.

Caitlyn looked at him defensively, "Are you suggesting that I imagined it? I'm telling you, I saw it! Earlier in the evening, I saw Percy open the textbook with the hidden cavity and take another book out from inside. And then I saw him return that 'hidden' book to the cavity and put the textbook back in the bookcase. When I found his body, that same textbook was lying next to him and it was empty. And he was also clutching a torn page in one hand, which was probably from the book. So it's clear that whoever killed Percy must have also stolen the book!"

"On the contrary, Miss Le Fey, that is not an assumption we can make at all. It is pure conjecture at this point. We do not know yet if Mr Wynn's death is indeed suspicious or if anyone else *was* present at the crime scene. So far, there is nothing to support your claim of Mr Wynn being killed during a 'robbery gone wrong'. There are no obvious injuries on him, and there are certainly no signs of a break-in at the Manor or an intruder anywhere on the estate last night."

Caitlyn bristled and was about to retort when James interrupted in a diplomatic voice: "Perhaps if Caitlyn could give us more information about this book, Inspector, it might help you appreciate its possible role in the events."

The inspector's expression changing to one of deference. It was no secret that James Fitzroy's position as local landlord and his quiet air of authority commanded great respect from the police, with Inspector Walsh always involving him deeply in any investigation. Now, the old detective gave a grudging nod and turned back to Caitlyn.

"You said you saw it—what kind of book was it?"

"I... well... I didn't really get a chance to look at it properly," admitted Caitlyn. "It was a small leather-bound volume, almost like a diary or a journal." She hesitated, then added in a rush, "I think it might have been a *grimoire*... a book of spells. And I think it might have belonged to my grandmother, the Widow Mags. I saw her handwriting on the torn page."

"We have that page as evidence. It appears to be part of a recipe for chocolate cake," said Inspector Walsh dryly. "Hardly the kind of thing that could inspire murder."

"But it's not just any old chocolate recipe," said Caitlyn quickly. "The *grimoire* would have contained all sorts of spells and magical recipes—"

Inspector Walsh's eyebrows climbed up into his hair. "You think Mr Wynn was murdered because someone wanted to steal a book of magical chocolate spells?"

Caitlyn flushed at the inspector's sarcastic tone. She'd forgotten that the old detective was notoriously dismissive of anything supernatural.

"Inspector, whether the book really is magical or not is immaterial," James spoke up quietly. "All that matters is that the *thief* thought it was, and therefore may have had reason enough to act violently. Caitlyn is giving us valuable information about potential motives."

Caitlyn flashed James a grateful smile. Next to him, the inspector stroked his moustache, then said:

"Yes, well, that may be so, Lord Fitzroy, but I am not convinced yet that there *is* a crime to have a motive for."

"But you should at least check everyone's movements to confirm their alibis, shouldn't you?" said Caitlyn. "Did you question all the other guests and the Manor staff last night?"

Inspector Walsh glowered at her. "I think I know how to do my job, young lady. And yes, interviews were conducted. My constables obtained statements from everybody on the premises last night. There are no obvious red flags. The staff can all vouch for each other. As for the guests..." He glanced at James, obviously uncertain about causing offence. "Well, they were all in their own rooms, until they heard your calls for help and went down to the Library. Do you remember seeing them arrive in the Library?"

Caitlyn cast her mind back, trying to remember the events of the night before. She could recall the stampede of people rushing into the Library, following her calls for help, but it was hard to remember the exact order in which everyone had arrived. James had been one of the first to arrive, instantly sizing up the situation and calmly asserting control. And there had been Mosley, of course, hurrying to follow James's instructions to notify the police and reassure staff. She could remember seeing Tori standing with an arm around Vanessa as the two girls huddled in a corner of the Library, their eyes riveted on Percy's still form. And Benedict looking pale and dishevelled—nothing like his earlier suave self, despite wearing stylish silk pyjamas—as he stood beside the girls, an expression of sick disbelief on his face. And then finally Katya, her long blonde hair tumbled around her shoulders, arriving at the door of the Library, her eyes widening in horror as she took in the scene.

"I think Tori and Vanessa were there first, followed by Benedict... and then Katya arrived last," she said, looking back up at Inspector Walsh. "There was quite a gap between her arrival and the others."

Inspector Walsh glanced down at his pile of statements again. "Hmm... Miss Novik said that she had retired early and was sleeping very deeply, which was why she didn't hear the commotion initially."

"Yes, she went to her room before anyone else," Caitlyn remembered. "But if she was alone there, there's no one to corroborate her alibi, is there?"

"There is nothing to disapprove it either," Inspector Walsh reminded her. "It is the same for Mr Danby. He, too, was in his room alone. He says he'd just fallen asleep when he heard the noise and came out to investigate."

"Benedict was the last person seen with Percy," James confirmed. "After dinner, they went for a nightcap in the Library, and then much later, I believe, Mosley saw them ascending the stairs together."

"Yes, Mr Danby maintains that he and Mr Wynn had drinks together in the Library and then they went up to bed, and this is corroborated by the butler." Inspector Walsh made a dismissive gesture. "In any case, why would any of these young people want to harm Mr Wynn? As far as I understand, they were good friends and spent a considerable amount of time in each other's company."

Caitlyn was silent. She had no good

answer for the inspector.

"Well, until I have good evidence to support a murder investigation, this will remain a non-criminal matter. Percy Wynn's death was tragic but not necessarily suspicious." Inspector Walsh stood up decisively. "Now, I have another case that requires my attention. I shall be in touch if there are any developments. Good day, Lord Fitzroy... Miss Le Fey..." He gave them each a courteous nod.

"I'll see you out, Inspector," said James, rising and accompanying the older man out of the room.

Chapter Fourteen

Caitlyn made her way slowly to breakfast, her thoughts spinning from the recent interview. In a way, she couldn't really blame Inspector Walsh for being sceptical about the possibility of murder. To all intents and purposes, it did look just like a heart attack—tragic perhaps, but hardly sinister. The only thing that suggested otherwise was the disappearance of a book that nobody had seen and no one knew about... Caitlyn sighed. No wonder Inspector Walsh had been so dismissive! From a policeman's point of view, it seemed like a clear-cut case: if there was no sign of outside intruders, then that meant that whoever had attacked Percy must have been staying on the estate, probably within the Manor. But if the staff were all accounted for, then that left only the guests. Why would any of his friends have wanted to harm Percy? To steal a so-called "spell book", which they wouldn't have even known existed?

Caitlyn came out of her thoughts to realise that she had been walking on autopilot and was now standing outside the Morning Room. Inside, she found a sumptuous breakfast buffet displayed on a sideboard and Tori, Katya, and Benedict already seated at the table, with Mosley hovering unobtrusively behind them. They all looked up as she entered, and the butler hurried to seat her.

"Please do help yourself from the buffet, Miss Le Fey. There is a selection of artisan breads and pastries, cheese, yoghurts, sliced fruit and berries, cereal, preserves, and stewed fruit... or should you wish to have eggs, I can have the kitchen prepare them to your liking. You can have a full English breakfast or you can opt for a choice of specific things to accompany the eggs. We have bacon, sausages, tomatoes, mushrooms, kippers, black pudding... oh, and Mrs Pruett has even made some kedgeree with smoked haddock from the local fishmonger, which is excellent, if I do say so myself," Mosley said, pausing for a breath at last and looking at Caitlyn expectantly.

"Uh..." She glanced over at the buffet, slightly bewildered by the exhaustive list.

"Perhaps madam would like tea or coffee first and some time to decide?" said Mosley, smoothly.

Caitlyn agreed and sat down with some relief. As soon as the butler had left the room, Katya turned to her and asked breathlessly:

"Was… were the police here again? I thought I saw that inspector from last night in the front hall, with James."

"Yes, Inspector Walsh was here, but he's just left."

Benedict looked up sharply. "Did you talk to him? Why was he back?"

Caitlyn hesitated under their expectant gazes. She wasn't sure how much she was supposed to reveal of her recent interview—or how much she *wanted* to reveal. Despite Inspector Walsh's scepticism, she couldn't help thinking that one of these young people *could* have been involved in Percy's death in some way.

"Um… he was just going over the statements. You know, tying up loose ends," she said, resorting to that old police bromide.

"So they don't think there was anything suspicious?" persisted Katya.

Caitlyn shook her head slowly. "I don't

think so. Inspector Walsh says that Percy very likely died of a heart attack."

"So you can relax—there isn't some crazy psycho running around, and you're not going to be murdered in your bed," said Tori sarcastically.

Katya ignored her and rose to go to the buffet, her expression relieved. Benedict, however, seemed more agitated than reassured by the news.

"Heart attack?" he said uneasily. "Are they sure? Percy was only twenty-six."

"Yes, and he was fairly skinny too," Tori added.

Caitlyn shrugged. "Inspector Walsh said young, slim people can have heart attacks too."

Tori frowned. "Yes, but still... Doesn't he think there could be *any* chance of foul play?"

"Do you know if Percy had any enemies?" Caitlyn retorted.

Tori shrugged. "Probably not. He was a quiet sort of chap. His life revolved around that bookshop of his. He's not from our Chelsea crowd—I think his family's from Norfolk or somewhere like that," she said, her lips curling contemptuously. "But Ness likes a 'project'," she added with a smirk. "So she took Percy under her wing. Tried to make him a bit trendier, more confident..." She snorted. "It was a lost cause, if you ask me. Percy was never going to be anything but a nerdy spod."

Glancing over at Benedict, she said: "Didn't I hear him asking you how to build more muscle to impress girls?"

"Nothing wrong with trying to bulk up," said Benedict defensively. "I showed Perce a couple of moves, gave him some tips on protein shakes and supplements."

"Did he seem all right when you left him last night?" asked Caitlyn. "It's just, you were probably the last person to see

Percy alive."

"He was fine," said Benedict. "We... we came up from the Library together and said goodnight and then went to our rooms..." His voice shook slightly and he cleared his throat, passing a hand over his eyes. "Christ, I can't believe that he died of a heart attack. He was the same age as me." He stood up abruptly. "I'm going to get some more fruit."

Caitlyn watched Benedict thoughtfully as he strode over to join Katya at the buffet on the other side of the room. He had seemed surprisingly upset about Percy. Was that just grief for a dead friend? Or discomfort at the reminder of his own fragile mortality, given their similar ages? Or was it something more... like a guilty conscience?

"Trying to play detective?"

Caitlyn jumped and came out of her thoughts to see Tori regarding her with a sly smile. She felt a prickle of dislike for the other girl, with her open snobbery and sneering manner.

"I thought you said the police *aren't* treating this as a suspicious death," said Tori.

"I'm just curious about what happened—aren't you?" Caitlyn shot back. "After all, Percy was your friend."

Tori wrinkled her nose. "I wouldn't go that far."

Caitlyn was taken aback by the other girl's cold attitude. Still, recalling Tori's contemptuous remarks about Percy's background and general person, perhaps she shouldn't have been surprised. Tori had probably never considered Percy "good enough" to be a true member of their clique, and she probably never saw him as a real person. To her, he had been nothing more than an amusing diversion.

Tori leaned forwards across the table and said in a stage-whisper: "If you're so keen to play Miss Marple... it's not Benedict you should be looking at—it's Katya."

"Katya?"

"Ohhh yes, Katya who says she was Sleeping Beauty last night..." Tori paused significantly. "Except that she wasn't."

"What do you mean?"

"Well, didn't she say in her statement that she went to bed early? Except that after dinner last night, I remembered that Katya had borrowed a Chanel eyeshadow from me. So I popped over to her room to get it and it was empty. She wasn't there."

Caitlyn looked at her in surprise. "What d'you mean, 'she wasn't there'?"

"She wasn't in her room. Her bed was empty. She had gone out," said Tori, enunciating each word slowly, like she was talking to a very stupid person. Then she gave a malicious smile and said: "So... it looks like the fabulous Miss Novik has been telling porkies to the police. Now, why would she do that? Why would she lie about where she was last night?"

Caitlyn glanced across the room to where Katya and Benedict were still busy at the breakfast buffet. "Are you suggesting that Katya might have something to do with Percy's death?"

Tori gave a languid shrug. "I'm just telling you what I saw."

"But why would Katya have wanted to harm Percy?"

"Who knows why that crazy cow does anything?" said Tori, scowling. "Katya's obsessed with magic and witchcraft and all that tripe. She's constantly banging on about moon rituals and channelling your inner goddess and crystal auras." She rolled her eyes. "And she's always having some hysterical fit or other because we didn't respect an ancient pagan tradition or something. So... maybe Percy just said the wrong thing and she freaked out and had a go at him."

Caitlyn glanced across the room again. Katya stood by the buffet, smiling and chatting with Benedict, with the morning sunshine glimmering on her long blonde hair as it cascaded over her shoulders. Even though she was obviously tired and bleary-eyed, somehow she still managed to look gorgeous, with the shadows under her eyes only seeming to accentuate her delicate beauty. Caitlyn thought of Pomona's comments about Tori's jealousy and wondered if this was just more vicious gossip.

"Have you mentioned this to the police?" she asked Tori. "If you really think that Katya might be hiding something, you should tell Inspector Walsh."

"Well, I didn't know what Katya had

said when I was giving my statement last night, did I?" said Tori sourly. "It wasn't until this morning that I heard her say she'd been sleeping the whole time and realised that she must have lied about her alibi."

Before Caitlyn could respond, Mosley returned, ushering Vanessa into the Morning Room. Tori sprang up at the sight of her friend and hurried over to greet her, followed by Katya and Benedict.

"Where have you been, Ness? We've been waiting for you," drawled Tori. "Don't tell me that you've only just got up?"

Vanessa shook her head. "No, I've been up for ages! I was out in the stables."

"I should have guessed," said Tori, rolling her eyes.

"I didn't realise everyone was at breakfast already, otherwise I would have come in sooner," said Vanessa, wandering over to inspect the buffet.

As the others followed her, Caitlyn realised suddenly that "everyone" wasn't here at breakfast: Pomona was still missing. She frowned as she glanced at the clock on the mantelpiece. Even with her cousin's usual habits, this seemed excessively late for Pomona. Surely she couldn't still be asleep?

Murmuring excuses, she left the Morning Room, but as she was about to ascend the stairs to the upper floor, she glanced through one of the front hall windows and caught sight of Pomona's bright red convertible, which was parked in the front driveway. She paused in her steps, noticing that the boot was open. The next moment, a figure emerged from behind the lid of the open boot: it was Pomona. Delighted, Caitlyn quickly changed course and headed out the front door of the Manor instead.

"Hi sleepy-head—when did you get

up? We're missing you at breakfast," she called, smiling a greeting as she went out to join her cousin. Pomona barely glanced up as she approached, standing instead with a perturbed expression and staring down into the boot of the car.

"Is something wrong?" asked Caitlyn, coming to a stop next to her cousin.

"Er..." Pomona finally looked up and met her eyes with a shame-faced look. "You know that bewitched garden hose we wrestled out of the Widow Mags's bedroom?"

"Yeah?"

"Well, remember I said I was going to keep it in the trunk of my car?" Pomona made a helpless gesture towards the rear of her convertible. "Um... It's kinda not there any more."

Chapter Fifteen

"What d'you mean it's not..." Caitlyn's voice trailed off as her gaze dropped to the empty boot of Pomona's car. "Oh my God, where is it?"

"I don't know! It was in there when I got back from Tillyhenge last night. I checked after I parked the car, before I went into the house. But just now, I came out to get some stuff I left in the trunk, 'cos I wanted to wear these new 'Hunter wellies' I bought—omigod, Caitlyn, did I tell you about them? Rubber boots are, like, so hot right now, and these are pink and super shiny and—"

"Pomie! Never mind your boots! What about the garden hose?" asked Caitlyn in exasperation.

"Oh... oh yeah... well, like I said, I opened the trunk to get my stuff and it was empty. I mean, the boots were there but the garden hose was gone."

"Are you sure you shut the boot—I mean, the trunk properly last night? Maybe you didn't push down hard enough and it was still slightly open—"

"Oh no. It was shut and locked. A hundred per cent."

Caitlyn raised an eyebrow and Pomona squirmed.

"Well, okay, maybe more like ninety-eight per cent..." She paused. "Or... er... ninety-two per cent." She paused again, then darted a look at Caitlyn. "Um... actually, thinking about it... it could be more like sixty-five per cent."

"*Pomie!*"

"How was I supposed to know that a garden hose would be such a good escape artist? Anyway, what's the big deal—it's probably just slithering around somewhere." Pomona waved a careless hand towards the grounds around the driveway. "It's not like it can bite anyone."

"No, but if any of the estate staff see it, they'll probably be terrified," said Caitlyn worriedly. She recalled the uneasy expressions of the customers in the chocolate shop yesterday when Leandra Lockwood had started talking about witchcraft and black magic. "I think people are slightly on edge because of the Samhain Festival... and anyway, even if you weren't superstitious, you'd probably be pretty freaked out if you saw a bewitched garden hose slithering around like a python!"

"Yeah, I guess," said Pomona

grudgingly. "But how are we gonna find 'Hosey Houdini'?" She gestured at the sprawling landscaped gardens around them. "The estate is enormous!"

"We've got to try," said Caitlyn urgently. "We've got to get it back before anyone sees it."

They started searching, fanning out from the parked car and making a circular sweep of each area as they moved slowly forwards. As they searched, Caitlyn filled Pomona in on the morning's events, including the talk with Inspector Walsh and the hints from Tori that Katya was hiding something.

"That girl's just jealous," said Pomona. "I wouldn't trust anything she says. She could be making the whole thing up out of spite just to get Katya in trouble."

"I did think of that," Caitlyn admitted.

"If anyone in that group is likely to be a murderer, it would be Tori," added

Pomona.

"Aww, come on, Pomie. What would be her motive? Why would she want to kill Percy? She might be a snob and think he's not good enough for their group, but that doesn't mean that she would want to *kill* him." Caitlyn sighed. "Inspector Walsh was right: why would *any* of them want to harm Percy? It just doesn't make sense."

Pomona shrugged. "Maybe they didn't mean to kill him. Maybe it was just a prank but the whole thing got out of hand. I mean, there *have* been cases of people dying of fright—like, literally 'scared to death'. Seriously!" she said indignantly, seeing Caitlyn's scoffing expression. "I saw a documentary about it on the Discovery Channel. It's called stress cardiomyopathy, or something like that."

"Okay, but even if that were true, what about the missing *grimoire*? Are you saying the person who played the prank then decided to steal the book? Isn't that a bit of a weird coincidence?"

"Well, maybe—*wait! What's that?*" Pomona froze and pointed to a small salvia bush nearby. Several of its bushy branches were rustling and moving in a suspicious way.

Pomona approached the salvia on tiptoe, stretching her arms in front of her, ready to grab her quarry. But just as she bent over to part the leaves, a ball of black fur shot out from beneath the bush and pounced on her ankles.

"*Aaaghh!*" Pomona reeled back and squealed in surprise. "Nibs! You little stinker—you nearly tripped me up!" she cried, making a grab for the kitten.

She caught hold of his collar but Nibs wriggled and fought, backing away until the collar slipped suddenly over his head. With a cheeky chirrup, the kitten turned and bounded off again.

"Wait till I catch him," muttered

Pomona with mock threat. Then she sighed and held up the empty collar in her hands. "Great. He isn't wearing his collar now."

"It's okay. All the staff on the estate know him," Caitlyn assured her. "He can't get lost. We'll just put it back on when we catch him."

Nibs popped out of the undergrowth further down the path and mewed cheekily at them, then scampered off again. He shadowed them as they continued to search the gardens, and Caitlyn hoped that the kitten's big doggie friend wasn't around as well. The last thing they needed was a huge English mastiff following them whilst they were trying to keep a low profile, searching for a bewitched garden hose!

They came at last to the large rear courtyard that surrounded the coach house restaurant and other nearby outbuildings. There were staff and estate workers moving around here, and the two girls tried to appear nonchalant as they wandered around, surreptitiously peering behind wooden barrels and looking under upturned wheelbarrows.

"This is a waste of time. We're never gonna find it," grumbled Pomona at last, stopping to lean against the side of one of the outbuildings. "It can't be anywhere around here that's obvious to see, otherwise we would have heard someone screaming. Same goes for the stables. And I don't know about you, but I'm starving," she added, pulling a face. "Let's go back and have breakfast first, then think about Plan B."

Caitlyn paused. Pomona was right, and she had to admit that her stomach was growling with hunger. Still, she hated abandoning the search. She gazed towards the other side of the courtyard, which led to the rear of the estate. There was a large stone barn in the distance.

"We haven't looked there," she

pointed. "Come on—let's just search that before we go in."

Pomona heaved a long-suffering sigh, but she followed along as Caitlyn walked up to the barn. It looked to be one of the outbuildings that had recently been converted into holiday accommodation as part of James's plans for modernising the estate. There was fresh paint on the door and windowsills, and the area in front of the building had been transformed into a small makeshift garden, with a gravel path leading up to a welcome mat outside the front entrance.

It looked like someone was already in residence: there was a pair of wellies by the front door, as well as a bicycle leaning against the side of the wall. The area around the door was also cluttered with decorative paraphernalia, such as several carved turnips sitting on the front steps and a wreath of dried autumn foliage, pine cones, and berries adorning the front door. Nibs trotted up to one of the carved turnips and sniffed it cautiously, then batted it with a paw, knocking it over on its side.

"Hey, stop that, you little monkey," said Caitlyn, reaching down to set the turnip upright again.

Pomona made an impatient noise. "Come on, Caitlyn—can we go? It's obvious Hosey Houdini isn't out here. There's nowhere, like, big enough to hide a big pile of rubber coils."

Caitlyn hesitated, glancing at the front door. "I wonder if we could look inside?"

Pomona sniggered. "Oh yeah, you're gonna go up and ring the doorbell and go: 'Hello! Have you seen a garden hose that thinks it's a snake?'"

Caitlyn turned away from the front door and pointed at the enormous elm tree to the side of the barn. "What about that?"

Pomona groaned, but she followed

Caitlyn around the side of the barn to the elm tree. Weather and age had twisted the trunk, making it lean sideways so that it looked almost as if part of it was lying on the barn roof. Caitlyn peered up into the canopy as Nibs scampered around her heels.

Pomona came up, cursing and grumbling as she tripped over the gnarled roots that sprawled around the trunk of the tree. She craned her neck to look up into the tree canopy as well and said:

"You're not seriously thinking that Hosey Houdini is up there? I mean, it might think it's a python, but it *is* still a garden hose at the end of the day. I don't think it can climb up into the branches like that python from *The Jungle Book*—"

They were interrupted by excited mewing, and Caitlyn looked back down to see Nibs perched on the edge of a large metal trough that had been left underneath the tree. This had obviously once been used for the horses or cows but was now abandoned. It was filled to overflowing from the recent rains, and Nibs was eagerly trying to dip his paws into the water.

"Nibs, stop that," Caitlyn admonished as the kitten nearly unbalanced and fell into the trough. She flashed back to the first time she saw Nibs, when she'd rescued the baby cat from drowning in a flooded quarry. Not wanting another accident, she hurried over to grab the kitten. But as she reached for Nibs, she looked down into the trough and gave an exclamation of surprise.

Submerged in the murky green water were several loops of rubber hose, coiled around itself in a cosy heap. A chain of air bubbles emanated every so often from the brass connector head, looking exactly like someone snoring.

"I don't believe it..." muttered Pomona, coming up next to her and staring at the tangle of rubber loops in the water. "Hosey Houdini is here, taking a freakin' nap!"

"Well, I suppose it makes sense, when you think about it," said Caitlyn with a laugh. "A garden hose would prefer to snuggle up in water."

Pomona gave her a sour look. "Honey, none of this makes sense. Why would—"

She broke off at the sound of footsteps approaching, and they both instinctively flattened themselves against the side of the barn. Caitlyn peered out cautiously. A slim figure was approaching them—it was Katya, and from the way she kept looking furtively over her shoulder, it was obvious that she didn't want anyone to see her coming. The two girls shrank back even more, hoping that they were out of sight. They were partially blocked from view by a large cotoneaster growing beside the barn wall, and Caitlyn was relieved to see Katya walk straight past them without a glance in their direction.

She approached the front of the barn with purpose, and her footsteps crunched on the gravel path leading up to the front door. Caitlyn ducked under the berry-laden branches of the cotoneaster and inched along the wall of the barn until she could peer around the corner of the building and get a view of the front door. Pomona followed at her heels, and they peeked around the edge of the barn wall.

Katya was standing in front of the front door, fussing with her hair. Then she knocked. There was a long pause before the door creaked open. Pomona gave a muffled gasp as a tall woman stepped out.

"You're late."

Chapter Sixteen

Caitlyn's eyes widened as she recognised the authoritative voice. It was Leandra Lockwood. It had taken her a moment to place her, since Leandra had exchanged her theatrical velvet dress and Gothic accessories for a more normal outfit of a sweater and black jeans.

"...sorry," Katya was saying breathlessly. "It was a bit difficult to get away without anyone noticing and I—"

"Hush. Come in first."

The two women disappeared and the front door shut behind them. Pomona ducked back under the cotoneaster, making her way along the wall towards the rear of the barn.

"Caitlyn! Over here!" she hissed, beckoning towards a large casement window.

Caitlyn hurried over, keeping herself hunched low. As she joined Pomona beneath the window, she was delighted to see that one of the frames had been left open slightly, probably to air the barn. Slowly, they raised themselves up so that their eyes were level with the window ledge. They were looking into a large modern kitchen with a stove and cabinets in one corner and a round table with chairs in the other. Leandra stood by the stove, her back to the window, and on the other side of the room, Katya leaned against the wooden table, fidgeting nervously. Their voices drifted out, unexpectedly loud and clear, through the open window.

"...did the police speak to you again

this morning?"

Katya shook her head. "No, but I don't think they suspect anything. I told that old inspector that I was sleeping in my room and he seemed to believe me."

"You're sure no one saw you leave the house last night?"

"I... yes, I'm sure."

"You shouldn't have come here. It was a silly thing to do."

"I wanted to see you! And out here, away from London, my parents will never know—"

"It was still very foolish of you. People talk, you know, especially the staff and villagers. They live on gossip. And don't underestimate the police. Be prepared to be questioned again. Especially if they decide that the death was suspicious after all." Leandra paused, then asked urgently: "The book that was stolen from the Library—the *grimoire*—have the police said anything about it?"

Katya gave a shrug. "No one seems to be talking about it. I don't think they're really focusing on it much, though, because the inspector doesn't believe in magic."

"More fool him," said Leandra contemptuously.

"I heard that the old witch in the village—the one who owns the chocolate shop—might be involved. There are rumours going around that the *grimoire* belonged to her." Katya looked at her earnestly. "Do you think that's true?"

"Don't worry about that old woman. Focus on this *grimoire*."

"Is it dangerous?" asked Katya, her eyes wide. "I overheard the staff talking about it. They're saying that it's a book of black magic with spells to summon demons and evil spirits—"

Leandra snorted disdainfully: "Knowledge is always dangerous, especially in the wrong hands. But in the right hands, when absorbed and deployed by the most talented witches, it can be used to accomplish incredible things. And this *grimoire*... it's an absolutely *priceless* repository of knowledge. It even has the potential to unlock realms beyond our understanding. Yes, darker, more powerful magic..." Her voice became wistful and she trailed off, as if lost in thought.

"How do you know so much about this grimoire?" Katya looked at the older woman curiously. "You sound almost as if you've seen it before."

Leandra hesitated, a distant look coming into her eyes for a moment, then she adopted a condescending expression and said: "I make it my business to know about such things. It is, after all, my field of specialty." She paused, seeming to collect herself, and added, with a return to her usual pompous tone: "Many poor ignorant souls are begging for guidance and yet have no one to look up to, no one to assuage their fears. They need someone who understands the complexity of magic rites and rituals, and who has a scholastic appreciation of ancient sacred traditions. And... and this *grimoire* offers not just spells or incantations but also pathways to revolutionising our understanding of the magical arts, through disciplined study and application, to reach new heights of enlightenment and capability."

Katya looked more confused than ever but before she could ask more, Leandra said, her tone brisk: "Now listen—the police must know more than they're letting on. That old inspector might be a tough nut to crack, but perhaps some of the younger constables would be easier to influence. You need to make them tell you more."

"But how do I do that?" asked Katya. "They'll never talk to me."

Leandra walked over to a small chest on the other side of the kitchen and rummaged inside for a moment, then at last pulled something out. She held it flat on the palm of her hand, and Caitlyn saw that it was a Celtic-style brooch with a fragment of dull, grey, weathered stone in its centre.

"This is the Silver Tongue Pin," said Leandra, handing it to Katya. "There is a piece of the Blarney Stone embedded in the centre—yes, the famous stone at Blarney Castle in Ireland, which bestows the gift of eloquence and persuasive charm upon those who kiss it. This brooch will work the same way: you simply have to kiss the stone just before you speak to someone, and you will gain the 'gift of the gab' and be able to persuade and influence them without effort."

"Really?" said Katya, her eyes shining. "That's... that's amazing! And you're trusting me with it? Oh Leandra!"

"I expect you to take good care of it, of course," said Leandra. "And make sure that you—"

She broke off suddenly and turned sharply towards the window. Caitlyn realised with horror that Nibs had jumped up on the ledge next to her and was mewing plaintively, obviously miffed at being ignored.

She jerked back from the window just as Pomona yanked her down, and the two of them crouched against the base of the wall, holding their breath. They heard Leandra approach the window and the creak of the hinges as the frame swung open fully. Caitlyn tensed. If Leandra leaned out, she would definitely see them crouched below...

"Oh! It's a kitten," came Katya's voice as she, too, joined Leandra at the window. "Isn't he gorgeous?"

Nibs let out a mew of greeting, and Katya cooed with delight as she reached out to stroke him.

"Look at him, with that pitch-black fur and those big yellow eyes—he's, like, the perfect witch's cat!" Katya laughed. "He hasn't got a collar. I wonder if he's a stray?"

"He looks too healthy to be living wild," commented Leandra. "In fact, he looks like a kitten I saw over at that chocolate shop in the village..." A bejewelled hand reached out and scooped Nibs off the window ledge, then the window was shut.

Pomona grabbed Caitlyn's elbow. "C'mon, let's get out of here..."

"What about Nibs?" Caitlyn asked.

"Oh, he'll be fine. We can just ask James to come and get him later."

With Pomona tugging her arm, Caitlyn reluctantly crept away from the window. They paused when they reached the horse trough beside the elm tree, and Caitlyn was dismayed to see that it was empty.

"Oh! The garden hose—it's gone!" she said. "Oh, Pomie! Now we'll never find it again."

But Pomona was barely listening. Instead, she seemed preoccupied, her brow furrowed.

"Who is that woman who lives in the barn? D'you know her?" she asked.

"Her name's Leandra Lockwood. I met her yesterday at the chocolate shop. She looked a lot more normal today; yesterday, she looked like a complete eccentric, with this long velvet dress and a big moon pendant and rings on all her fingers. She told me she's a 'witch'—" Caitlyn made air quotes with her fingers and rolled her eyes. "—and she gave me this big lecture on Samhain traditions."

"Is she on vacation? Is that why she's staying here?"

"No, she said she's taken early retirement—apparently, she was a professor at one of the London colleges—and she's just leased the barn conversion as a temporary base until she finds somewhere to buy—"

"I think I saw her at one of Thane's parties in his London penthouse!"

"Thane Blackmort?"

Pomona nodded eagerly. "Yes! I'm sure she was there."

"Is this like you're ninety-eight per cent sure or you're sixty-five per cent sure?"

Pomona ignored this and continued excitedly: "That must be why she's in Tillyhenge! She was sent here by Blackmort to look for the *grimoire*. She probably murdered Percy to get her hands on it!"

"Whoa—slow down," said Caitlyn. "Aren't you jumping to conclusions a bit?"

"Hey, she was asking about the

grimoire, wasn't she? You heard her— she sounded like she had a really personal interest in it. She's going on about how valuable the *grimoire* is and how it should be in the 'right' hands—her hands, in other words. Plus, she was telling Katya to, like, pump the police for information."

"That doesn't mean that she's connected with Blackmort or even Percy's death. She could just be generally nosy or keen to find the *grimoire* as a collector—"

"A *collector*?"

"Well, maybe not a collector exactly, but you know, for more academic reasons. I mean, Leandra is such a pompous know-it-all and always going on about being an expert on witchcraft and the occult. So maybe she wants the *grimoire* just to study it, you know?"

Pomona made a rude noise. "Nobody wants a book like that just to study it!"

"Okay, but regardless, Leandra wasn't even in the Manor house last night—"

"How do you know? She could've easily gotten Katya to let her in. That girl is totally under her thumb. Katya lied about her alibi, right? She wasn't sleeping in her room. Well, maybe she sneaked down to let Leandra into the Manor. That's why there was no sign of a break-in—"

"No, no, you heard what Katya said just now: she sneaked *out* last night to come to the barn. That's why she lied to the police. She obviously didn't want them to know that she was here with Leandra."

"Well, she could have come here and then they could have gone back to the Manor together," Pomona said stubbornly. "Maybe Katya remained as lookout and Leandra went into the Library."

"Wouldn't someone have seen her?

Benedict and Percy were together in the Library until just before midnight. In fact, we heard them come up, didn't we? And Mosley was still around too—he confirmed that he saw the boys going upstairs. It wasn't that long after that we went down ourselves. Surely if Leandra was sneaking around downstairs, *somebody* would have seen her?"

Pomona shrugged. "The Manor was pretty dark by then. All the main lighting had been dimmed, especially in the Library. Maybe Leandra managed to sneak in there and hid in the corner and nobody noticed. Or..." Pomona held a hand up excitedly. "Or maybe she used magic to make herself invisible!"

"What? That's ridiculous!" scoffed Caitlyn. But even as she said it, she had an uneasy recollection of that moment the night before when she had been sure she sensed a presence in the Library, someone brushing past her... Pushing the memory away, she said:

"Leandra's not a real witch, remember? She's obviously just one of these self-appointed gurus who peddles folk magic and dodgy trinkets, pretending they're ancient talismans with amazing powers. I mean, look at all the rubbish she was saying about that 'Blarney Stone brooch'! And then she takes advantage of impressionable young women like Katya, who think she holds the key to hidden knowledge and power. It's all just a show to puff up Leandra's ego. She can't really work magic."

"She could have, like, siphoned powers from Blackmort," Pomona suggested. Her hand crept to her throat and she added earnestly, "Like the way I did, when I was wearing that Black Diamond choker he gave me..."

Caitlyn was silent. Thane Blackmort was an enigmatic billionaire who had repeatedly tried to buy part of the Fitzroy estate, despite James's continued refusal of his offers. It might have been purely a shrewd acquisition for Blackmort's property development business—after all, the area was prime real estate in the Cotswolds. But since that part of the estate contained the hill with the stone circle, Caitlyn always wondered if the mysterious businessman had a more nefarious reason for coveting the land.

Still, it wasn't so much Blackmort's aggressive business dealings that unsettled her—it was his sinister charisma. Caitlyn had always known that Pomona had a thing for "bad boys" and had grown used to her cousin falling for a series of rebellious rockstars and rogue mavericks—so it had hardly been surprising when the notorious "Black Tycoon" captivated Pomona. With his piercing blue eyes and dark, saturnine good looks, not to mention the aura of mystery and sinister rumours that surrounded him, Blackmort had been like romantic catnip for her impulsive cousin.

But Caitlyn had quickly realised that Thane Blackmort was nothing like Pomona's past boyfriends—there was a real malevolence to him that filled her with dread. And it had been torture to watch Pomona change as she'd sunk deeper and deeper under his influence. Even worse, Caitlyn hadn't been able to *prove* her suspicions and fears. With his wealth, power, and clever manipulation, Blackmort had been protected, and it had been almost impossible for Caitlyn to convince others that her cousin was being held captive by Dark Magic.

Caitlyn shifted uncomfortably as unpleasant memories flooded her mind. Pomona had displayed frightening powers of Dark Magic when she had been under Blackmort's influence— magic taken from a cursed diamond choker that had been a gift from the billionaire. *But Pomona's free of*

Blackmort now, and the whole thing is over, Caitlyn reminded herself with a mental shake. Her cousin had broken free of Blackmort's seduction and seemed to have recovered from her time under the curse, none the worse for wear.

Making an effort to bring her thoughts back to the present, Caitlyn said gently, "Pomie, do you think maybe... well, maybe you're being paranoid? I mean, it would be understandable after what happened to you. But that doesn't really mean that Blackmort is involved in everything. Maybe you're just imagining a connection that isn't there—"

"He's involved," Pomona insisted. "I'm telling you, Leandra isn't who she says she is, and I'll prove it to you!"

Chapter Seventeen

By the time they got back to the Morning Room, the others had finished breakfast and were lingering over their coffees. Vanessa beamed as they came in and said:

"Oh good, you're back. We were just talking about what to do this afternoon. Would you like to join us in a ride around the estate?"

Tori noticed Caitlyn's hesitation and said with a sneer: "You *do* ride, I take it?"

"Um... a bit. Not very well," Caitlyn confessed. She had only been on horseback a few times since arriving in Tillyhenge—usually under James's gentle guidance. The thought of having to display her poor horsemanship to Vanessa's circle, who had probably all been born on horseback, was enough to make her cringe. She knew it was silly, but somehow she still wanted to impress James's sister and to be seen as worthy of him.

"Hey, I think you're pretty good on horseback, considering that you never had lessons," said Pomona loyally.

"Oh yes, I forgot—you Americans don't learn how to ride," said Tori, curling her lips in a superior smile.

Pomona looked at her evenly. "No, I guess all those cowboys out West are just hanging on for dear life all the time."

Tori scowled whilst Benedict burst out laughing, looking pleased at her discomfiture. There was an awkward silence, then Caitlyn cleared her throat and asked:

"Um... do you know where James is? I thought he'd be having breakfast with you."

"He said he had a teleconference in his study," Vanessa replied.

"Oh." Caitlyn tried not to show her disappointment. Last night's hectic events had left them with no chance for a private moment, and she had been looking forward to seeing James and spending a bit of time with him this morning.

"Would you like some coffee, Miss Sinclair?" asked Mosley, hovering next to Pomona.

"Ooh, yeah—can you make me a cup in one of those cute French press things?"

Mosley looked befuddled for a moment, then said, "Ah... do you mean a cafetière, ma'am?"

"Yeah, you don't see those much back in the States, and I always feel like a cool coffee geek when I get a cup brewed from one," said Pomona, grinning.

Benedict chuckled. "I love the way you make that sound so exotic. Cafetières are a bog-standard way most Brits make coffee at home—if they're not using instant coffee, that is."

"I never drink instant. It's vile," said Tori disdainfully. "I have an espresso machine that grinds fresh beans, froths milk—the works."

"Well, bully for you," said Benedict, his tone sarcastic.

Tori ignored him, turning instead back to Pomona and saying with a sly smile, "You're lucky since you probably wouldn't know the difference between the different types anyway. America is notorious for having the worst coffee in the world, after all. Most places just have a huge jug of burnt stale coffee that sits on a hot plate all day and tastes like battery acid."

Pomona opened her mouth indignantly, but before she could retort, Katya spoke up:

"Poor Percy," she said, biting her lip. "He loved his coffee. Vanessa—isn't that how you two met?"

Vanessa looked uncomfortable. "Um… yes, you know the story."

"Percy told me you bumped into each other in the café down the street from his bookshop—is that right?" said Katya. "The place where he always used to get a morning latte."

Vanessa nodded, looking like she didn't really want to talk about it.

Tori smirked. "Percy and his morning latte: a love story with a bitter end—"

"For God's sake, Tori, give it a rest!" snapped Benedict, erupting from his chair. "The poor sod only died last night. Show some bloody respect, can't you?" He tossed his napkin down. "Excuse me."

He stalked from the room. Caitlyn felt an unexpected wave of liking for Benedict. She had thought him self-centred and materialistic, but so far, he seemed to be showing more genuine regard for Percy, and distress about his death, than anyone else in the group.

There was a strained silence at the table after Benedict's departure as they all tried to pretend that everything was normal. Mosley discreetly returned with a cup of freshly brewed coffee for Pomona, who shot Tori a pointed look before picking up the cup and drinking it with great relish. Tori scowled and got up from the table with bad grace, muttering "Come on!" to Vanessa before flouncing out of the room.

"Man, I'd like to smack that cow," muttered Pomona.

"Hush..." said Caitlyn, glancing up to check if Vanessa had heard.

Thankfully, James's sister had already risen as well and was following her best friend out of the room, leaving them alone with Katya. Caitlyn felt her shoulders relax. She hadn't realised how tense she was under Tori's sardonic eye; it was a relief to have a break from the girl's company. *She's such an unpleasant character—it wouldn't be a surprise if she was a murderer*, mused Caitlyn as she sipped her tea. Still, much as it would have been satisfying to see Tori arrested, she couldn't think of any likely reason why Tori would have wanted to harm Percy.

She ate quickly and then, leaving Pomona regaling Katya with wild stories of life in Hollywood, she left the Morning Room and went in search of James. Recalling Vanessa's mention of her brother's teleconference plans, she decided to try his study first. The door was shut when she arrived, and she knocked hesitantly. There was no answer. She tried again, leaning close to the door to listen for any sound of voices. Nothing.

Maybe he's gone to meet the estate manager already, she thought absently as she patted her pocket for her phone to ring James. It wasn't there. She cursed under her breath as she realised that she must have left her phone in her bedroom upstairs. Not wanting to waste time running back upstairs to find it, she looked thoughtfully at the closed study door. She didn't like the thought of going in uninvited, but on the other hand, she knew that there was an internal phone on James's desk. She could use that to call other areas of the estate and ask the staff to help her locate him...

Caitlyn turned the knob and opened the door, then gasped in surprise. The room wasn't empty. There was someone hunched over in the corner behind

James's desk. The figure jerked upright and whirled around, hastily tucking one hand behind their back. Caitlyn saw a swirl of blonde hair and enormous grey eyes.

"Vanessa?"

"Caitlyn!" Vanessa clutched her chest with her other hand and giggled. "Darling, you nearly gave me a heart attack!"

"Sorry, I didn't mean to startle you. I didn't realise there was anyone in here. I knocked just now..." Caitlyn trailed off, but the unspoken question hung in the air.

Vanessa looked at her innocently. "You did? I didn't hear you. You must have knocked very softly."

"I suppose I must have." Caitlyn hesitated. "Um... what were you doing?" She felt abashed quizzing Vanessa in her own house, and yet there had been something about the way the other girl had jumped which made her blurt out the question.

Vanessa casually slipped the hand that was behind her back into her jeans pocket and sauntered around the desk to join Caitlyn. "Oh... I was looking for sweets," she said airily.

Caitlyn blinked in surprise. "Sweets?"

"Yes, I had a sudden hankering for Liquorice Allsorts so I thought I'd check to see if James had a stash in his office." She leaned in and gave Caitlyn a conspiratorial smile. "He has a terribly sweet tooth, you know. He always used to keep sweets in the drawers of his desk in his room, so I thought he might still be doing the same thing, even if he is 'lord of the manor' now." She covered her mouth and giggled like a schoolgirl.

Caitlyn stared at Vanessa. It was strange to think that James's sister was in her mid-twenties—a couple of years older than Caitlyn—and yet somehow she felt so much younger. Even Evie, who was only eighteen, didn't seem quite so much like a ditzy schoolgirl.

Vanessa grabbed Caitlyn's wrist. "You won't tell him I was looking through his drawers, will you? James can be a bit square, you know. He's really touchy on things like 'invasion of privacy' and all that rot." She made a face. "He'll read me the Riot Act if he found out that I was going through his desk."

"I'm sure he wouldn't mind you looking for sweets—"

"You don't know what he's like. Besides, everyone seems so on edge at the moment, because of what happened last night..." She squeezed Caitlyn's hand. "Please don't tell James I was here! Promise?"

"Er... I promise," said Caitlyn uncomfortably.

Vanessa beamed at her. "I like you, Caitlyn. Much more than my brother's past girlfriends."

"Oh." Caitlyn flushed. "Um... thank you. But I'm... er... I'm not sure I'm really his girlfriend, as such."

"What do you mean?"

"Well... it's... it's a bit complicated. I mean, we've only known each other for a few months and... um... it's not like we've been going on dates or anything like that so... um... I don't know if it's really official—"

"You mean, you're just bonking each other?"

"*What?* No!" cried Caitlyn, aghast. "No, no, of course not! We haven't even—I mean..." She faltered, flushing bright red.

Vanessa shrugged. "Darling, it's no big deal. Lots of my friends have similar arrangements. Actually, maybe if Benedict and I had been like that, we wouldn't have broken up. He was a bit of a bore as a boyfriend, really—always rabbiting on about his weight training and his protein shakes and supplements or talking about how much dosh his father's antique business made at the last auction." She rolled her eyes, then gave Caitlyn a cheeky grin. "Although, he was great if you fancied a bit of 'rumpy-pumpy'—"

"Um... yes, well... James and I are definitely *not* like that," said Caitlyn, taken aback by Vanessa's candid revelations. "We're good friends and we care about each other and—"

"Yes, but it's obvious that you're more than just friends! I could tell, even before I met you, by the way my brother talked about you. Even the way he says your name. You're special to him." She tilted her head to one side and looked at Caitlyn, her grey eyes wide and serious. For a second, she seemed much older. "Do you love him?"

"Oh! Er... I... um..." Caitlyn stammered, her cheeks on fire. She was beginning to wish that she had never come into the study. She was also beginning to see why James would lecture his sister on the importance of privacy—the girl seemed to have no filters or boundaries!

"I... er... he's very special to me too," she said lamely at last. Desperately, she tried to change the subject. "So... um... are you still going riding this afternoon?"

"I don't know. Tori's gone off in a bit of a strop, and Benedict and Katya didn't seem too keen on the idea," said Vanessa, looking crestfallen. Then she brightened. "Maybe I'll suggest a spot of clay pigeon shooting instead! Do you shoot?"

"Er... no," said Caitlyn. Why couldn't the British aristocracy dabble in "normal" hobbies like cycling or baking or playing board games?

"Oh, don't worry. I'll ask James to teach you. He's a crack shot," said

Vanessa, waving a careless hand. "Well, I'd better go and find Tori and see if her mood's improved. I'll see you later!" She gave Caitlyn an artless smile, then sashayed out of the room in a cloud of that familiar, sweet perfume.

Alone in the study, Caitlyn breathed a small sigh of relief and sank down into a chair. She felt drained after that encounter with Vanessa. She also felt vaguely uneasy, although she wasn't sure why. Perhaps it had been Vanessa's blunt appraisal of her relationship with James. Or perhaps it had been the other girl's happy preoccupation with fun activities for the afternoon. It felt so wrong and disrespectful when Percy had only died yesterday.

And it seemed especially strange behaviour from someone who should have been grieving Percy on a particularly personal level. *Or did I read the signs wrong?* wondered Caitlyn. She had been so sure, watching Vanessa at dinner last night, that James's sister had looked frustrated and resentful when Percy had devoted all his attention to Katya. She had been certain that Vanessa had harboured romantic feelings for the young bookdealer. But if Vanessa had been in love with Percy, shouldn't she have been devasted by his death? How could she seem so frivolous and uncaring?

Caitlyn gave her head a shake, feeling suddenly bad for her judgemental thoughts. People showed grief in different ways, she reminded herself. Perhaps Vanessa's excessive gaiety was her way of coping with the shock of Percy's death; it didn't mean that she wasn't really grieving for him, inside. The British upper class were notorious for maintaining a "stiff upper lip" and never showing emotions in public, weren't they? Maybe Vanessa's behaviour was a natural result of her upbringing. Besides, listening to her talk about her mother's early death, it seemed that Vanessa had learned to adopt a very philosophical attitude towards grief and dying...

The door to the study opened, interrupting her thoughts, and she sprang up from the chair just as James stepped into the room.

"Caitlyn!" His face broke into a smile as he regarded her with surprised pleasure. "I was just wondering where you were. I popped into the Morning Room just now but you weren't there."

Caitlyn smiled shyly at him. "I came to look for you, actually. Vanessa said you might be in here having a teleconference—"

"Yes, I finished that about half an hour ago and was going to come and join you all in the Morning Room, but then Lisa wanted to see me urgently," James explained. He frowned slightly. "She's worried because there's been some unrest amongst the staff. People seem to be very uneasy about the Samhain Festival, for some reason. Some of the staff are even refusing to be involved with any of the preparations. Lisa is concerned because we have had a very positive response to the advertising and we're expecting a lot of visitors to the estate. With the festival just two days away, it would be very difficult to hire enough external staff at such short notice."

James shook his head and heaved a sigh of frustration. "I just don't know what's got into people! I know some of the villagers can be a bit superstitious, but this seems to be beyond all reason. Everyone seemed fine about it when we first mooted the idea of a Samhain Festival, but now it's as if fear and paranoia have suddenly spread through the village and the estate. Even those that you'd expected to be fairly sensible and have modern attitudes seem to be

acting like they've stepped back into the Middle Ages." He stopped and gave Caitlyn an apologetic smile. "Sorry... I didn't mean to offload my troubles on you like that—"

"No, no, I want to listen! I mean, I want you to feel like your troubles are my troubles and that we share everything—" Caitlyn broke off, embarrassed. She looked down, not meeting James's eyes, her cheeks burning.

James reached out gently and pulled her to him, dropping a kiss in her hair, and Caitlyn sighed happily, her embarrassment dissolving. She slipped her arms around him and leaned into his chest. He was warm and solid, and it felt wonderful to be enveloped in his arms.

"Thank you," James said softly. "It means a lot to me to hear you say that."

"You know, maybe you take your responsibilities too seriously, James. I mean, you're a wonderful landlord and everyone on the estate appreciates your dedication, but that doesn't mean that you should feel personally responsible for everyone's actions. People often don't have the same standards of behaviour—"

"Yes, even my own sister, it seems," said James dryly. "I've been trying to speak to her all morning. There are decisions that need to be made with regards to Percy's funeral and contacting his family and things like that. As his friend, Ness should be the one overseeing that, but all she seems to be concerned about is organising activities for the weekend." He sighed with frustration.

"Maybe it's her way of coping," Caitlyn suggested gently, repeating her own earlier thoughts. "I mean, maybe she's keeping busy so she doesn't have to face the horror of what happened."

James gave her an ironic look. "That's

nice of you—a lot of people would just say that my sister is very immature. And they'd probably be right. Ness is sweet, but she was always spoilt, even when my mother was still alive. After Mother passed away... well, I think both Father and I felt sorry for her, so we indulged her even more. It has probably resulted in her growing up a bit too used to getting her own way." He paused, then added ruefully: "Her thoughtlessness has been quite shameful sometimes. I remember she once took a tray from the family silver collection just so she could use it to display her entry in the school cake sale. She said she wanted her cake to stand out more," said James with exasperated disbelief. "The staff spent a panicked day searching for it, thinking that it had been stolen, and we were practically calling the police and the insurance company before she confessed."

"I suppose lots of people do

thoughtless things when they're children."

"She was twelve by then—hardly a child," said James, shaking his head. "The most terrible incident was when she lost out on a pony that she'd set her heart on. The breeder had promised it to us, but the parents of one of her classmates made a successful counter-offer just before the filly was due to be delivered. Quite reprehensible, but not illegal, and there was nothing we could do about it. Still, Ness was furious, and the next week at school, she spiked the other girl's tea with some alum powder that she'd found in the cook's supplies."

"Alum powder?"

"It's a pickling agent. Horribly sour and astringent. Luckily, the girl wasn't allergic or anything, otherwise it might have ended very badly. Still, the parents kicked up a terrible fuss, claiming that Ness had tried to kill their daughter. Which was all nonsense, of course," said

James impatiently. "I'm sure Ness didn't mean any real harm. She was probably just miffed and decided to 'punish' the other girl. It was spiteful, I grant you, but I don't think there were really any sinister intentions. Ness just isn't aware of the implications of her actions sometimes."

"When was this?" asked Caitlyn, somewhat shocked by the story.

"Several years ago, when she was still in her early teens." James sighed, then he ran a hand through his dark hair and gave Caitlyn a smile. "Maybe you're right, though. Maybe I'm being unfair and judging Ness by the past. She's in her twenties now, after all. I'm sure she's changed and matured."

But what if she hasn't? thought Caitlyn suddenly. An uncomfortable idea popped into her head. What if Vanessa had been outraged that Percy had rejected her affections? Would she have resorted to a similar method to punish him—only this time, by using a substance that resulted in a heart attack?

Chapter Eighteen

Caitlyn pulled back, horrified at the direction that her thoughts had taken and hoping that none of it had shown on her face. Hurriedly, she said to James: "Have you heard anything more from the police?"

"I just had a call from Inspector Walsh, actually, and you'll be pleased to hear that he *is* considering opening an official inquiry into Percy's death. He has already put some of his men on to investigating Percy's background, and he's also asked my permission to do a search of the Manor. Of course, a lot depends on the results of the autopsy. The report hasn't come through yet, but if it concludes that Percy died of natural causes, then the case will be closed."

James tilted his head and looked at her curiously. "Why are you so sure that Percy's death might be suspicious? Aside from the fact that this... er, *grimoire* is missing, there don't seem to be any other anomalies."

Caitlyn hesitated, wondering if she should mention Katya's furtive tryst the night before. After all, the girl *had* lied to the police and given a false statement about her whereabouts. But on the other hand, it wasn't really a crime to sneak out to meet someone. Katya might have wanted to keep her assignations with Leandra a secret for other reasons. With Percy's death not even confirmed as suspicious yet, it seemed petty to "rat" on her to the police simply because of Tori's spiteful insinuations.

"You said Inspector Walsh was

checking Percy's background. Is there anything special there? What about his family?" she asked instead.

"He doesn't appear to have any immediate family. Percy's mother passed away when he was young and his father a few years ago, and he had no siblings or other close relatives. There is a distant cousin who lives in Norwich, who will have to be informed, but aside from that... It seems that Percy lived a very quiet, simple life which revolved entirely around his bookshop. And that appears fairly kosher. Inspector Walsh told me they are conducting all the usual checks, but so far, there seem to be no scandals, financial shenanigans, or any other kind of notoriety. In fact, the only bit of fame was when the shop was featured in a lifestyle magazine a few months ago. The article was about an heirloom Percy had inherited and how it's helped him establish his rare books business."

"Oh! The heirloom is a dowsing pendulum, isn't it?" said Caitlyn.

"Yes, how did you know?" said James, looking surprised. "Apparently, Percy found it when he was going through his late father's things, and he claimed that it's a powerful divination tool, enabling him to find rare and valuable antique books. He certainly seemed to build up a successful catalogue in a very short space of time, and his bookshop had quickly become known as having one of the best rare book collections in London."

"Percy had that pendulum with him last night," Caitlyn explained. "I saw him using it in the Library just before the others arrived. That's how he found the *grimoire*, actually. I... I didn't like to mention that when I was speaking to Inspector Walsh because... well, you know, he's so sceptical about magic."

James smiled. "You know, Inspector Walsh might seem a bit gruff and dismissive sometimes, but he does listen when you talk. He might not admit it, but he's impressed by your contributions to the police investigations in the past."

"He didn't seem very impressed this morning," said Caitlyn dryly.

"Well, suggesting that Percy was murdered for a book of magical chocolate spells is probably a *bit* too much for Inspector Walsh's down-to-earth sensibilities," said James, looking amused. "But to give him his credit, he *has* instructed his men to include the *grimoire* in all their investigations."

"What about the dowsing pendulum?" asked Caitlyn suddenly. "Now that I think about it, I didn't see it when Pomona and I found Percy. Did the police find it when they moved his body?"

"No. As far as I know, Inspector Walsh didn't mention anything that fitted that description."

"So where has *that* gone?" Caitlyn mused. "Did the murderer take it along with the *grimoire*?"

James raised his eyebrows. "So you are convinced that it *is* murder, are you?"

"I... yes," said Caitlyn slowly. "I know there's no evidence so far for any kind of foul play but... but I just feel it in my gut. Percy's death wasn't natural."

"If we accept that it *was* murder and that you're right about the motive to obtain the *grimoire*..." James paused for a moment, thinking. "You know, I can't help wondering if this whole thing might be linked to Daniel Tremaine."

Caitlyn squirmed at the mention of the man's name. Tremaine had been a British government agent who had been murdered at the Mabon Ball held at Huntingdon Manor not two months ago. In fact, Caitlyn herself had discovered his body in the Portrait Gallery. She still shuddered at the memory of seeing his limp form impaled by a witch's stang—a pronged metal staff which had been driven into his chest with almost supernatural force. There had been several suspects, but in the end, they had all been cleared of guilt, and the mystery of Tremaine's death had never been solved. The police were convinced, though, that a red-haired woman who had been caught on camera going into the Portrait Gallery just before the murder was the culprit.

A woman who had been identified by the Widow Mags as her daughter Tara.

But that doesn't mean that my mother was *the murderer*, Caitlyn reminded herself quickly. She was sure that her mother could never be so ruthless.

She realised that James was looking at her expectantly. "Um... why do you think there's a link?"

"It's just too much of a coincidence

that both deaths should have happened here, at the Manor, within a month of each other. And both events seem somehow linked to your family. In this case, to the Widow Mags and her *grimoire*, and in Tremaine's case..." He paused, glancing at her. "To your mother. In fact, she could be the common link between both murders."

"There could be a dozen reasons why Tara was at the crime scene the night of the ball," Caitlyn said quickly. "There's no proof that my mother had anything to do with Tremaine's murder. And there's definitely nothing linking her to Percy's death! I mean, she's not even here!"

"Would you know if she was?" challenged James.

Caitlyn frowned. "What do you mean?"

"Well, you are the one who told me about her extraordinary abilities with 'glamour magic'. She was even able to fool everyone at the ball into thinking that she was Pomona! So we don't know if she *is* in the vicinity or not. She may be using magic to disguise her appearance."

Caitlyn raised her chin defensively. "I would know my own mother."

"Would you?" James asked, his voice gentle. "You were left as an abandoned baby. You've never known her, never even met Tara face-to-face... How do you know that you could recognise her?

"And if you think about it, it all makes sense," said James eagerly, warming to his theory. "We know that Daniel Tremaine was a member of a secret society of witch hunters sanctioned by the British government; an organisation that was devoted to hunting down and destroying witches and tools of witchcraft... such as a *grimoire*," said James significantly.

"I thought Tremaine came to Huntingdon Manor to try to recruit you to join the society, so that you could take your father's place," said Caitlyn, recalling with distaste the man's words about James's duty to the Crown as the current bearer of the Fitzroy title.

"Yes, that might be one reason he came, but I suspect that he was also under orders to locate and retrieve a specific item," said James. "Tremaine obviously used the distraction of the Mabon Ball to steal into the Portrait Gallery unobserved, and it's likely that he was searching for something when he was killed. I wouldn't be surprised if that 'something' was this *grimoire*. After all, my father's famous occult collection would be the obvious place to look for a book of spells. Tremaine just never thought that my father would hide a book in literally the one place where books are kept: the Library.

"And we know that your mother was

involved with Tremaine's murder in some way," James continued doggedly. "You cannot deny that. She was seen at the crime scene. Which likely means that she was searching for the same thing that Tremaine was. That makes perfect sense if that 'thing' was a *grimoire* which used to belong to her own mother. Now, if you're saying that Percy's death is linked to the *grimoire* as well... Well, don't you agree that it's very likely your mother is also involved?"

"Yes," said Caitlyn, in a small voice. She took a deep breath. "Actually, it's even more complicated than you realise: Tara stole the *grimoire* from the Widow Mags over twenty years ago and ran away from home. I think that's the reason she's been sort of... well, disowned. Apparently, stealing another witch's *grimoire* is one of the worst acts a witch can commit, and in this case it was a double betrayal because Tara violated her own mother's trust. I think it's why the Widow Mags won't talk about her or even mention her name."

James whistled softly. "Why did she steal it?"

Caitlyn sighed. "I don't know exactly. I tried to ask the Widow Mags about it and got nowhere. But I know my mother was a very gifted witch. She was almost like a... a 'witch prodigy', you know? And I remember Bertha telling me that, because Tara's natural talents were so strong and she could do the kind of advanced magic that took other witches years to learn, she got quite arrogant.

"And she was apparently obsessed with the *grimoire*," Caitlyn added, recalling what Evie had shared in the chocolate shop kitchen the day before. "Bertha told Evie once that Tara was always trying to have a peek at the *grimoire* but that the Widow Mags would never let her have access to it. So maybe... maybe Tara stole it just to make a point. You know, to show that she *can*."

"There has to be more to the story," argued James. "I can't believe that the Widow Mags would have reacted so strongly just because her rebellious teenage daughter decided to challenge the 'house rules' and show off that she could access something that was forbidden. For one thing, why did Tara run away from home and never return? You don't do that lightly, even when you're a cocky, headstrong adolescent."

"I don't know, okay?" Caitlyn burst out. "That's what I've been trying to find out ever since I arrived in Tillyhenge, and I just can't seem to get any answers! I've tried asking the Widow Mags, I've tried asking Bertha—and no one will tell me anything!"

She stopped, appalled, as she realised that she had just been yelling at James's face. "Oh God... I'm... I'm sorry," she stammered, her face contrite. "I didn't mean..."

"It's okay," said James gently. "It's good to have someone you can vent your frustrations to sometimes. I'm not just here for the romantic dinners, you know." He gave her a whimsical smile. "I'm here for the rough patches and rants too."

"Oh James..." Caitlyn threw her arms around him, feeling both humbled and overwhelmed with love and gratitude.

James turned and sank into the armchair next to them, pulling her with him so that she fell into his lap.

"James!" Caitlyn gasped, laughing.

"I've been wanting to do this since last night," he murmured, leaning towards her.

Tenderly, he brushed a tendril of hair off her forehead, then his fingers slid down, a feather-light caress along her jaw, until they reached her chin. He tilted her face up and lowered his head. Caitlyn held her breath, her eyes fluttering shut as heady anticipation filled her. She leaned towards him, waiting for the feel of his lips on hers...

... and instead, felt a huge wet tongue slurp against her cheek.

"Yeeuugghh!" she gasped, opening her eyes and jerking backwards, almost falling off James's lap.

"Bran!" cried James in exasperation as he regarded the slobbery English mastiff standing by their armchair.

Bran wagged his tail and panted amiably, one long string of drool dangling from his baggy lips. Then he whined and came forwards again to lick Caitlyn's face.

"Ughhh! No, Bran... I love you too, but no licking!" she cried, hastily ducking sideways.

"Blast, I didn't shut the door properly," James said, glancing over at the study door, which was still slightly ajar. "I can put him back out and—"

"No, no, it's okay," said Caitlyn, hastily scrambling off his lap. A wave of embarrassment swamped her, and all her old insecurities came rushing back. How could she have let herself sit on James's lap? Had she forgotten how much she weighs? What if James had been feeling squashed by her enormous hips?

She got to her feet and James followed suit, his expression chagrined at the sabotaged romantic moment. Bran came up to Caitlyn again and shoved his huge head into her stomach, causing her to nearly double over.

"Bran!" said James sharply, trying to grab the mastiff's collar. "Stop that! What are you doing?"

The huge dog snuffled deeply in the folds of Caitlyn's jersey dress, leaving a trail of drool, then he looked up at her with soulful eyes and whined questioningly.

"Oh! He's looking for Nibs!" said Caitlyn with sudden understanding. She was also reminded that the kitten was still at Leandra's place. Crouching down next to the mastiff, she smiled and patted his giant head.

"He's not here, Bran, but don't worry, I know where to find him. I'll go and fetch him right now!"

Chapter Nineteen

In the event, Caitlyn didn't get further than the rear courtyard before she was distracted from her kitten-fetching mission by the sound of angry voices. They were coming from the coach house restaurant and Caitlyn turned in that direction, curious to see what the commotion was about. Her eyes widened as she approached and spied her aunt Bertha surrounded by a group of people. Everyone seemed agitated, but her aunt's voice rose shrilly above the others.

"...think it's an utterly despicable

prank!" seethed Bertha. "Do you realise how long it took me to collect all the different kinds of wood required for the bonfire? And now it's all gone! A stack of wood like that doesn't just go missing by itself. Someone's taken it. I want to know who."

Bertha glared at the crowd, her arms akimbo and her usually smiling face replaced by an expression of outrage. The crowd, which seemed to be mostly made up of the staff who worked in the restaurant and the outside areas of the estate, shifted uneasily and exchanged glances, but nobody spoke.

"Come on—one of you must have seen something!" Bertha insisted. "The bonfire wood was stacked right here, in front of the restaurant." She turned to one of the men. "Neil, I know you always come in early. Was the pile of wood here when you arrived this morning?"

Neil shrugged sullenly. "Don't know nothing about the wood. Don't look at it."

"It's just as well that it's gone," the woman next to him added.

"Yeah, we should never have had it here!" shouted another woman. "Disgusting, filthy, pagan stuff. We want no part in such demonic rituals!"

There were mutters of agreement through the crowd and everyone began talking at once.

"Yeah, black magic—that's what you're doing with that bonfire. We'll be cursed for sure!"

"Witchcraft, that's what it is! It ain't natural!"

"It's the devil's work. You'll be inviting all manner of evil!"

"I heard the bonfire wood is bewitched! Would give you a hex if you even looked at it!"

Bertha made an exasperated noise. "Oh, for Goddess's sake! Samhain is nothing more than an ancient harvest festival. For the pagans, it was simply a time to mark the end of the summer season and the start of the long winter months. It has nothing to do with demon worship or black magic!"

"It's a festival to call back the dead. Don't deny it!" said a woman, thrusting her chin out.

"It is a time when we *honour* the dead," corrected Bertha. "And the rituals can be a lovely way to remember the loved ones that we have lost—"

"We don't need them old druid ways here!"

"Yeah, all this meddling with Samhain has already brought evil onto the estate," declared the first woman. "Look what happened last night!"

"What do you mean?" asked Bertha, puzzled.

"We heard that a man was murdered by black magic because he was reading a witch's book!"

"That is incorrect," came a calm, authoritative voice.

Caitlyn turned in surprise to see James striding towards the group with Mosley at his heels. A murmur of consternation ran through the crowd and several members of the staff bowed their heads deferentially as James approached. It was obvious that they viewed their boss with great respect and liking, and were keen not to displease him.

James stood in front of Bertha and scanned the crowd, letting his gaze linger on each person so that he met their eyes and addressed them personally.

"It is true that one of the Manor guests was found dead in the Library last night," he said quietly. "But so far, the police believe that he died of natural causes—probably a heart attack. It is a tragic occurrence, but there is nothing sinister about it."

There was a murmur of surprise and speculation, and the crowd seemed to subside, looking slightly shamefaced.

"Yes, and the Samhain Festival we are planning this Sunday is just a bit of fun, that's all!" added a tall, fashionably dressed woman who had followed James out of the Manor. Caitlyn recognised her as Lisa, head of the Manor's marketing team. "It's no different to a farm open day, really. It's just that it'll run into the evening," she said, smiling brightly at everyone. "Just a bit of a laugh."

Mosley hurried to urge people back to their jobs and most of the staff members began to disperse. But as Caitlyn walked over to join the others, she was troubled to see that a few of the staff members had remained huddled together, whispering and throwing dark glances in Bertha's direction.

"...I don't understand—what were they talking about? What witch's book? What happened last night?" Bertha was asking James.

"A young man—one of my sister's friends—was found dead in the Library last night," James explained. "The police think that he probably suffered a heart attack. However, he was found with a torn page in one of his hands. It looked like a page from a book of recipes—a recipe for chocolate cake, to be exact. I think some of the staff must have overheard the police constables talking, and you know how quickly gossip spreads on the estate."

Bertha still looked bewildered. "But what does that have to do with witches—"

"I think rumours have got around that the book might have belonged to the Widow Mags, due to the chocolate connection," Lisa said, rolling her eyes. "It's just silly, superstitious nonsense."

"Oh." Bertha's expression changed. She turned back to James. "Have you got the page? Can I see it?"

He shook his head. "Unfortunately, it's in police custody. Although Inspector Walsh is not treating the death as suspicious at the moment, he is nevertheless retaining everything as evidence, just in case."

"Anyway, the important thing is that we need to rebuild the bonfire," said Lisa briskly, obviously keen to turn the focus back to the Manor's upcoming event. "It has played a key role in our promotional material for the Samhain Festival; everyone is keen to see the bull being driven between the dual bonfires. We must have it! Do you think you might be able to collect all the necessary wood again by the Festival, Bertha?"

"I suppose so," said Bertha with a sigh. "I'm too busy today, but I should be able to spare some time tomorrow morning."

"I can assign some staff members to help you search the estate for the right trees, to save time," James offered.

"Probably better if we don't involve them," said Bertha dryly. "I'll ask Caitlyn and Evie to help me, thanks." She turned and started to walk away, then stopped as she saw Caitlyn. "Oh my Goddess! I didn't realise you were standing there, dear."

Caitlyn hurried over to her aunt and said in a low voice: "Aunt Bertha, where's the Widow Mags?"

"I imagine she's in the chocolate shop, as usual—why?"

Caitlyn looked again at a couple huddled together a few feet away from them. It was Neil and one of the female staff members who had spoken up. They were talking in low voices, but Caitlyn caught the words: "...*don't care what they say, I'll bet that old witch in the village has something to do with it...*"

She turned back to Bertha and said urgently, "I think we should go back to Tillyhenge and make sure Grandma is okay."

Bertha glanced at James and Lisa, but they had moved away and were earnestly discussing something whilst Lisa pointed to the front of the restaurant. "All right. Come on, I can drive us back."

As soon as they were in the privacy of the car, Caitlyn blurted: "I think the police are wrong. I think there *is* something sinister about Percy's death, and I think it's got something to do with the book that he was holding at the time—the one that the torn page came from. Pomona and I saw that page. It contained part of a handwritten recipe." She paused significantly. "It looked like the Widow Mags's handwriting."

Bertha shot her a sideways look. "You think—"

"You think so too," said Caitlyn. "That was why you asked James to see the torn page, wasn't it? You suspect that the stolen book is Grandma's long-lost *grimoire*."

"Well, it might just be a coincidence."

"No, it isn't! The book obviously contained chocolate recipes in the Widow Mags's handwriting, and I'm sure I saw the word '*grimoire*' on the cover. I was with Percy when he first found it, earlier in the evening, you see, although he put it back in the bookcase before I had a chance to look at it properly. I was planning to go back to the Library late last night to check it out again. That's why Pomona and I found Percy's body," she explained.

Bertha looked bewildered. "But... why would Mother's *grimoire* be in the Fitzroy family library?"

"I don't know. But I'm sure it's connected somehow to Percy's death."

Caitlyn looked eagerly at her aunt. "Evie told me that you mentioned Tara used to have a 'thing' for the *grimoire*, that she was obsessed with it. And the Widow Mags told me that her *grimoire* is gone, that it's been stolen. It was Tara who stole it, wasn't it?"

Bertha raised startled eyes to her. "How did you know...?"

"It's obvious! I knew she had to have done something truly terrible to be ostracised by her own family, and this is one of the worst acts that a witch can commit, isn't it—to steal another's *grimoire*? It's the ultimate betrayal. Is that why she ran away and disappeared?"

Bertha hesitated. "Caitlyn, you know Mother doesn't want me to talk about Tara—"

"Why not? I have a right to know! I'm sick and fed-up of being shut down every time I try to ask about her!"

Caitlyn cried furiously. "You said just now that Samhain is a time when we remember the loved ones we've lost— were those just empty words? Have you just completely cut Tara from your lives and forgotten her?"

There was silence in the car after her outburst. Then Bertha said, in a quiet voice:

"No, of course we haven't forgotten her." She stared out the window for several minutes, her eyes distant and unfocused, as if looking into the past. "But it's not as simple as you think. For one thing, Tara herself has chosen not to return, and I think that hurts as much as her betrayal in stealing the *grimoire*."

"How do you know that? How do you know she is deliberately refusing to come back?" asked Caitlyn. "Maybe something's happened to her, maybe she can't—"

"No, she is all right," Bertha reassured

her. "Don't tell Mother, but I've been using divination spells to check on Tara over the last twenty-two years. It took me a while to find her—she was hidden by some kind of veil—but I did find her eventually."

"So you've known where she was all this time?" asked Caitlyn excitedly.

Bertha shook her head. "The divination spells I use are not very powerful. I can't see Tara directly, only sense her presence. So I didn't know exactly where she was or what she was doing—but I knew that she was alive and that she was safe and well. In fact..." She paused thoughtfully. "Recently, I feel like her presence has been stronger, as if she is here, near us."

"She is!" exclaimed Caitlyn. "That's what the police footage showed, didn't it? She was at the masquerade ball last month."

Bertha gave her a wry smile. "Yes, I

have to say, when Mother told me about seeing Tara in the security camera footage, I wasn't really surprised. I'd sensed, somehow, that she was here, somewhere on the estate."

Caitlyn frowned. "But I don't understand—why haven't you seen her or heard about her if she's around? The village isn't that big and you know how fast things travel on the local grapevine, especially when there's gossip about a newcomer. Why haven't you caught a glimpse of her or heard any—"

"Oh, you don't know how skilled your mother is at the art of glamour magic," said Bertha, with a rueful laugh. "It's one of her special talents. Once, when she was just a toddler and I was babysitting her, Tara glamoured herself when I went to the loo. I had a complete panic when I returned, thinking that someone had stolen my baby sister and replaced her with a huge turnip! I can still remember her giggling at me when she revealed her glamour."

"A turnip?" said Caitlyn, smiling at the mental picture.

Bertha nodded, her face softening in reminiscence. "Tara had a thing about turnips. She loved them mashed, roasted, boiled in soup... and she especially loved carving them for Samhain. She would enchant a chisel and then use magic to create the most amazing lanterns—not just the usual faces but also beautiful scenes of fairy grottos or mythical beasts playing..."

She trailed off, lost in thought for a moment, then sighed and looked back up at Caitlyn, her eyes serious. "Anyway, what I wanted to say is that Tara could be hiding in plain sight. With her skill at disguising her appearance and fooling the eyes, even *I* wouldn't be able to recognise her. She could be right here, with us, and we would never know."

Chapter Twenty

Caitlyn was quiet on the rest of the drive back to Tillyhenge, her mind whirling as she mulled over what her aunt had told her. The thought that her mother could be here in Tillyhenge, or somewhere on the Huntingdon Manor estate, was both thrilling and nerve-wracking. Caitlyn had yearned for so long to find her mother and yet now that it was becoming a genuine possibility, she felt suddenly terrified.

When Barbara Le Fey had died six months ago and Caitlyn had discovered that she was adopted, she had spent hours fantasising about finding her "real" mother and meeting her at last. While Barbara had been kind and generous, the American actress had always remained a distant figure, lavishing Caitlyn with material luxuries but rarely offering any deep emotional warmth. So Caitlyn had imagined the joy of finally having a mother figure she could really bond with.

But since arriving in Tillyhenge and slowly learning more about the woman who was her mother, Caitlyn was beginning to realise that her fantasy of Tara was wildly different from the reality. Bold, confident—arrogant, even—and ruthless in getting what she wanted, Tara was nothing like the saintly, maternal figure that she had built up in her imagination. And now that there was a real chance to meet her at last, Caitlyn felt torn between anticipation and apprehension.

As the car drove into the village, she

was pulled out of her thoughts by the sight of a crowd on the village green. It looked like a group of people encircling something... or some*one*. Caitlyn peered over the heads of the crowd, trying to see what they were fixated on, then gasped as she caught sight of a hunched figure in black.

"It's the Widow Mags!" she cried. "Quick, stop the car!"

Bertha slammed on the brakes and Caitlyn threw herself out of the car. The sound of horrible jeering laughter filled her ears as she ran towards the circle, and when she'd finally pushed her way to the front of the crowd, she was horrified to see the Widow Mags being hemmed in on all sides by hostile villagers.

"What did you do to that young man, you old crone?" hissed one woman. "We know you had something to do with it!"

"Yes, you can't hide in your shop

now!" yelled another man. "There are no potions or concoctions here to save you."

"I always said them chocolates in your shop were cursed. You were using them to bewitch us, so you could bind us to your will, weren't you?"

"Well, look who's trapped now!" shouted another voice, accompanied by more jeering laughter as the crowd jostled closer to the Widow Mags.

"Yeah, let's see you try to hex us!" taunted a man standing near Caitlyn.

"Filthy witch!" spat a woman. "Demon worshipper!"

"We want you gone from this village! Get out!" cried another shrill voice, and the next moment, Caitlyn saw a hand raise to hurl a plum at the Widow Mags.

She cried out in alarm as the dark, ripe fruit flew through the air, straight for the Widow Mags's head. But just when it would have smacked into her face in a mess of pulp and purple juice, the old witch raised a hand and the plum transformed in midair into a shower of delicate plum blossoms which fell harmlessly to her feet.

There was a collective gasp and several people took steps back. Nervous whispers rippled through the crowd.

"Did you see that—?"

"What happened?"

"Is that... did she...?"

"Your magic tricks don't scare me, witch!" snarled a woman, stepping out of the crowd to confront the Widow Mags.

Caitlyn's heart sank as she recognised Vera Bottom, the sister of dairy farmer Jeremy Bottom. Vera was a sour, sanctimonious woman who seemed to divide her time between spreading spiteful gossip and intimidating the other villagers with warnings about witchcraft and black magic. She had already tried several times to sabotage the Widow Mags's chocolate shop and Bertha's herbal business, and now she looked smug as she faced the old witch, surrounded by her fellow hecklers.

"Let me pass," said the Widow Mags, in a quiet voice.

"Not until you confess!" hissed Vera. "What did you do to that young man? I heard that he was reading a witch's book—you hexed him, didn't you? "

"That's rubbish!" shouted Bertha, shouldering her way to the front of the crowd. "My mother had nothing to do with the death up at the Manor."

"And why should we believe *you*?" shouted a belligerent voice. "You're as bad as her, with your herbal poisons and Satanic candles—"

"Oh, for Goddess's sake...! Those are organic soy candles with pure essential oils and dried herbs. There's nothing 'Satanic' about them. Any *child* could see that," Bertha said contemptuously.

The man bristled and grabbed Bertha's arm.

"Take your hands off my daughter," snapped the Widow Mags, rounding on him. "Or you will regret it."

Vera narrowed her eyes. "Are you threatening us, you old hag? How dare you! We are the true residents of Tillyhenge, and we have a right to protect ourselves from you and your filthy witchcraft!"

The crowd surged in again, emboldened by Vera's words, and closed in around Bertha and the Widow Mags. Caitlyn felt herself being shoved to the back of the circle and a wave of dread came over her. She could sense the mood getting ugly, the hysterical fear of the villagers turning into mob fury, and she didn't know what to do.

A spell, she thought. *I need a spell! Something to distract their attention!*

She scrunched her eyes shut, trying to recall all the incantations and enchantments that she'd been taught in the past few months. But her mind felt paralysed, blank with panic and fear. Caitlyn opened her eyes again, looking wildly around and wishing desperately that James had come with her and Bertha. Or even Inspector Walsh with his sceptical—

There was a sudden cry of alarm and a different kind of fear spread through the crowd.

"It's them constables!"

"The police are here!"

People began to disperse, turning and rushing away. Vera looked undecided for a moment, her face flushed with angry frustration, then she scowled and hurried away down the street, disappearing around the corner. Caitlyn felt a wave of relief as she saw the familiar uniform of a British police constable crossing the village green, accompanied by a middle-aged man with greying hair and a trim moustache.

"Inspector Walsh, I'm so glad to see you!" cried Caitlyn, almost having to restrain herself from hugging him as the old detective came up to join her.

"Eh?" The inspector looked startled by her vehemence. "Is something wrong, Miss Le Fey?"

"There was a crowd here and some of the villagers were—"

"—talking about the death at the Manor last night," the Widow Mags cut in.

Caitlyn turned to look at her grandmother in surprise. "They weren't just talking!" she said indignantly. "They were hostile and abusive, and should be—"

"I'm sure Inspector Walsh has more important things to attend to than dealing with village gossip," growled the

Widow Mags. She gave the detective a nod. "Now, if you'll excuse me, I need to be getting back to my shop—"

"Actually..." The inspector cleared his throat. "I've come to see you, Widow Mags. I'd like to ask where you were last night, between the times of half past eleven and midnight."

"I was in bed, in my room behind the chocolate shop."

"And is there anyone who can corroborate that?"

"If you're asking if anyone was with me, then no. I was alone."

"Wait... why are you asking all this?" demanded Caitlyn, looking at the CID detective. "You're acting like my grandmother is a suspect. But you just told me this morning that the police are treating Percy's death as non-suspicious. You said that he died of a heart attack."

"He did. However, I have since

received the preliminary results of the autopsy, which suggest that his heart attack was artificially induced by some kind of toxin."

Caitlyn stared at him. "Are you saying Percy was poisoned?"

Inspector Walsh nodded. "According to the pathologist, the post-mortem findings are consistent with death from cardiac arrest and respiratory failure— due to ingestion by mouth of some poisonous substance."

"What poisonous substance?" asked Caitlyn.

"That remains to be determined. Specimens of the stomach and intestinal contents, as well as liver tissue, have been submitted for analysis. But I am not waiting for the results—I have opened an official inquiry," said Inspector Walsh grimly. "This is now a murder investigation."

Chapter Twenty-One

Caitlyn felt her heart thud uncomfortably in her chest. Even though she had been frustrated by the inspector's dismissive attitude that morning and had wanted the police to take things seriously, she still felt unnerved to hear the case officially elevated to murder. And she felt her unease grow as she saw that several of the villagers were still hanging around, unashamedly eavesdropping on their conversation. The fact that the police had confirmed the murder and were questioning the Widow Mags about her alibi would only add fuel to the already smouldering fire of the villagers' distrust.

Inspector Walsh turned back to the Widow Mags. "Several villagers have reported that Percy Wynn was seen visiting your chocolate shop yesterday evening before arriving at the Manor."

Caitlyn made an impatient noise. "That's just Vera Bottom and her cronies trying to stir up trouble again!"

Inspector Walsh raised his eyebrows at her. "Are you saying that they're lying?"

"No, Percy did come to the shop," Caitlyn admitted. "But he never saw my grandmother. She had already gone out. It was me he talked to."

"And did he purchase some chocolates?"

"Y-yes," said Caitlyn reluctantly. "Although that wasn't the reason he came into the shop. He was asking for directions to Huntingdon Manor Then he saw one of our special displays and bought a couple of packets of Florentines before he left."

"These Florentines—did they contain berries?"

"They contained wild autumn berries, such as elderberries and sloe berries," said the Widow Mags. "Why?"

Inspector Walsh looked thoughtful. "Elderberries, eh? And sloe berries—the fruit of the blackthorn bush, isn't it? And they are both fairly large, round, dark berries, aren't they?"

"Well, elderberries are a bit smaller and sloe berries are more oval in shape... but what is your point?" asked the Widow Mags impatiently.

The inspector looked smug. "My point is that the deadly nightshade plant—also known as belladonna—has berries which look very similar: large, round, and black. And those berries are high in atropine, which is one of the types of poison that can give you a heart attack."

"You think I poisoned that young man with my Florentines?" growled the Widow Mags.

"Oh, maybe not deliberately," said the inspector hastily. "I mean, they do look very alike. Perhaps you just made a mistake—"

"Are you suggesting that I don't know the difference between elderberries, sloe berries, and belladonna berries?" demanded the Widow Mags, sounding more offended to be accused of berry ignorance than to be accused of murder.

"Well, it would be understandable if you made a mistake when you were foraging. The light might have been fading, and your eyesight might not be what it used to... uh..." Inspector Walsh trailed off, quailing under the Widow Mags's fierce gaze. He cleared his throat. "Er... *ahem*... yes, well... It was just a suggestion."

"Surely Percy wouldn't have been the only person who bought those Florentines, Inspector?" Bertha spoke up. "There were several packets in the shop display. If the Florentines did have poisonous berries in them, wouldn't other customers have reported being ill too? You haven't had any reports from local hospitals or poison centres, have you?"

"No," the inspector admitted. "That was one of the first things we checked."

"And did you check the packets that Percy bought?" asked Caitlyn. "They're probably still in his room at the Manor. Surely you can examine them and see if they contain any belladonna berries?"

"My men are at the Manor now, conducting a thorough search of the premises," said Inspector Walsh.

"You should be questioning all the guests at the Manor again, as well as double-checking their alibis," said

Caitlyn.

The inspector frowned. "What are you saying, Miss Le Fey?"

"Katya Novik. She told you that she'd gone to bed early and was asleep in her room the whole time until she heard the commotion. But she's lying."

"And how do you know that?"

Caitlyn hesitated, thinking of the conversation that she and Pomona had overheard when they were eavesdropping through Leandra Lockwood's barn window. But something in her balked at mentioning it to the inspector. For one thing, it would mean having to confess her and Pomona's snooping, and for another, it seemed like an unwarranted invasion into Katya's private life. After all, it wasn't a crime for Katya to see Leandra in secret—whatever her reasons—and Caitlyn squirmed at the thought of revealing the girl's personal affairs.

"Miss Le Fey?" Inspector Walsh looked at her impatiently.

"Um…" Caitlyn suddenly thought of another way to question Katya's alibi without mentioning Leandra. She disliked being part of Tori's spiteful chain of gossip, but it seemed to be the lesser of two evils. "Tori—Miss Fanshawe-Drury—told me that she popped over to Katya's room last night to get something after everyone had retired, and it was empty. There was no one there. So Katya lied to you about her whereabouts last night."

Inspector Walsh raised his eyebrows. "Miss Fanshawe-Drury didn't mention this to me when I interviewed her."

"It wasn't a murder investigation at the time, so maybe she didn't think it was important."

"Hmm… well, I'll speak to Miss Fanshawe-Drury again. But it comes back to motive. Why would Miss Novik have wanted to harm Mr Wynn?"

Caitlyn hesitated again. "I... I think Percy liked Katya. I was watching them at dinner last night and it looked like he was trying to flirt with her, but Katya didn't seem very keen. Maybe she began to find his attention annoying—"

"And decided to murder him?" said Inspector Walsh incredulously.

Caitlyn flushed. It did sound a bit ludicrous when put like that. "Maybe she didn't intend to kill him. Maybe it was an accident."

"And what about your theory about the stolen book—how does that fit into this?" Inspector Walsh continued. "I thought you were convinced that Mr Wynn was murdered because someone wanted to steal a book of magic spells?"

"What book is this?" the Widow Mags interrupted. "Is this the 'witch's book' that the villagers were talking about?"

Inspector Walsh gave an impatient

sigh. "Yes, Percy Wynn was holding a piece of paper in one hand when he was found, and your granddaughter here—" He nodded at Caitlyn "—thinks that it was a page torn from a book hidden in the Manor Library. She believes it's a book of spells, a—what d'you call it—a 'witch's *grimoire*'?" He reached into his jacket and withdrew something from an inner pocket, which he held out to the old witch. "Do you recognise this?"

The Widow Mags stiffened as she stared down at the plastic sleeve containing the torn page that had been in Percy's hand. Next to her, Bertha drew a sharp intake of breath.

There was a long silence. Then the Widow Mags gave a curt nod and said: "It looks like a page torn from a *grimoire* that once belonged to me."

Inspector Walsh raised an eyebrow. "'*Once* belonged'?"

"The *grimoire* was stolen from me,

many years ago," said the Widow Mags.

"And you had no idea that it was in the Fitzroy library?"

"I have not seen it in twenty-two years."

"Inspector, that book is very valuable to our family and we must get it back," said Bertha urgently.

Inspector Walsh gave Caitlyn a grudging nod. "Well, you may be right, Miss Le Fey, in suggesting that this 'grimoire' holds the key to this case. *Not* because it is a magical book or any other such nonsense," he added quickly. "But simply because it is an item that may have represented enough value to someone to motivate them to commit murder. So if we can find out who wanted that book, that may lead us to Percy Wynn's killer."

Inspector Walsh turned back to the Widow Mags. "Do you know anyone who might have had a specific interest in this book?"

"I cannot give you a list of names. That would be an impossible task," said the Widow Mags. 'The *grimoire* contains knowledge of immense power. There are many who would wish to own it and use it for their own ends."

Including your own daughter? thought Caitlyn suddenly. If the *grimoire* had been hidden in the Library all these years, then that meant that after Tara had stolen it from the Widow Mags, she must have lost it somehow. Was she now trying to get it back? Caitlyn thought suddenly of Bertha's earlier words: *...you don't know how skilled your mother is at the art of glamour magic... Tara could be hiding in plain sight... disguising her appearance and fooling the eyes...*

A wild idea popped into Caitlyn's head: could Katya Novik be Tara in disguise? Had her mother assumed a false identity as Vanessa's friend to come to the Manor and search for the *grimoire*? It would fit with Katya's lies about her whereabouts last night. She hadn't been in her room sleeping—she had been downstairs in the Library with Percy! After all, Percy had already been trying to show her the *grimoire*—perhaps she decided to take him up on his offer after all, and then... and then what? Killed him?

No, it's a stupid idea, Caitlyn chided herself. Katya couldn't be Tara. It just didn't feel right. She had sat next to Katya, had talked to her and watched her—and nothing about the girl had felt anything like the woman described as her mother. Besides, wouldn't Tara have glamoured herself as someone closer to her own age?

"Miss Le Fey?"

Caitlyn blinked and came out of her thoughts to see Inspector Walsh looking at her expectantly. "I'm sorry?"

"I was asking if you had anything to add with regards to the *grimoire* and who might have been interested in it."

"Well, Katya Novik is really into magic and witchcraft. In fact, her friends said that she was 'obsessed' with the occult. Maybe she tried to take the *grimoire* from Percy by force and, like I said, there was an accident or something. You need to question her again. And... and there might be others too."

"Others?"

"Um..." Caitlyn hesitated, thinking of Leandra Lockwood and feeling even more like a spiteful village gossip. She didn't particularly like the woman and found her patronising, melodramatic, and annoying, but none of those things were reasons for Leandra to be a murderer. "Well, there are others living in the village and on the estate who have a strong interest in witches and the occult," she said at last, opting for vague references rather than naming names.

"You should question them."

"That could mean all of Tillyhenge at present," said the inspector dryly. "We've had an inordinate number of phone calls recently from people in the local area, all concerned about supernatural activity. Everyone seems to have become an expert on witchcraft and the occult suddenly." He gave an irritable sigh. "Well, if you think of anything else, please let me know."

As soon as Inspector Walsh had walked off with his constable at his heels, Bertha turned to the Widow Mags and began anxiously checking her for signs of injury.

"I'm fine, I'm fine... stop fussing!" snapped the old witch, brushing her daughter's hands way.

"Those villagers could have really hurt you," fretted Bertha.

"Yes, why didn't you let me tell Inspector Walsh what really happened?"

demanded Caitlyn. "That wasn't just a couple of people having a malicious gossip—they were practically a lynch mob!"

"Oh, stop exaggerating, girl," growled the Widow Mags. "They were nothing more than a clot of nitwits with more hysterical imagination than sense."

"Just because they're stupid doesn't mean that they're harmless!" said Caitlyn. "In fact, people who are ignorant and scared are the worst. They're so self-righteous and defensive, and all they want to do is destroy what they don't understand, because they think that puts them in control. We should have reported it to Inspector Walsh—"

"And what good would tattling to the police have done?" said the Widow Mags. "It would have just got the villagers even more riled up and added grist to their mill." She waved a hand. "Least said, soonest mended."

"But..."

"I said—*stop fussing!*" The Widow Mags glowered at her. "We've wasted enough time on this hullabaloo. We need to get back to the chocolate shop—there's work to be done." She turned and began hobbling up one of the lanes leading away from the village green.

"Do you think you should stay at the chocolate shop?" asked Caitlyn, rushing after the old witch and putting a protective hand under one of her elbows. "I'll be staying at the Manor this weekend so you'll be there all alone."

"I've been alone a long time," said the Widow Mags. "I don't need anyone to babysit me."

"Yes, but what if—"

"I am not helpless!" The Widow Mags yanked her elbow out of Caitlyn's grasp. "Stop treating me like an old woman."

"But you *are* an old wo—er, I mean..."

The Widow Mags glared at her. "I can take care of myself, girl. I was doing it for years before you showed up." Whirling, she stalked off down the lane, muttering under her breath: "Young people... always thinking they're the first to come up with every idea in the book and that the world will stop without them..."

"Mother..." Bertha hurried after her. "Mother, I think Caitlyn is right. I know there's always been some unpleasantness in the village, but this time... well, I've never seen so many people so agitated before. Maybe it isn't a good idea to be living at the chocolate shop alone. You could come and stay at the herbal shop with me or you could go back to the Manor with Caitlyn and stay there for a few days, just until things calm down. I'm sure James—"

"I'm not going anywhere," snarled the Widow Mags. "I'm not letting a gaggle of village imbeciles drive me from my home. Now if you don't let the subject drop, I'll have to use a Babble Ban spell on you!"

Caitlyn and Bertha exchanged frustrated looks and gave up.

Chapter Twenty-Two

Leaving her aunt to return to her herbal store, Caitlyn followed the Widow Mags meekly through the winding lanes of the village back to *Bewitched by Chocolate*. When they arrived, they found Evie manning an empty shop and looking very bored.

"There hasn't been a single customer," she complained as the Widow Mags took her place behind the counter. "I don't understand why it's so quiet."

Caitlyn wondered uneasily if Vera and her cronies were doing something to sabotage business for the chocolate shop. She felt a surge of angry indignation. After months of hard work, they were finally turning things around at *Bewitched by Chocolate*: building a name for the Widow Mags's luxurious, handcrafted confectionery and enjoying a steady flow of customers. She couldn't bear to think of it all being undone by a couple of spiteful women and their petty bigotry.

The Widow Mags didn't seem bothered by the lack of customers, however. Instead, she said, with satisfaction: "Good... the less people, the better. Then I can get on with making some chocolates in peace."

The old witch began heading to the kitchen, then paused and made an irritable sound. "Ah... warts and widdershins! I was supposed to stop at the village post office shop to get some cream for my next batch of ganache." She glared at Caitlyn. "All that fussing by you and Bertha made me forget."

"I can pop back to get it now," Caitlyn offered soothingly. "I won't be long."

She left the shop and began retracing her steps along the winding, cobbed lane. As she walked, her thoughts drifted back to the recent interview with Inspector Walsh. *So Percy's death is murder after all*, she thought grimly. *And Katya? Am I wrong to think that the girl's illicit meeting with Leandra Lockwood had nothing to do with the murder?*

Caitlyn began to regret not being more specific in recounting her suspicions to Inspector Walsh. Had she been too nice in trying to respect Katya's privacy? She recalled the expression of hero-worship on the girl's face. Katya was obviously completely under Leandra's influence and would do anything to impress the older woman. What if she *had* been trying to get hold of the *grimoire*—not for herself, but for

Leandra?

And Leandra—what was *her* motive? Caitlyn recalled the woman's sharp interest in the *grimoire* during that eavesdropped conversation. Was that just idle curiosity borne of her general obsession with the occult or was there a more sinister reason?

"Caitlyn! Wait!"

Caitlyn snapped out of her thoughts and turned around to see Evie running down the lane towards her. The younger girl arrived in a flurry of lanky limbs and frizzy red hair, her eyes bright and excited.

"I told Grandma that I'm coming to help you," she said breathlessly.

"Oh, thanks, Evie." Caitlyn smiled at her young cousin, thinking that she was obviously desperate for a change of scene to relieve the boredom of the shop.

But as Evie fell into step beside her,

Caitlyn realised that there was another reason why the younger girl was so keen to speak to her.

"Guess what?" Evie said, her voice quivering with excitement. "I cracked it!"

"Cracked what?"

"The Truth Nougat! I finally figured out how to make the spell infuse the mixture, and I've even made some pralines filled with the Nougat."

She dug into her pocket and pulled out a packet wrapped in foil. Carefully, she unwrapped this to show Caitlyn a small pile of chocolate pralines. The rich aroma of cocoa and roasted hazelnuts wafted up from the glossy brown chocolates.

"Now, I just need to find someone to test it on," said Evie. She looked hopefully at Caitlyn. "I don't suppose you'd like a little taste?"

"Er..." Caitlyn felt caught between a

rock and a hard place. She loved Evie and wanted to show support, but her past experiences with her young cousin's spells had also made her more than a little wary!

Before she could think of a diplomatic reply, their attention was distracted by a voice calling to them, and they looked up to see Pomona in the distance, waving madly. The American girl was standing on a corner of the village high street with a group of people, and Caitlyn quickly recognised them as Vanessa and her friends. They had obviously decided to have an outing to Tillyhenge instead of going riding that afternoon. Benedict was peering with interest into the window of an antique shop whilst Katya, Tori, and Vanessa were huddled in front of a village boutique on the opposite side of the street, their heads bent as they admired some handknitted mittens on display. They all looked up as Caitlyn and Evie joined them. Tori raised an eyebrow and said in an amused voice:

"Well, well, if it isn't Miss Marple... had a busy morning hunting for clues?"

Caitlyn felt her cheeks reddening, but she kept her voice even as she said: "We should all be keeping our eyes open, since Percy's death is now officially a murder inquiry."

"*What*?" Benedict stared at her. "Bloody hell—I thought you said the police thought it was a heart attack?"

"They still do, but I just saw Inspector Walsh again and he says the toxicology report suggests that Percy's heart attack was triggered by some kind of poison."

Caitlyn eyed the group carefully, observing their reactions. They all looked suitably horrified—even Tori had lost her trademark smirk—but she wondered just how genuine everyone's expression was. After all, shock was one of the easiest reactions to fake.

"So... what's gonna happen now?"

asked Pomona.

"Well, Inspector Walsh has sent some of his men over to the Manor. They're going to search the rooms and question everyone again," Caitlyn said.

"What? Search our rooms?" cried Katya, looking alarmed.

"They can't do that!" said Benedict angrily. He turned to Vanessa. "You need to speak to your brother, Ness!"

Vanessa shrugged. "They probably have a search warrant. Anyway, James told me this morning that he'd already given the police permission to search the whole Manor house if they wanted to."

"Why so worried, Ben?" asked Tori slyly. "Do you have something to hide?"

Benedict flushed. "No, of course not! It's just... we're being treated like common criminals, and it's preposterous to suggest that one of us might have hurt Percy!"

"Yes, what about the staff?" demanded Katya. "The police should be looking at them."

"They all have alibis," said Caitlyn simply. "They were mostly together in the kitchen and they can all vouch for each other."

"Shame you went up to bed so early, Katya, and there's no one to vouch for *you*," said Tori, with a malicious smile. "That's a long time you were alone that's unaccounted for."

Katya paled slightly. "I… I was tired," she said. Then she glanced at Benedict and added defiantly, "Anyway, I wasn't the only one who was alone in my room."

"Ah, but Benedict insists that he tucked up Percy nice and safe in bed before he went to his own room," said Tori, turning her mocking gaze to the young man next to her.

"What about you? Where's *your* rock-solid alibi, then?" challenged Benedict.

"Tori was with me," said Vanessa quickly. "We were chatting in her room until we heard the commotion downstairs. Anyway, it's silly, us getting in a stew over this," she added brightly, obviously trying to repair the camaraderie in the group. "I'm sure the police are really good at their jobs and they'll get to the bottom of things." She glanced over at Evie, who had been hovering shyly behind Caitlyn, and smiled at her. "Hello, I don't think we've met?"

"I...I'm Evie," stammered Evie, squirming slightly as the attention of the group shifted to her.

"Oh, sorry—yes, this is Evie," said Caitlyn, quickly making introductions. "She's my cousin."

"I thought Pomona was your cousin?" said Tori.

"I'm the sassy American cousin;

Evie's the sweet English cousin," said Pomona, with a wink. "Evie's mom, Bertha, owns this really cool herbal shop in the village. It's just off the other end of the high street. We should go check it out! It's called *Herbal Enchantments* and it's got all these awesome things like scented soy candles, and organic bath salts. and herbal creams, and shampoos..."

"Ohhh, I love candles," said Katya, her eyes lighting up. "Let's go and see this shop now."

"Yes, I've been looking to get a new organic shampoo," said Tori, in agreement with Katya for once.

Benedict didn't seem to share the girls' enthusiasm for retail therapy. "I don't know... maybe we should get back," he said, looking towards the village green where he had parked his car.

"Yes, it'll be time for tea soon,"

declared Vanessa, turning in the direction of the green as well.

"Bloody hell, you two are a pair of wet blankets," Tori complained. "We've only just got here; we haven't even looked around the whole village yet. It sounds like the Manor's going to be crawling with police anyway. Not sure I want to be standing around watching PC Plod go through my undies. We can have tea in the village pub, can't we? And then afterwards, we can pop into that chocolate shop that Percy was talking about—"

"That's on the outskirts of the village," said Vanessa quickly, pulling a face. "I don't want to trek there. I've worn the wrong shoes for walking and my feet are already killing me." She stretched out a foot and gestured to the dainty ankle boots she was wearing. "I just want to flop down on a sofa and have a cup of tea. But *not* the stuff they serve in the village pub. I want proper leaf tea, in a china cup—and no one can serve a cup of tea like Mosley!"

That was certainly true. Still, Caitlyn was slightly surprised by Vanessa's outburst. Up till now, it had been refreshing to see that—despite her aristocratic background and privileged upbringing—James's sister had never behaved like a wealthy "spoilt brat". So Caitlyn was taken aback by her suddenly petulant manner. Still, people do get cranky when they're tired, she reasoned, and it was true that none of them had got much sleep last night.

The others seemed to share her thoughts. After exchanging some looks, they shrugged and agreed, and began walking towards their car. Katya offered Evie a friendly smile and fell into step beside the younger girl as they followed Tori, Benedict, and Vanessa. Caitlyn started after them, but Pomona caught her arm and held her back so that they fell behind the group.

"So who does Inspector Walsh suspect?" she asked in a low voice.

Caitlyn shrugged. "You know what he's like. He's keeping his cards close to his chest at the moment."

"Did you tell him about Leandra?" demanded Pomona.

"Um... not specifically," Caitlyn admitted. "But I did tell him that he should question people living in the village and on the estate who have a strong interest in witches and the occult."

"Caitlyn!" Pomona groaned. "That could be anybody! You should have told him our suspicions about Leandra."

"They're not *our* suspicions—they're *your* suspicions. You're the one who was concocting this wild fantasy about Leandra not being who she says she is."

"Aw, come on! Don't tell me you don't think there's something 'off' about that woman."

Pomona is right—there is *something 'off' about her*, Caitlyn admitted to herself. She thought back to her first meeting with Leandra outside the chocolate shop. Something about the retired academic had put her on edge, although she couldn't explain what. Maybe it had been the way Leandra had looked at her so intently, as if she were trying to see right into the depths of Caitlyn's heart...

Now who's being paranoid and over-imaginative? she chided herself. Still, Caitlyn couldn't shake off her sense of disquiet. It was almost as if she were missing something about the woman, some vital truth that was just out of her reach...

Then she drew in a sharp breath, her heart pounding. "Oh my God..." she whispered.

"What?" said Pomona.

Caitlyn shook her head wordlessly,

still grappling with the thought whirling through her mind. Yes, Pomona was right in saying that Leandra wasn't who she said she was, but it wasn't because some mysterious billionaire had recruited her and given her the ability to fool others—it was her own magic!

The conversation with Bertha that morning echoed in Caitlyn's mind: "...*you don't know how skilled your mother is at the art of glamour magic... It's one of her special talents... With her skill at disguising her appearance and fooling the eyes... she could be right here, with us, and we would never know...*"

Could Tara have disguised herself as Leandra Lockwood? Now that she thought about it, so many things seemed to fit. The way Leandra had been hovering outside the chocolate shop and even Bertha's herbal shop—if Leandra really was Tara, then it would make sense that she would be drawn back to her family, in spite of herself, perhaps to check out her sister's business or revisit her old home.

And old habits would show, too, despite her best intentions. Caitlyn thought of the row of beautifully carved turnips outside Leandra's barn, and then heard Bertha's voice in her head again: *"...Tara had a thing about turnips... she especially loved carving them for Samhain. She would enchant a chisel and then use magic to create the most amazing lanterns..."*

If Leandra was really Tara, then it would also explain the intense curiosity that she had shown towards Caitlyn, such as those nosy questions about her relationship with James Fitzroy. It was natural that Tara would want to know about her grown-up daughter's personal life. And her impersonation would have given her the perfect excuse to approach and observe, without being exposed herself.

Caitlyn became aware suddenly that Pomona was talking to her.

"...hello? Earth to Caitlyn?" Pomona waved a hand in front of her face. "Are you okay?"

She blinked and refocused on her cousin. "Yes... sorry, Pomie... I was... listen, I'm sure Leandra isn't the murderer."

"Why not?"

"She just can't be."

Pomona gave her an irritated look. "You can't just say that without giving a reason. You're dissing all my ideas and saying they're stupid, but at least I've got reasons to back up my theories, whereas you—"

"All right!" Caitlyn glanced ahead to make sure that the others were still busily talking and not paying them any attention. Then she took a deep breath and said, keeping her voice low: "I'm sure Leandra can't be the murderer because… because I think she's my mother!"

Chapter Twenty-Three

Pomona stopped in her tracks and gaped at her. "Wait—*WHAT*? You think Leandra's your mom?"

"Shhh!" hissed Caitlyn. "Keep your voice down!"

Pomona made a visible effort, saying in an incredulous whisper: "You're telling me that your mom's actually some uptight academic who's been teaching college kids in London this whole time?"

"No, no, no," said Caitlyn impatiently. "There probably *is* a London academic called Leandra Lockwood, but I don't think she's the woman staying on the estate. I think that's Tara, who's used glamour magic to disguise herself as 'Leandra' so that she can remain incognito and move around Tillyhenge without anyone recognising her."

"Holy guacamole! Leandra's your mom? Are you, like, really sure?"

"Well, I'm not *sure,* but... you know when I first met her, I did wonder about her... but then she looked at me so blankly that I thought I must be wrong. And she acted so pompous—you know, all those lectures about Samhain and going on and on about magic rituals and ancient traditions..." Caitlyn shook her head in reluctant admiration. "Except when you think about it, that could actually be a clever smokescreen! I mean, Leandra's academic background is the perfect cover story. It would explain how she has all this knowledge about magic and the occult, but at the same time, her ridiculous obsession with superstitious trinkets and her sermonising about magic is exactly the opposite of how a real witch *would* act! So it means that anyone with a genuinely magical background, such as her own family, would never consider her a *real* witch—so her real identity can't be discovered."

"I don't know..." Pomona still looked unconvinced. "You're saying you think the woman is your mom because she doesn't act like your mom?"

"It's not just that! There are other things too. For example, we know Tara was here during the masquerade ball last month, right? And Bertha told me that she thought Tara could still be in the village or on the estate, just disguised by glamour magic. She said Tara could be 'hiding in plain sight'—well, impersonating Leandra Lockwood would be the perfect way to do that! Plus, Leandra would be around the right age. Oh, and also there were the turnips—"

"Huh? Turnips?"

Caitlyn nodded eagerly. "Bertha told me that Tara used to love carving turnips for Samhain, and you remember all those carved turnips outside Leandra's barn?"

"I don't know, Caitlyn. That's kind of random. I mean, lots of people probably carve turnips for Samhain. And what about the real Leandra? What's happened to her?"

"I don't know; she's probably still in London or something," said Caitlyn dismissively. She took a deep breath. "I think she's Tara. And that means that Leandra can't be the murderer because my mother just wouldn't do that!"

Pomona didn't say anything for a moment, then she gave Caitlyn a hesitant look and said: "Are you sure? I mean... I know it sucks to hear this but... maybe you don't really know what your mom's capable of."

"How can you say that, Pomie? You

know your own mother would never do certain things—"

"Yeah, but I've lived with my mom my whole life. I *know* her. You don't know Tara at all," said Pomona awkwardly. "All you have is this fantasy of who you'd *like* her to be."

Caitlyn clenched her teeth. "And all *you* have is a fantasy too! The whole theory about Leandra murdering Percy to get her hands on the *grimoire*—possibly to give to Blackmort—could just all be in your head."

"Okay, so you have a better idea?" challenged Pomona.

"Yeah, I do. I don't think we should be obsessing over Leandra. We should be looking at other suspects."

"Like who?"

Caitlyn glanced at the group walking ahead. "Like... like Tori, for instance."

"Vanessa vouched for her,

remember? She said that the two of them were chatting in Tori's room."

"Well, she could have been lying to cover up for her best friend."

"Yeah, but what motive would Tori have?" demanded Pomona. "If it had been, like, *Katya* who'd gotten murdered—sure, no question! Tori hates Katya's guts. She's jealous of Katya for being thinner and prettier, and because Vanessa likes her. But Percy's different. Tori had no reason to kill Percy."

"Well... maybe Tori wanted the *grimoire* and Percy got killed by accident."

Pomona made an impatient sound. "Gimme a break! Tori is, like, so snarky about any magic stuff. There's no way she's gonna be interested in any *grimoire*. You're clutching at straws, Caitlyn, 'cos you wanna find someone else to frame for the murder. You don't want Leandra to be involved because you think she's your mom."

Caitlyn shifted uncomfortably, not wanting to admit—even to herself—that Pomona might be right. "I'm not," she insisted. "I really do think we can't just focus on Leandra and not consider anyone else—"

"What are you two conspiring about?"

They looked up to see that the others had stopped walking and were waiting for them to catch up. They had been so engrossed in their discussion that they hadn't noticed they were already by Benedict's parked car on the village green.

Tori wagged a finger at them and said, with that familiar supercilious smile: "Naughty! Naughty! Don't you know that it's bad manners to whisper and gossip when there are other people around?"

Caitlyn hurriedly straightened away from Pomona, trying to keep her expression cool and unbothered. She knew that Tori was just baiting them; nevertheless, she felt embarrassment wash over her. There was nothing like being castigated for bad manners in public to make you feel small.

"We weren't conspiring," she said, trying not to sound defensive. "We were just discussing some private matters."

Tori gave a scornful laugh "Private matters? Since when did Americans keep anything private?"

Pomona's eyes flashed. "And since when did being British give you the right to be a condescending bi—"

"Okay, okay, let's not get our knickers in a twist, eh?" said Benedict, hurriedly, stepping between the two girls. "Er— Ness, didn't Mosley say something about putting on a special 'high tea' this afternoon?"

"Yes, Mrs Pruett finally came 'round to my idea of a picnic," said Vanessa, with a dimpled smile. "Not in the Portrait

Gallery like I wanted, though—it'll have to be in the Conservatory. But still, it should be more fun than another boring formal meal in the Dining Room."

"Sounds good," said Benedict, rubbing his hands with relish. "Is she going to lay on some traditional nosh? I fancy steak and kidney pie... mm, devilled eggs would be good too."

He turned and began getting into the driver's seat of the parked Range Rover, obviously energised by the thought of the food that awaited them back at the Manor. Tori and Vanessa followed suit, climbing into the back seat. Katya cast a last longing look back at the cobbled street leading to Bertha's herbal shop, then reluctantly went around the other side of the car and got into the passenger seat next to Benedict.

"Man, I'd so like to wipe that smirk off Tori's face," muttered Pomona under her breath as the car doors slammed shut next to them.

"You know she's doing it on purpose, Pomie," Caitlyn admonished gently. "I think people like Tori get a kick out of provoking others and watching them squirm. The best thing you can do is not react. Don't let her see that she's got to you."

"No, the best thing I can do is make *her* squirm," said Pomona, jutting out her bottom lip. Then she heaved a sigh and said, "Well, I'd better join them if I want a lift back to the Manor." She looked at Caitlyn and Evie expectantly. "What about you guys? I'm sure you could both squeeze in with us."

"Oh... I'm not... I mean, I'm sure they don't want *me* at the 'high tea'," stammered Evie shyly.

"'Course we do! James *especially* told me to invite you if I saw you. It's gonna be a fun, casual affair, with a few other staff members from the estate, so it won't just be Vanessa and her friends." Pomona paused, then added with a teasing smile: "I know Chris Bottom will be really disappointed if you don't come."

"Chris is going to be there?" Evie's voice had gone up several octaves.

Pomona nodded, grinning. "Yup. You know James really likes him. Says Chris is great at helping with odd jobs around the Manor... What does he call it— 'dogsbody'? Anyway, Chris is invited, along with the other members of James's core team." Pomona winked at Evie. "Six o'clock in the Conservatory. So you've got, like, two hours to get all dolled-up, honey."

"*Two hours?*" Evie wailed, her hands going up to her frizzy red hair. "Oh my Goddess... I... I wonder if I've got time to wash my hair? And what about the spot on my chin? Maybe I can put a clay mask on it while I'm washing..." Still muttering frantically to herself, Evie hurried away and disappeared down the lane towards Bertha's herbal shop.

"I wish I had time to wash *my* hair," said Caitlyn wistfully. "But I've got to get some fresh cream for the Widow Mags, and then I've got to pack an overnight bag—"

They were interrupted by the tooting of a car horn and turned to see that Benedict had wound down his window and was jerking an enquiring thumb towards the back of the car. "You getting in, Pomona?"

The American girl nodded, then turned back to Caitlyn. "We could wait for you while you go and get your stuff from the Widow Mags's cottage," she offered.

"No, don't worry," said Caitlyn quickly. "I'll just take the shortcut over the hill back to the Manor."

Caitlyn waved the car off, then hurried to the village post office shop to pick up a tub of cream before heading back to *Bewitched by Chocolate*.

Back at the cottage, she found the Widow Mags engrossed in making a new batch of Florentines. The old witch barely looked up when Caitlyn poked her head around the kitchen doorway.

"Um... I'm heading back to Huntingdon Manor and I'll probably stay there all weekend. Will you be okay?" asked Caitlyn hesitantly.

"Of course, I'll be okay," said the Widow Mags tartly. "What do you think I am, a pot of soup? I don't need you keeping an eye on me all the time."

Caitlyn bit her lip. "You could come back with me..." she tried again.

"Stop fussing, child, or I will really give you something to worry about!"

Caitlyn swallowed an exasperated sigh and gave up. As she hurried up the spiral staircase to her attic room, she consoled herself with the thought that although the Widow Mags might look like a frail old woman, she was still a very powerful witch. Even if her fingers were stiff and arthritic now, the spell power that exuded from them was undiminished.

Besides, what can I do? thought Caitlyn with a wry smile. *I've barely mastered how to enchant a ladle to stir a cauldron of hot chocolate. The Widow Mags probably has more of a magical arsenal in her little finger than I can muster with my whole body!*

Chapter Twenty-Four

Twenty minutes later, Caitlyn left *Bewitched by Chocolate* with a small overnight bag and set off across the hill behind the cottage. This was the shortcut that she had described to Percy and, despite involving a vigorous climb, it was actually a quicker route to the Manor. In fact, she was soon descending the other side of the hill with the sprawling grounds of the main estate below her. As she scanned the outbuildings, she caught sight of the stone barn and recalled guiltily that she hadn't gone to retrieve Nibs yet. In all the excitement with Bertha's conflict with the Manor staff, followed by the "mob attack" on the village green and Inspector Walsh's visit, she had completely forgotten about the little kitten.

Changing course, Caitlyn made her way down the hill and, instead of heading for the main Manor house, she walked between the outbuildings until she reached the barn. It looked quiet, and when she knocked on the door, she got no reply. Leandra was obviously out.

Annoyed at the wasted trip, Caitlyn was about to turn away from the door when a faint sound caught her attention. She paused, cocking her head to listen. *Was that the high-pitched mew of a kitten?*

"Nibs?" she called, turning back to the barn door.

She strained her ears, trying to catch that faint sound again, but heard nothing. Still, Caitlyn was sure she hadn't imagined it.

"Nibs? Nibs, are you okay?" she called, leaning close to the door.

Silence.

Caitlyn bit her lip, wondering what to do. She could go and look for Leandra to get access to the barn, but she had no idea where the woman was. She turned and glanced across the rear courtyard, scanning the area. Leandra might have left the estate and gone to one of the nearby towns. And in the meantime... *What if Nibs is caught in something or trapped somewhere? What if he's injured and in pain?*

Caitlyn turned back to the door, and before she realised what she was doing, she was holding a hand out to the knob and whispering: "*Aperio!*"

It was one of the first spells she had learned when she'd arrived in Tillyhenge, and now—just as she had that first time—she gave a little gasp of surprised delight as the knob turned of its own accord and the door clicked open.

Stepping inside, she paused for a moment, looking around and getting her bearings. The barn had been completely renovated, with a spacious interior that retained the high, vaulted ceilings, timber beams, and exposed stone walls of the original building, but also—judging from the cosy temperatures and lack of draughts, as well as the beautiful polished wooden floorboards—incorporating modern features like raised floors and underfloor insulation. Most of the space was open plan, spread over a sitting room, kitchen, and dining area, but there was a connecting door at the far end which she assumed led to the bedroom. It was strangely neat and immaculate, almost like a showhouse, with very few of Leandra's personal belongings.

"Nibs?" she called softly, sweeping

her gaze around.

No reply. She began making a circuit of the room, looking under tables, behind cupboards, and even lying down flat on her stomach to peer underneath the sofa. There was no sign of the kitten. Finally, Caitlyn made for the connecting door at the end of the room. When she stepped through, she was surprised to find that the rear of the barn building was bigger than she'd expected, with several rooms leading off a small T-bar corridor that ran perpendicular to the doorway. She hesitated and was about to turn to the right when she thought she heard a faint thump coming from the left branch of the corridor that ended at a closed door.

She hurried down the corridor and knocked hesitantly on the shut door. She felt a bit silly—it was obvious that Leandra wasn't home—but at the same time, it felt rude just barging through a closed door without knocking. As expected, there was no answer, and a moment later, she stepped inside what looked like a study, furnished with bookcases along the walls and a desk by the window. Unlike the main living area, which looked like a picture in a holiday rental brochure, this room looked messy and lived-in. There were folders, academic textbooks, and piles of papers everywhere, accompanied by canvas bags and half-opened cardboard boxes stacked haphazardly around the bookshelves. By the window stood a cabinet filled with a jumble of divination crystals, scented candles, bundles of dried herbs and incense sticks, velvet pouches, carved medallion necklaces, and other mystical paraphernalia.

As Caitlyn surveyed the clutter in the room, she felt a surge of doubt. Her theory that her mother had used glamour magic to impersonate Leandra had seemed to fit perfectly. But now, looking around, the mess seemed such a realistic representation of a typical academic's workspace that she began to wonder if her guess was wrong after all. If Tara was pretending to be Leandra, would she bother with so much paraphernalia?

She began searching the room, calling softly for the kitten. "Nibs? Nibs, where are you?"

A faint mewing sounded behind her, and she whirled around to find herself staring at the desk, with its jumble of books and papers, and a half-drunk mug of coffee next to an open laptop. There was no kitten amongst the mess of things atop the desk... so she walked around the side, peering over the back of the leather executive chair, bending to look into the footwell... but there was no kitten on the chair behind the desk, no kitten on the floor beneath the desk, and no kitten in between any of the boxes of files piled next to the laptop.

Her gaze drifted down to the deep

drawers lining one side of the desk. Could Nibs be in one of the drawers? Surely not!

Still, she found herself reaching out and carefully sliding each of the drawers open. As she had expected, she found nothing in them except a mess of papers and stationery, old diaries, planners, copies of academic journals, and pamphlets from various small religious organisations.

As she was about to shut the bottom drawer, she noticed a small slip of paper tucked into the side of the interior panel. There was some writing scribbled on it, something that looked like a foreign alphabet. Then, as she looked again, she paused, her heartbeat quickening.

No, those weren't letters from a foreign alphabet—they were symbols.

Almost unconsciously, her hand crept up to her throat, where she wore a ribbon around her neck strung with a simple runestone. This was the only thing that had been with her when she was found as an abandoned baby, and it had always been her most precious possession, her only link with her past. Now, she drew it carefully out from where it was always tucked under her shirt and stared down at its surface. It was engraved with markings similar to those on the slip of paper. Not exactly the same, but close enough for her to know what the writing on the paper was: witch's runes.

She reached into the drawer and tried to pull the slip of paper out, but it was wedged tight, one end tucked beneath the base of the drawer. Caitlyn dropped to her knees so she could lean down and peer at the drawer from underneath, but to her surprise, the other end of the paper was not sticking out from the underside of the drawer.

She straightened up again, frowning. Then it came to her: *Of course! The drawer must have a false bottom!* Quickly, she emptied the drawer of all its contents, then felt around the flat inner base. It seemed solid, but when she gave it a little wriggle, it shifted beneath her fingers. She wriggled it again, harder, and suddenly the sheet of plywood slipped sideways and lifted up.

Caitlyn peered underneath it. There was a shallow compartment filled with papers, documents, envelopes, and folders. The slip of paper with the runes was tucked vertically down one side of the concealed space, its end wedged between two brown envelopes. Caitlyn reached in and was about to pull the slip of paper out when her gaze fell on the topmost envelope. It was a plain brown manila envelope with the name "Carla Dowlenook" scrawled across the top— but what *really* caught her eye was the corner of a photograph protruding from one ripped side. Two faces peeked out, and her heart skipped a beat as she thought she saw James in the photograph.

Caitlyn yanked the envelope from the drawer and shook the photograph out into the palm of her hand. She stared at it, her mind a jumble of confused thoughts.

No, it wasn't James after all. This man was older, although he shared the same strong jaw, grey eyes, and calm, authoritative air. As she peered closer, Caitlyn realised who it was: James's father—the old Lord Fitzroy.

As she recalled the oil painting of James's father hanging on the wall of the Portrait Gallery, she noticed a strong resemblance to the man in this photograph. This was obviously taken many years ago, as evident from the faded quality of the photograph and the fact that the senior Lord Fitzroy looked a lot younger—somewhere in his fifties, perhaps. He was standing next to a much younger man, who looked to be in his late twenties.

Their expressions were solemn, but there was a sense of camaraderie between the two men, and something in the way the younger man stood slightly behind James's father suggested a respectful deference, like that of an apprentice with his master.

Who is he? Caitlyn wandered. Then, as she brought the photograph closer to examine the young man's face, she felt her pulse begin to race. The young man was handsome, with dark hair and a sensitive mouth that spoke of a gentle, compassionate nature. But it was his vivid hazel eyes which held her attention and made her heart thud uncomfortably in her chest. Because she had seen eyes exactly like his before... every time she looked in the mirror.

Chapter Twenty-Five

Caitlyn stared at the photograph, her thoughts whirling even more wildly than before. *What does this mean? Who is this man who has the same eyes as me?* An idea, bold and thrilling, sprang to her mind, but before she even had time to consider it properly, the sound of footsteps in the corridor outside broke into her thoughts.

Caitlyn jerked her head up and pressed the photo reflexively to her chest. *Is Leandra back?*

She hesitated only a split second before tucking the photograph into the waistband of her jeans and pulling her sweater down to hide it from view. Then she dropped the brown manila envelope back into the hidden compartment, slid the false bottom on top, and piled all the contents haphazardly back into the drawer. She'd barely slammed the drawer shut and straightened up from the desk when the door to the study opened.

Caitlyn whirled to face it, but to her surprise, instead of Leandra, she saw a wrinkled old man in an ancient suit framed in the doorway.

"Viktor!" she cried, sagging with relief. "What are you doing here?"

"Looking for my fangs—what do you think?" said the old vampire grouchily. He shuffled into the room and began rummaging through the clutter. "I'm sure I had them at breakfast... yes, one got stuck in a stewed prune... and then that Pruett woman came in, rabbiting on about dirty old tramps stealing food from the Manor—why she was telling *me*, I have no idea! Really, it was enough to give a bat an echo-ache... Hmm, you know, now that I think about it, I could have dropped the fangs when I climbed out of that upstairs bedroom window, but unlikely, I think..." He paused at last and regarded Caitlyn curiously. "What are you doing here, my dear?"

"I'm searching for Nibs. Have you seen him, Viktor?"

"Eh? Who's Nibs?"

"Nibs, my kitten! You know: little ball of black fur, big yellow eyes—"

"Ahh, yes, the feline kit. Tiny little fellow, isn't he? Nearly tripped me up, running around my ankles chasing a blasted belladonna berry—"

Caitlyn did a double take. "Chasing a *what*?"

"A belladonna berry. Fruit of the deadly nightshade plant. Not one of the nicer fruits, I might add. Very much an acquired taste," said Viktor, making a face. "Highly toxic, you know. Mind you, I once met a vampire who'd developed quite a tolerance to them. Used to have a couple with his gin and tonic before supper. But of course, he shifted into a lesser long-nosed bat, and they're always eating agaves and cacti stuffed with toxins, so he's got a cast-iron stomach—"

"I know what belladonna berries are," cut in Caitlyn impatiently. "I'm just wondering how on earth Nibs ended up playing with one! Where was this? Where did you see him?"

"Hmm… let me see now." Viktor stroked his knobbly chin. "It was when I was looking for a place to have a nap after breakfast this morning. In one of the guest bedrooms."

"The one you were sleeping in last night?" asked Caitlyn quickly, thinking of Katya.

"No, no, that one is too full of hysterical females. Never having a kip in there again," said Viktor irritably. "No, I found a room further down the corridor that was completely empty. Had police tape across the doorway, which is marvellous at keeping everyone out. Well, that's when I saw your kit. He was just outside the bedroom next door, chasing the berry about."

Caitlyn stared at him, almost unable to believe what she was hearing. "You saw Nibs outside Percy's room, playing with some belladonna berries? But where did the berry come from?"

Viktor made a tutting sound. "Well, obviously the room next door. The girl who brought the bundle of belladonna berries must have dropped one without realising."

Caitlyn felt like her head was spinning. "*What girl?*"

"One of those bleating females who

arrived yesterday."

"Which one? Viktor, which one was she?" asked Caitlyn urgently. "What did she look like?"

Viktor furrowed his brow. "Eh? Wasn't really paying much attention. I was more interested in the basket of fruit in her room. Mmm, Shropshire Damsons as big as apples, can you believe it? There's nothing like these old English varieties. I can remember when they first came out in the 1670s... ah, I was a much younger vampire then and had just developed a taste for plums—"

"*Viktor!* Never mind the plums—what about the girl?"

"The girl? What about her?"

"You must remember *something* about what she looked like?" said Caitlyn desperately.

Viktor gave a helpless shrug. "One human girl looks much like any other."

"Well, what about her hair? Was it the same colour as mine?" asked Caitlyn, holding up a strand of her fiery red tresses.

"Oh no, certainly not. It was gold-coloured. Quite lovely, actually, now that I think about it. Made me think of a leprechaun I once knew. Always had a soft spot for girls with gold hair. Not that hair is real gold, of course, but old Seamus liked anything yellow and glittery..."

Caitlyn's mind was racing. Both Katya and Vanessa had gold hair just like Viktor described. Which one of them had brought belladonna berries to the Manor? And were those what had poisoned Percy?

"Do you remember anything else about the girl?" she asked hopefully. "What was she wearing?"

Viktor looked at her in bewilderment. "She was wearing clothes."

Caitlyn hung on to her patience with an effort. "Yes, but what kind of clothes? How did she dress? Was she wearing a skirt? Jeans? What colour top?"

"Hang about, let me think..." Viktor mused for a moment. "Hmm... don't remember the colour, but there were lots of sparkly whatsits on her jumper."

Sparkling whatsits? Caitlyn flashed back suddenly to the first night she'd met Vanessa and how she had admired the girl's soft white sweater, embellished with a delicate pattern of gold sequins. But surely Viktor couldn't have seen Vanessa? What was James's sister doing with belladonna berries?

"Viktor, how do you know this girl brought belladonna berries—"

"I told you..." said Viktor tetchily. "I saw her take them out of her handbag. She came into her room and took a little bundle of fabric out of her bag, and when she unwrapped it, I saw that there were several belladonna berries in there. She counted them, then wrapped them up again and put them under the pillow on her bed."

"Yes, but what I meant was: how did you happen to see all this?" asked Caitlyn. "Why were you in Vanessa's—I mean, why were you in this girl's room?"

"It was the basket of fruit," said Viktor, as if it were obvious. "I could smell those Damson plums from the top of the staircase. They have the most wonderful perfume, you know. Some people call them sharp and bitter, but I say that's because they haven't developed the palate for the more robust plums—"

"Er... yes, Viktor, going back to the girl," interrupted Caitlyn. "Didn't she see you if you were standing there, drooling over the plums in her fruit basket?"

Viktor bristled. "I do not drool! I was merely admiring them and trying to decide which one to eat first." Then he added in a grudging tone: "I was also in my bat form, so perhaps she did not notice me."

Ahh, that explains it, thought Caitlyn. If Viktor had shapeshifted into his other form—a small, fuzzy brown fruit bat—he would have been much easier to miss, especially if the room had been dark.

"When was this, Viktor?" asked Caitlyn. "When were you in the room?"

Viktor heaved a long-suffering sigh. "I *told* you. It was when this new lot of visitors arrived and went up to their rooms."

That would have been just before dinner on Thursday night... *Which was last night*, Caitlyn reminded herself. It was hard to believe that not twenty-four hours had passed since Vanessa and her friends had arrived at the Manor and Percy had been murdered. So much had happened since then.

She turned back to the old vampire. "Listen, Viktor, did you see—"

Caitlyn broke off as she heard the sound of footsteps outside in the corridor again. These were quick and purposeful, unlike Viktor's shuffling steps earlier, and they were approaching rapidly. Caitlyn darted out from behind the desk and hurried towards the study door, but just as she reached it, it swung open to reveal Leandra Lockwood standing in the doorway.

"What are you doing in here?" she cried in surprise.

Caitlyn stared at her. All she could think was: *Is this woman really my mother?*

Once again, she searched Leandra's features desperately for some sense of familiarity, some sign of resemblance. She only had a vague sense of what her mother might look like—she had never seen a proper photograph of Tara aside some faded childhood pictures in the Widow Mags's family photo album and a fuzzy image from the security camera footage at the recent masquerade ball. The one thing she knew was that Tara had red hair, just like herself. Leandra's hair was certainly the right colour (although she admitted to herself that the vivid crimson shade could also have come out of a bottle). Caitlyn scanned the woman's face again. She knew that Tara was likely to be completely glamoured, with her real features hidden, but surely some vestiges of her real face, her personality, would peek through?

"Miss Le Fey—are you all right?"

Caitlyn blinked and realised that Leandra was eyeing her worriedly. It reminded her of their first meeting. "Er... yes, sorry, I'm fine..."

Leandra was glancing around, obviously trying to see if anything had been disturbed, and Caitlyn suddenly remembered the photograph tucked into her waistband, hidden under her sweater. Even though she knew there was no way Leandra could see the stolen photograph, she had to restrain herself from adjusting her sweater nervously.

Leandra had swung her gaze back to Caitlyn and was now regarding her expectantly, obviously waiting for her explanation. Caitlyn gulped, trying to think of a good excuse for breaking into the woman's house, but before she could speak, Viktor tottered forwards and thrust his head out on his scrawny neck.

"Have you seen my fangs?" he asked Leandra.

"I... I beg your pardon?" said Leandra, taking a step back.

Viktor gestured vaguely. "Thought I might have dropped them around here. Probably slipped out of my mouth while I was flying—wouldn't be the first time, you know; confounded dentists, never know what they're doing. Of course, the fangs are most likely outside on the ground somewhere, but you never know with teeth... turn up in the most unlikely places... thought it was worth popping in here to check."

"Is this some kind of joke?" said Leandra, looking as if she didn't know whether to be baffled or annoyed.

"Joke? This is no joke, my good woman," said Viktor, looking affronted. "Those fangs are my third pair, and I'm garlicked if I'm going back to the dentist again for another replacement!"

Still muttering grumpily, the old vampire shuffled out of the door and disappeared down the corridor. Caitlyn started to follow, grateful that Viktor seemed to have distracted Leandra. But her relief was short-lived, for the older woman grabbed her arm before she could slip out of the room and said:

"You still haven't answered my

question, Miss Le Fey. What are you doing in my study?"

"I... er..." For a split second, Caitlyn thought of lying, then she remembered Nibs. "Actually, I was looking for my kitten. I came to pick him up, but then you weren't home and... er... the front door was slightly ajar so—"

Leandra frowned. "That's impossible. I remember locking it."

"Maybe the lock didn't quite latch or something... you know how it is with these old buildings."

"But this barn has been completely modernised and renovated. They even installed new flooring and insulation, and replaced all the doors and windows. It would have been impossible for you to get in, unless you're a professional burglar or—" She gave Caitlyn a knowing smile. "—you used magic."

For a moment, Caitlyn was struck dumb. Was the woman joking? Or was

Leandra trying to tell her something else?

"Um… er… well, even modern locks have problems sometimes, don't they?" stammered Caitlyn at last. "Er… anyway, I'm sorry for bothering you, but if you could just get Nibs, I'll be on my way—"

"I don't have your kitten. I don't know why you thought you would find him here."

Caitlyn stared at the older woman in surprise. "But he has to be here! You must have seen him. You're the one who—"

She broke off, realising that she couldn't accuse the woman of having grabbed Nibs earlier without revealing that she and Pomona had been eavesdropping under the barn window.

"Yes?" Leandra was looking at her quizzically.

"You must have seen him," said Caitlyn weakly. "He… he was playing around your barn here earlier."

"Ah, well, I did see a black kitten which might have been yours. He'd crawled onto my kitchen windowsill. But I put him out the front door hours ago and I haven't seen him since."

Caitlyn was taken aback. She had been so focused on fooling Leandra and hiding the fact that she had been snooping in the woman's study that it had never occurred to her that Leandra would deny having Nibs. Something of her distress must have shown in her face because Leandra seemed to soften slightly and said:

"Look, if I see your kitten I'll be sure to let you know. Don't worry—I'm sure he's fine. He's probably just out, playing in the Manor grounds somewhere. Have you checked the stables?"

"N-no," Caitlyn admitted. "I just thought... well, I thought he'd definitely be here. And earlier, when I was outside your front door, I was sure I heard him crying—"

"You must have been mistaken," said Leandra, shaking her head. "But we can search the house again, if you like."

She turned and led the way out of the study, and Caitlyn followed dumbly as they went from room to room. She had to admit that Leandra made a commendable effort to let her search the whole barn, opening wardrobes and storage cupboards, and encouraging her to look behind furniture and in corners. The kitten was nowhere to be seen.

Finally they returned to the main room. Caitlyn expected to be shown the door but to her surprise, Leandra hesitated, looking as if something was on her mind. But after a moment, all she said was: "I'm sorry I can't invite you to stay for tea but I have some work I need to get to."

"I thought you were retired," said

Caitlyn, following her reluctantly to the front door.

"That doesn't mean that I can't continue my own studies, my personal growth," said Leandra loftily. "And now, more than ever, there are those who require my knowledge and expertise to guide them during this perilous time around Samhain."

She opened the front door and Caitlyn had no choice but to step outside. As she was walking out the door, though, Caitlyn strained her ears, hoping to catch that faint mewling again. But she heard nothing. Feeling troubled but unsure what to do, she bade Leandra goodbye and left. And despite the other woman's claims of needing to get to work, she was aware that Leandra stood in her doorway for a long time, watching her as she slowly walked away.

Chapter Twenty-Six

Mrs Pruett had put on an impressive high tea: everything from dainty finger sandwiches with traditional fillings like egg and cress, smoked salmon and cream cheese, and wafer-thin roast beef with horseradish sauce, to curried devilled eggs, miniature steak-and-ale pies, and—the *pièce de résistance*—a Coronation quiche filled with spinach, broad beans, fresh tarragon, and cheddar cheese, encased in a crisp, light shortcrust pastry. The savoury dishes were accompanied by a selection of petits fours, traditional buns, and teacakes, as well as a basket of freshly baked scones. Mosley presided over a side table offering perfectly steeped tea, coffee, and—for those who were feeling particularly indulgent—glasses of champagne.

Everyone exclaimed over the lavish spread and were quick to help themselves, piling their plates high from the buffet laid out at one end of the Conservatory. But Caitlyn found herself without much of an appetite. Her mind kept returning to what had happened in Leandra's barn. *Can that woman really be my mother?* thought Caitlyn uneasily. She didn't want to believe it. And yet what she had told Pomona was true: so many things *did* fit.

And then there was that photo she'd found. Caitlyn's heart beat faster again at the memory of the young man who shared her eyes, and she finally acknowledged the idea that she hadn't dared to consider fully earlier: *Could he be my father?* If that was the case, then the fact that Leandra had a photo of him just cemented the idea that she was Tara.

Perhaps it was silly of her to expect any flicker of recognition or familiarity. After all, she had been a newborn baby when she was abandoned twenty-two years ago; she'd had no memory or experience of her mother, so why would she expect some kind of connection now?

And if Caitlyn was honest with herself, she had to admit that her unease was probably more due to the fact that she didn't like Leandra Lockwood. She recalled Leandra's pompous pontificating about the Samhain Festival and made a face to herself. The woman could be intensely irritating and she recoiled from the thought that such a patronising bore could be her mother.

But the whole pompous, superior academic thing could just be an act, she reminded herself. Yes, thinking about it,

Tara wouldn't just rely on physical appearance to maintain her disguise— she would make sure to adopt a false persona too. It would certainly explain Leandra's melodramatic manner and ridiculously sanctimonious attitude towards the Samhain Festival rituals: surely no normal person could behave like that? It had to be an exaggerated act!

Feeling exhausted by her tormented thoughts, Caitlyn tried to turn her mind in another direction. But the first thing she thought of was what Viktor had told her in Leandra's study and her mind balked anew. This was a different kind of uneasy thought—and one that was harder to swallow. *Could it really have been Vanessa with the belladonna berries?* she wondered for the umpteenth time. But what did that mean? She shied away from the obvious conclusion. No, Vanessa couldn't be involved with Percy's murder... could she?

"Is the food not to your liking, madam?"

Caitlyn looked up to see Mosley hovering over her, a bottle of champagne cradled with a napkin in one hand, and an expression of dismay on his face as he eyed her sparsely filled plate.

"Oh no, Mosley—the food is great," said Caitlyn. "I... um... I'm just not very hungry."

"Perhaps a glass of champagne would help to whet the appetite," suggested Mosley.

Caitlyn hesitated, then shook her head. Her mind was muddled enough without adding champagne on an empty stomach. "No, thank you, Mosley, I'm fine. And the food really is delicious," she assured the butler with a smile.

She glanced around the room after Mosley left and noted that she seemed to be the only one who wasn't enjoying the convivial atmosphere. Vanessa and her friends were sprawled out on the wicker furniture at one end of the Conservatory, plates of food expertly balanced on their laps as they talked and laughed amongst themselves. Beyond them, Caitlyn could see Evie—looking very pretty with her usually frizzy red hair wrestled into a gleaming half-knot and her lanky frame enveloped in a soft velour dress—standing next to a tall, good-looking teenage boy with sun-bleached blond hair and a ready grin. Her young cousin was smiling shyly, her cheeks pink with pleasure, as Chris Bottom offered her some quiche from the buffet.

On the other side of the Conservatory, James stood with his personal assistant and a few other members of his office staff, listening as Lisa, the Manor's marketing coordinator, talked and gesticulated passionately. She seemed to be venting about some aspect of the Samhain Festival preparations, and James nodded sympathetically as he listened. Then he glanced up and caught Caitlyn's eye across the room. He gave a faint jerk of his head towards Lisa, then sent her a helpless smile, wordlessly apologising for not being able to join her. Caitlyn smiled back and nodded to show that she didn't mind.

Rising from her seat, she decided that she should try to fill her plate with more food, if only to mollify Mosley. As she reached the buffet, she was accosted by Pomona enthusiastically waving a circle of bun-like bread slathered with butter.

"Omigod, have you tried the English muffins?" she said, thrusting the half-eaten muffin out to Caitlyn. "I mean, when they first told me this was a 'muffin', I was like: Er, you Brits don't know how to bake a muffin... But then I tasted it and was like: This is seriously out of this world! So soft and chewy... I don't care what they call it—it's delicious!"

Caitlyn laughed. "Yeah, I've had some of Mrs Pruett's muffins before—they're pretty amazing."

Pomona sidled closer, cast a glance around, then said in a low voice: "Hey… you know, I've been thinking about what you said earlier. Maybe you're right. Maybe Tori isn't, like, as innocent as she pretends to be. I mean, I still can't work out why she would have wanted to murder Percy, but I agree that she *could* have. Remember how quickly Vanessa jumped to give Tori an alibi when Benedict called her out earlier? I'll bet anything you like that Tori was lying about where she was last night and Vanessa is covering up for her."

"Or—" Caitlyn broke off, swallowing the words that sprang to her lips. *Or it was* Vanessa *who needed to have a cover for her movements on the night of the murder, and that's why she rushed to vouch for her best friend—because it would have provided her with an alibi too.*

"Or what?" said Pomona.

"Uh... nothing," muttered Caitlyn. A part of her desperately wanted to share her suspicions about Vanessa with Pomona, but another part wanted to just push the whole idea out of her head, to ignore the possibility of James's sister being involved.

Pomona gave her a quizzical look, then shrugged and continued: "Yeah, well, the problem is how to get Tori to tell us the truth. I just wish there was, like, some way to force her to tell us what she was really doing last night!"

"We could use my Truth Nougat."

They looked up to see that Evie had joined them at the buffet.

"Huh? But I thought you couldn't make it?" said Pomona.

"I can now!" said Evie eagerly. "I was just telling Caitlyn about it before we saw you back in Tillyhenge. I managed to make the spell work." She dug into her pocket and pulled out the foil-wrapped lump again. "Ta-da! Roasted Hazelnut and Chocolate Pralines filled with Truth Nougat and sprinkled with crunchy almond brittle."

"Wow! Those look awesome, Evie," said Pomona, peering into the foil packet. "And they smell amazing!"

Caitlyn put a hand on her arm. "Pomie... I don't think this is a good idea—"

"Aww, come on! Don't you wanna know if Tori is lying about her alibi? This would be the perfect way to make her talk," wheedled Pomona.

"But you haven't tested those pralines yet, Evie," said Caitlyn anxiously. "You're not even sure if the Truth Nougat works or if it's safe—"

"Exactly! That's why we need to try it out on someone," said Pomona, grinning. "You don't wanna submit a dud to the Samhain Gourmet Glory contest, do you?" Her eyes gleamed as she turned to look across the Conservatory. "And I know just the person to test it on."

Chapter Twenty-Seven

Caitlyn wondered how they were going to get Tori alone, but it seemed that luck was on their side. Soon after everyone had eaten their fill, James and his team left to have a meeting in his study, leaving them alone with Vanessa and her friends. The fresh air and exercise earlier in the village, combined with the lavish tea and warmth of the Conservatory, had cast a soporific mood over the room. Vanessa yawned and stretched one leg out from the sofa.

"Ugh... my jeans are damp at the bottom," she said, regarding the hem with distaste. She stood up from the sofa. "I'm going up to change into a dry pair."

"I'll come as well," said Katya, standing up and stretching. "I think I might have an early night."

"What—another one?" said Tori, with a smirk. "Let's hope none of us get murdered tonight."

Katya flushed, but she flounced out of the room without answering.

"That's not funny, Tori," said Benedict tightly. He got up and stalked out of the room.

"Tori... that was a bit mean," said Vanessa reproachfully.

"Oh, for God's sake, if Benedict wants to go off in a strop because I made a little joke about Percy, then that's *his* problem," said Tori, rolling her eyes. "It's called dark humour. What does he want us to do otherwise? Wail and cry all the time?"

"No, but..." Vanessa sighed. "Oh, never mind. Are you coming up with me?"

"Uh-uh, I'm happy where I am," said Tori, idly flicking through an issue of *Country Life* magazine.

"Okay, see you in a bit."

Pomona exchanged looks with Evie and Caitlyn as they were left alone with Tori, then she grinned and whispered: "It's showtime!" Before Caitlyn could stop her, she plucked the foil packet out of Evie's hands and sauntered over to sit next to Tori. The other girl pointedly ignored her, continuing to peruse her magazine, but Pomona was undaunted. Leaning over to look at the open magazine, she gushed:

"Wow—check out those tweed pants! You know, you English people always somehow make wearing boring things look really cool."

Oh wonderful, thought Caitlyn with an

inward sigh. *She's really going to make friends with back-handed compliments like that!*

Tori gave Pomona a sour look and deliberately turned away so that her shoulder blocked the view of the magazine. But Pomona hadn't developed her thick Hollywood skin for nothing. She ploughed on, ignoring Tori's obvious snub.

"Hey... I love your jacket! Where did you get it from?"

For a moment, Caitlyn thought that Tori wasn't going to reply at all, but obviously ignoring a direct question was too rude, even for the Sloane set. "Barbour," she said curtly.

"Ahh... I love British brands: Liberty, Hobbs, Mulberry, Harris tweed, and—omigod—don't get me started on Hunter boots!" Pomona chattered on. "So, what new stuff have you got from the fall collections?"

"I don't follow trends," said Tori disdainfully. "I only invest in classic pieces."

"Oh-kay... what about make-up?" Pomona tried again. "You gotta change that up sometimes, right?"

Tori sniffed. "I favour the natural look."

Pomona persisted, undaunted. "How about hair? You always had your bangs like that?" She tilted her head to one side and regarded Tori critically.

The other girl put a hand up reflexively to her forehead, finally beginning to look a bit discomfited. "Yes, I like my fringe like this."

"Oh, it looks good on you!" Pomona assured her. "Only someone with such a... er... generous forehead could carry it off."

Tori scowled. "What's that supposed to mean? Are you saying that my forehead is too big?"

"Oh no, honey! I mean, who doesn't wanna have a high forehead, right? Isn't it supposed to be, like, a sign of class and privilege?"

Tori gave her a sneering look. "It's not a matter of privilege—it's a matter of birthright. My family have been part of the reigning nobility since Anglo-Saxon times, long before America was even colonised! We've owned properties and country estates across England... we've had an influence on industrial reforms, politics, the arts... we've contributed to countless charitable causes—"

Pomona's hand shot out, offering the foil packet of pralines. "Chocolate praline? They're homemade. Cocoa and roasted hazelnuts—yum!"

"Uh..." Tori looked down distractedly, obviously disorientated after being interrupted mid-flow, and absentmindedly grabbed a praline. She popped it into her mouth before continuing her tirade: "...and we've maintained traditions and ceremonies that are core to the nation's identity, shaping the very fabric of British society!"

She paused at last to catch her breath and chew the praline in her mouth. Caitlyn watched tensely as Tori swallowed the chocolate bonbon. Nothing happened.

"How does the Truth Nougat work?" she said to Evie under her breath.

"I... I think you need to ask her a question."

Pomona must have thought the same thing because she leaned close to Tori and asked: "Tell us the truth, Tori—what really happened on the night of Percy's murder?"

Tori stared at her in surprise. Her jaw worked spasmodically for a moment, then she blurted: "I still practise kissing on my pillow."

"Huh?" Pomona frowned at her. "Well,

good for you, but you didn't answer my question. Did you and Vanessa really stay in your room the whole time?"

Tori's eyes darted left and right, and she made a choking sound. Her jaws spasmed, as if she were trying to keep her mouth shut, but she seemed unable to stop herself.

She said through clenched teeth: "I pick my nose at traffic lights."

"Whoa!" said Pomona, leaning back. "That's, like, TMI—'Too Much Information'—okay? I'm not interested in your boogers. I'm interested in what you were doing on the night that Percy was murdered! Were you really with Vanessa?"

"I buy fake designer handbags and then show them off as real," said Tori, her eyes wide with dismay.

"Hey!" said Pomona, looking really angry now. "Quit playing games, okay? D'you think you're funny? That's not—"

"Wait, Pomona..." Caitlyn put a restraining hand on her cousin's arm. She lowered her voice. "I think she can't help herself. I think the Truth Nougat is making her speak."

"Well, of course it's making her speak. It's supposed to make her tell the truth—"

"No, no, I mean—I think the magic has gone wrong somehow. It *is* making her tell the truth—just not the truth *you* want. She's telling the truth about all her guilty little secrets instead."

"Oh my Goddess, I'm sorry!" said Evie, in a small voice. "I really thought I'd got the spell right this time."

Caitlyn gave Evie's shoulder a squeeze, then turned back to look at Tori, who was sitting there, staring at them in horror, her hands clamped over her mouth. "Never mind. But we need to figure out a way to undo the spell."

Evie bit her lip. "I don't think you can

undo it. I think the effect eventually wears off as your stomach digests the Truth Nougat, but I don't know how long that will be."

"You mean it might be hours?" said Pomona, looking gleeful.

Tori's eyes bulged in alarm. She looked at the girls pleadingly and choked, trying to speak, but all she managed at last was to croak: "I secretly enjoy the smell of my own sweaty gym clothes."

"This is terrible. We can't leave her like this—she'll be blurting out horribly embarrassing personal things to everyone," Caitlyn said, giving Tori a compassionate look.

"Why not? It would serve her right," said Pomona, with no sign of remorse. "It's about time that someone made *her* squirm for a change."

Caitlyn turned back to Evie. "If we can't undo the spell, how about trying to neutralise the effect of the Truth Nougat in her stomach? You know, like how you can drink milk to help neutralise acids that cause indigestion—"

"Ginger!" said Evie suddenly. "Mum always says that a cup of ginger tea *'cures all that ails ye'*—it works for sore throats and nausea and indigestion and bronchitis—"

"Does it work for 'truth-blab-itis' too?" sniggered Pomona.

Caitlyn ignored her. "It's worth a try. Run to the kitchen and get some ginger tea. Quick!"

It seemed to take ages, although it was probably just a few minutes, before Evie was back, carefully carrying a steaming mug. The fresh, pungent aroma of ginger filled the air as she approached. She held the mug out to Tori.

"Here..." she said gently. "Try to drink it all."

The other girl recoiled.

"Tori, it might fix the problem," said Caitlyn earnestly. "Please, we're just trying to help you."

Tori gave her a dirty look, then she grudgingly took the mug, screwed up her face, and gulped down the ginger tea. They all eyed her expectantly when she finally lowered the mug.

"Um... how d'you feel, Tori?" asked Caitlyn. "Can you talk?"

Tori cleared her throat, then opened her mouth hesitantly. "I... I don't kno— *Oh my God!* I can talk normally!" She clutched her throat, laughing with relief. Then she rounded on them accusingly.

"What did you do to me?" she demanded. "You put something in that chocolate, didn't you? That's... that's like poisoning and assault! I'm going to report you to the police."

Before Caitlyn could respond, Pomona pushed in front of her and jabbed a finger in Tori's chest. "And I'm going to report *you* for giving a false alibi!"

"Wh-what d'you mean?" said Tori.

"You lied to Inspector Walsh," said Pomona, advancing and forcing Tori to lean back. "You told him that you and Vanessa were together, but in fact, you were downstairs in the Library with Percy, weren't you? You got Vanessa to cover for you—"

"What? NO! You've got it backwards, you stupid cow," said Tori furiously. "Ness isn't covering for me! *I'm* the one who's covering for her—" She broke off, a look of angry chagrin crossing her face.

Caitlyn stared at her. "Vanessa? You were covering for Vanessa? Are you saying *she* was the one who went down to the Library?"

"It's none of your sodding business," Tori spat at them. "But you're bonkers if you think Ness could have anything to do with Percy's murder!"

Shoving Pomona out of the way, she stumbled past them and ran out of the Conservatory.

"Wow," said Evie, letting out a breath. "That was like watching a detective show on telly, Pomona. You were brilliant!"

Pomona grinned and swept a mock bow. "Thank you, thank you."

Caitlyn, however, was barely listening. Instead, she was fighting the sickening realisation that her suspicions about Vanessa could be correct.

"Hey Caitlyn—you okay?" said Pomona, turning to her. "You look kinda weird."

Caitlyn turned troubled eyes on the other two girls. "Do you realise what Tori just said? It was *Vanessa* who lied about her alibi, not her! So that means when Vanessa jumped to say that she and Tori were together, it was actually to provide herself with a cover story. It means that

Vanessa could be guilty."

Pomona sobered. "Hang on, hang on... Much as I hate to admit it, Tori kinda has a point. You're nuts to be suggesting that James's sister had something to do with Percy's murder!"

"I know it sounds crazy," Caitlyn admitted. "But think about it: you said Tori had no motive for wanting to hurt Percy. That's true... but *Vanessa* did. She liked him, but he didn't return her feelings; he was besotted with Katya instead. And you know what they say about 'a woman scorned'."

"You're suggesting that Vanessa murdered a guy she had a crush on, just because he didn't like her back? Jeez, and you say *I* jump to conclusions!" complained Pomona.

"Maybe it was an accident," Evie suggested. "Maybe Vanessa didn't really mean to kill him, but something went wrong?"

"Yes!" said Caitlyn. "Yes, maybe Vanessa just wanted to do something spiteful, to punish Percy, and it backfired on her. It wouldn't be the first time she's done something like that either. Listen to this…" She recounted the story that James had told her about Vanessa's hapless classmate who had made the mistake of "snatching" the girl's coveted pony.

"I don't know… that's still a big jump," said Pomona, although she was starting to sound less doubtful.

"There are other things too," Caitlyn continued quickly. "Like Vanessa seems very blasé about Percy's death, when you'd expect it to be a big shock for her, *and* I caught her snooping in James's study earlier today. She said she was just looking for sweets, but now that I think about it, I'm sure she was lying."

"What was she doing then?"

Caitlyn thought back to the earlier

scene in the study. "I don't know. She was behind James's desk, in the corner of the room. I remember seeing her put her hand quickly behind her back, as if she was hiding something. Actually, I thought I caught a glimpse of something glittering, you know, like gold. I thought that maybe James keeps some of the family jewels in a safe in his study and Vanessa was helping herself..." Caitlyn frowned. "But it doesn't make sense: if Vanessa *was* just helping herself to jewellery from the family safe, why did she need to be so furtive about it? She begged me not to tell James that she'd been in there."

Pomona threw up her hands. "Maybe she wanted to wear some fancy diamond necklace that's a family heirloom and she thought James wouldn't approve. Honestly, Caitlyn, I think you're reading too much into this."

"No, I'm not. There's something odd going on with Vanessa, I'm sure of it..."

Caitlyn paused as another thought struck her. "Oh my God... you know what? I just realised something else: the Library! That's where I'd smelled her perfume!"

The other two girls looked at her blankly.

"This morning, when I saw Vanessa just before breakfast, I noticed that she was wearing this really lovely fragrance," Caitlyn explained. "The thing is, the fragrance seemed really familiar, like I'd smelled it before somewhere, but I couldn't figure out where. Vanessa said she hadn't been wearing it when they arrived at the Manor, and I wasn't sitting close enough to her at dinner to be able to smell it, so I couldn't work out why it seemed so familiar."

Pomona shrugged. "Maybe you smelled it in Duty Free at the airport or—"

"No, no, Pomie—that's the whole

point! Vanessa said that it was a *custom* fragrance. James gave it to her for her birthday, and it was made up especially for her by a perfumery in Paris. So it's unique. There's no way I could have smelled it before. But I was *sure* that I had... and now I've just remembered where!" Caitlyn looked at them excitedly. "Last night, in the Library. You know, when you and I went looking for the *grimoire*, just before we found Percy's body... *that's* where I'd smelled this same perfume! Which means that Vanessa was in the Library last night, probably just before we got there!"

Caitlyn was disappointed to see that neither Evie nor Pomona looked very impressed.

"I'm not sure if the police would take that seriously," said Evie at last, with an apologetic look.

"Yeah, you can't accuse someone of being at a crime scene just because you think you smelled their perfume there," scoffed Pomona. "You need proper proof, like… like some solid thing that proves Vanessa was in the Library last night."

She leaned forwards, her expression unusually serious. "But the thing is, Caitlyn—even if you *do* manage to prove that Vanessa was in the Library last night, whatcha gonna do? Tell James that you think his baby sister is a murderer?"

Chapter Twenty-Eight

Caitlyn couldn't wait for everyone to retire for the night so that she could speak to James in private. She hovered in the background as James said goodnight to his sister, watching the fond way he smiled at her, and wondered once more how she could ever voice her suspicions about Vanessa to him. The easiest thing would have been to say nothing, but now that the idea had taken root, it seemed to grow and fester inside her.

Could Vanessa really be involved in Percy's murder? Caitlyn wanted to recoil from the idea, to reject it outright, but she couldn't help thinking of all the odd coincidences she had mentioned to Evie and Pomona, which pointed to Vanessa being at the scene of the crime.

Still, just because she was there doesn't mean that she murdered Percy, Caitlyn reminded herself. *There might be another, perfectly innocent reason for James's sister being in the Library last night. Maybe I should wait until I have more concrete evidence before jumping to conclusions...*

But even as she had that thought, the sceptical voice in her head piped up: *If it was innocent, then why did Vanessa lie and pretend that she was with Tori the whole time?*

Caitlyn sighed. She knew that if this had been anybody else but James's sister, she would have already been beating a path to Inspector Walsh's office. After all, weren't there a wealth of suspicious coincidences already?

Vanessa's perfume in the Library on the night of the murder, her past history of seeking revenge on those she resented, her best friend Tori covering up for her false alibi, her own furtive behaviour in James's study—and finally Viktor's account of seeing her with belladonna berries. But still, the thought of facing James with her accusations made her cringe inside...

"Would you like a nightcap?"

Caitlyn blinked and looked up to realise that she and James were alone in the hallway. He was smiling at her and nodding down the hall in the direction of his study.

"I've got some excellent port... and Mosley's stoked the fire in my study."

"Um... yes, I'd love that," Caitlyn said, falling into step beside him as he led the way.

Once in James's study, she stood and watched distractedly as he poured dark ruby port from a crystal decanter, her mind in a tumult as she agonised over what to do.

No, I'll wait a bit longer, Caitlyn decided as James turned towards her and held out a glass of port. She knew she was taking the coward's way out, but after everything that had happened that day, she felt too drained to face a confrontation with James as well. *I'll just ask him about the photograph tonight. I won't say anything about Vanessa. After all, another day can't matter, can it?*

"Finally... I've been looking forward to this moment all evening," said James, with a smile, breaking into her thoughts as he came over and slid one arm around her waist.

He pulled her close and dropped a kiss on her forehead. Caitlyn felt herself blush and reflexively look around to check that they were alone, even as she savoured the feeling of being held in James's arms. It was still hard to believe sometimes that he had chosen *her* over all the sophisticated society beauties in his circle.

"Actually, I wanted to come and find you as soon as I heard about the 'mob' in Tillyhenge earlier today," said James, a frown creasing his handsome face. "Did they hurt you? Did anyone—"

"No, no, I'm fine," Caitlyn assured him.

"And the Widow Mags?"

"Well, someone tried to throw a plum at her, but she transformed it into plum blossoms before it hit her," said Caitlyn, with a wry smile.

James laughed. "Good for her! I would have liked to have seen that."

Caitlyn looked up, feeling a rush of love for him. It was both heartwarming and humbling to see how readily James accepted magic in his life now. He had always been a man of hard science and fact; she could remember how leery he had been of anything to do with the paranormal when she'd first met him. And yet, somehow, he'd managed to put aside a lifetime of scepticism, simply because he had accepted that she was a witch and that magic was in her blood. It was as if he was ready to embrace it all, just because it was a part of who *she* was. It made her ashamed of her own continued cynicism and instinct to doubt—despite having conjured magic spells herself!

"What is it?" asked James, searching her eyes.

Caitlyn gave him a sheepish smile. "Nothing. I was just thinking that you put me to shame. The way you've just accepted magic and witchcraft, when I'm still always rolling my eyes whenever Pomona talks about memory spells and fairy creatures."

"Well, I think a healthy scepticism of what Pomona says may not be a bad thing," James said, chuckling. "And it's not terrible to have a doubting nature or a questioning mind, Caitlyn. It can be a strength rather than a weakness."

He led her over to one of the leather Chesterfield sofas and sat down, patting the space next to him invitingly. Caitlyn smiled and dropped down, nestling close to his side. James leaned over and brushed his lips across hers in a feather-light kiss.

"I've missed you," he murmured. "I feel like I've hardly seen you lately..."

"I... I've missed you too," said Caitlyn shyly, looking up at him with her heart in her eyes.

"Do you know how much gentlemanly restraint I have to exercise when you look at me like that?"

"What if... what if I don't want you to be so gentlemanly?" Caitlyn said breathlessly.

James drew in a sharp intake of breath, then crushed her to him. For a long moment, there was no sound but the soft crackle of the fire in the grate as Caitlyn surrendered herself to the kiss. At last, they broke apart and James reluctantly let her go, although he kept one arm draped around her shoulders.

I never want this moment to end, thought Caitlyn dreamily, snuggling closer and leaning her head against James's chest.

James, however, was staring pensively into his port glass, and his face darkened as his mind returned to what they had previously been talking about.

"I thought that kind of stupid 'witch vigilantism' in Tillyhenge was over," he said, his voice thick with disappointment. "I know things got a bit hairy around the time of the Mabon Ball, but I really thought my efforts had calmed things down after that and we were making good progress. In fact, there seemed to be increasing acceptance and goodwill towards the

Widow Mags in the village." James shook his head in frustration. "I just can't believe how easily people have fallen back into blind prejudice and bigotry!"

"It's not your fault," Caitlyn consoled him. "I think it's just easy to go back into old habits when people are stressed. It's like they reach for what's familiar. And I don't know why, but something's really scaring the villagers at the moment. Even Inspector Walsh has commented on it. He said the police have received a lot more distress calls about witchcraft activity in the area."

"Maybe this Samhain Festival wasn't such a good idea after all," said James with a sigh. "When Lisa and the marketing team pitched it to me, it seemed like a great concept: a way to respect the old traditions, bring the community together, and also generate income for the estate and its tenants, as well as raising Huntingdon Manor's profile for tourism and entertainment.

But then the staff started raising objections... and Percy's death happened... and now it's an official murder inquiry!"

He rose from the sofa and began to pace the room. "I did talk to Lisa earlier today about cancelling the Festival, but she was adamant that we should go ahead. She said it would harm the villagers and tenants of the estate more than anything if we cancelled—they'd lose the extra stock they'd prepared, bookings for accommodation and dining, business from visitors shopping..."

"I think Lisa's right," said Caitlyn. "And I actually think that it would make things worse from the fearmongering point of view if you cancelled the Festival now."

James stopped and looked at her in surprise. "What do you mean?"

"Well, don't you think it would be sending a tacit signal to the community that Samhain is dangerous after all? It would be giving in to their fears. Whereas if you just continue as normal and don't make a big deal of anything, it might make them feel a bit silly for 'overreacting'," Caitlyn explained earnestly. "I mean, other towns don't cancel Christmas markets or Easter fairs just because a death happened in the local area. They're just seasonal events that are not connected to anything bad which may have happened."

James gave her a lopsided smile and came back to sit down next to her. "Thanks. It's good to have a voice of reason I can trust. And what you said does make sense." He leaned back on the sofa again and let out another sigh. "It would help if the police could make some progress on the case! At the very least, determine how Percy was poisoned and with what. All the uncertainty and unknowns just lead to endless speculation and superstitious gossip."

"I thought the police were searching the Manor all afternoon," said Caitlyn. "Haven't they found anything?"

"Nothing of consequence. I know the Forensics team have been talking to the kitchen staff and trying to examine any of the glassware, crockery, and utensils that Percy might have used or been served from, but—" He gave a rueful laugh. "—unfortunately, this is where Mosley's efficient running of the household has worked against us. Everything was thoroughly washed up and tidied away last night, after dinner was completed, so the chance of finding any trace of specific toxins on Percy's dinnerware is pretty slim."

"Um... are the police searching *all* the rooms in the Manor?" asked Caitlyn in a carefully casual voice. "Like, for example, the rooms belonging to the... er... owners as well as the guests?"

"I imagine so. I gave Inspector Walsh *carte blanche* to search where he wished. My bedroom certainly isn't off limits." James regarded her curiously. "Why?"

"Oh... nothing. I just wondered." Caitlyn thought of Inspector Walsh's deference towards the Fitzroy family. Would he see Vanessa as a possible suspect? Or would he consider James's sister above suspicion and therefore not bother to search her room?

"Is something wrong?"

Caitlyn looked up to see James watching her quizzically. Those keen grey eyes of his always seemed to see right through her, and right now, she didn't want him to guess at her thoughts. Hastily, she attempted to change the subject.

"No, nothing's wrong," she said, with a bright smile. "Listen, James, there's something I need to show you." She pulled the photograph she had taken from Leandra's study out of her skirt pocket and handed it to him.

"Where did you get this?" he asked, staring at it.

"Er... never mind that for now. Tell me, is that your father?"

"Yes. This must have been taken at least twenty years ago. That's the Library, I think—look, can you see the bookshelves in the background?"

"And the young man standing next to your father? Do you recognise him?" asked Caitlyn.

James frowned at the picture, then his face brightened. "It's him! The young man I told you about—the one who was here when I came to Huntingdon one summer. Remember, I told you I didn't live here when I was a child: my mother preferred our townhouse in London, and my father would divide his time between the estate and our London home. But that summer, Ness had just been born, and my mother was so busy with the new baby that she didn't have much time for me, so my father brought me with him when he came up here."

He tapped the photo. "And this young man was here... He worked with my father, I think—they used to sit in his study for hours. But when he was free, he used to spend time with me, teaching me various things like how to read a compass or how to play chess..." He smiled in reminiscence. "I really looked up to him and remember wishing that *he* could be my father because I'd never had someone spend so much time with me like that."

"What was his name?" asked Caitlyn eagerly. "Can you remember?"

James furrowed his brow. "Something beginning with 'N'... Neville? Neil? Or... Nigel... no, wait—Noah!" he said, snapping his fingers. "Yes, that was it! Noah."

"Noah what?"

James shook his head regretfully. "I don't remember. I only ever saw him that one summer. I didn't come up to the estate again the following summer or the year after that, and by the time I returned, he was gone. I never saw him again, and to be honest, I'd quite forgotten about him until you showed me that parchment with the rune symbols a couple of months ago."

"Yes, and you said Noah told you stories, didn't he? About witches and monsters and magic and vampires..."

"Yes, he had the most incredible imagination," said James with a laugh.

"What if... what if it wasn't his imagination?" asked Caitlyn breathlessly. "What if he was actually telling you the truth?"

James looked bewildered. "What do you mean, 'the truth'?"

Caitlyn took a deep breath. "Look, we

know that your father was a member of a secret society of witch hunters. You said this young man was a 'colleague'— what if he was another agent within the society? Like... maybe a young trainee that your father was mentoring?"

James still looked puzzled. "I suppose that's possible, but I don't understand why you're suddenly so interested in him—"

"Because I think..." Caitlyn hesitated. She had been afraid to voice the idea out loud, even to herself, but she couldn't contain it any longer. "I think he might be my father."

Chapter Twenty-Nine

"Your *father*?"

Caitlyn nodded. "The timing fits perfectly! This young man was here just about the time my mother would have been around sixteen or seventeen years old, and with the Manor so close to the village, they could easily have met and fallen in love.

"And the rune symbols he'd drawn on that parchment—you said it was just a prop for a game he played with you, and that it didn't have any special meaning, but..." Caitlyn paused, thinking out loud. "But even if they were just gibberish, he must have drawn those symbols based on something he'd seen—right?"

She reached beneath the collar of her top and pulled out the runestone necklace that she always wore. "This was with me when I was found as an abandoned baby. I think it belonged to my mother. And the symbols on that parchment match these on my runestone," she said excitedly. "Not exactly, but very closely... Well, what if that's what happened? Maybe this young man—this Noah—had seen the runestone necklace on my mother's neck several times, and so when he was creating the 'secret symbols' for your game, he decided to base them on the runes he'd seen on my mother's necklace. It all fits!"

"It's one possibility," said James cautiously. "But we're not even certain this Noah really was a member of that secret society—"

"It all fits!" Caitlyn insisted. "And if

Noah was a 'witch hunter', then he would have been the last kind of man my mother should have fallen in love with."

"So you think that's why your mother ran away? To be with him? But then where is he now? Why did she abandon you? And why did she murder Daniel Tremai—"

"We don't know for sure if she did," said Caitlyn quickly.

"The evidence from the camera footage from the ball is pretty irrefutable," said James. "Tara is seen at the crime scene just at the time that Daniel Tremaine was killed, and she is the only person who was with him."

"But the footage only shows her going into the Portrait Gallery. It doesn't show what actually happened in there. We don't know if she actually killed Tremaine," Caitlyn argued.

"Caitlyn..." James looked at her with compassion. "I know you don't want to consider the possibility that your mother could have murdered someone. God knows, I can relate! I grappled with denial myself when I found out that my father was a member of that despicable secret society of witch hunters. But in the end, I had to face the truth that parents might not be the saintly idols one imagines them to be; that just because someone is 'family', it doesn't necessarily mean that they can't do evil." He paused, then added gently, "You might need to face that truth as well."

Caitlyn was silent. She wanted to argue, to deny what James was saying, but she couldn't find the words. Instead, she cleared her throat and ploughed on, pretending that she hadn't heard what James had just said: "I don't think Tara ran away just because of Noah. I think the *grimoire* is involved as well, somehow. She stole it from the Widow Mags at around the same time."

"So I was right," said James, jubilant. "I said Tara was involved in this case. It's very likely that she's here, in the vicinity—in hiding, perhaps—and that she's searching for the *grimoire*. In fact, it could very well have been her with Percy in the Library last night. It would explain the mysterious circumstances of his death, with his heart attack brought on by magic rather than some kind of overdose—"

"No!" said Caitlyn. "No, there are lots of ways that Percy could have been poisoned. You're the one who's usually convinced that there's an ordinary, non-magical explanation for the murders—why are you jumping to a supernatural cause this time?"

"There are no other suspects, Caitlyn—"

"Yes, there are! Katya, for instance!"

"Katya?"

"Yes, I didn't get a chance to tell you

earlier, but Katya wasn't in her room like she told the police. Tori told me that she went to Katya's room to get some make-up and it was empty. So Katya lied about her alibi. She wasn't sleeping in her room. She'd actually sneaked out of the Manor last night, after dinner."

"Sneaked out where?"

"To—" Caitlyn broke off suddenly as she realised that if she mentioned Katya going to see Leandra, she would be dragging the latter into the murder investigation as well. And if the young man in the photo really was her father... well, it seemed to confirm that Leandra was Tara in disguise—why else would she have a photo of Noah? So mentioning Leandra would only validate James's suspicions about her mother.

"Yes?" said James, looking puzzled at her hesitation.

"Um... somewhere on the estate," Caitlyn mumbled. "Anyway, the point is she lied about her alibi."

"People often lie about their alibis," said James with a shrug. "It's not uncommon. But it's usually just something they're trying to hide—some small misdemeanour that's completely unrelated to the murder."

"You can't be sure of that. If someone gives a false alibi, it could actually be because they're guilty. Don't they say, 'There's no smoke without fire'?"

"They also say: 'A shadow does not always mean there's something lurking'," said James with a wry smile. "Why are you so certain that Katya could be involved in Percy's murder?"

"It's not just her. There are others who lied about their alibis. Tori also said—" She broke off and bit her lip.

James raised an eyebrow. "Tori said what? You're not suggesting that *she* might be involved as well? Look, I know Tori can be a prickly shrew at times, but

I've known her almost as long as I've known my own sister. She and Vanessa have been inseparable since primary school." He gave a droll laugh. "Ness would probably have your guts for garters if you suggested that her best friend might be a suspect."

Caitlyn hesitated, then on an impulse said: "James, have you noticed anything odd about Vanessa?"

"About Ness?" James looked surprised. "She's a bit more manic than usual, perhaps, but not really. Why?"

Caitlyn avoided answering directly. "Don't you think it's a bit strange that she seems so happy and carefree? Percy was her friend. Wouldn't you expect her to be less blasé about his death?"

He thought for a moment. "I suppose... although just because Ness isn't crying her eyes out, that doesn't mean that she isn't upset." He gave her a dry smile. "It's not the British way, you know, to wear our hearts on our sleeves."

"I know, but..." Caitlyn took a deep breath. She felt like a worm, but the suspicions had been festering so much inside her, she felt as if she would burst if she didn't share them. Ignoring her earlier decision to say nothing, she blurted: "I... I think I caught Vanessa snooping in your study yesterday. I went in to find you and she was behind your desk, searching for something... or maybe getting something. Do you have a safe in the study?"

"Yes, there's a safe behind one of the paintings, but I don't keep much in there. Just some documents—"

"Jewellery?"

"No, most of the Fitzroy family jewels are in the bank vault." He shook his head, clearly bemused. "What does this have to do with Vanessa?"

"I... I thought she might have been

trying to get something out of the safe. She jumped when I walked in, like she'd been caught doing something furtive."

Caitlyn hesitated, then blundered on. "Did you know that Vanessa had a crush on Percy? But he didn't like her back—he liked Katya—which really annoyed her. I saw her watching them at dinner... and then I thought of that story you told me, you know, about Vanessa putting the alum powder in her classmate's tea to get back at her—"

James's face darkened suddenly and his brows lowered in a frown. "Are you suggesting that my *sister* might have something to do with Percy's murder?"

"I... I don't know," said Caitlyn miserably. "It's just... there are lots of little things that don't add up. For example, Inspector Walsh mentioned that Percy may have been poisoned by belladonna berries, and Viktor told me that he saw Vanessa take a bundle of belladonna berries out of her handbag on the day she arrived. Why would she have brought belladonna berries—"

"I can't believe you're saying this," James cut in. His grey eyes had gone chilly, his face hardening.

"You said yourself that Vanessa behaved badly in the past," Caitlyn pointed out. "You said that she could be spiteful when she didn't get her own way."

"There's a big difference between a bit of childish spite and murder," James bit out. "What you're suggesting is preposterous! It's ludicrous to think that Vanessa might be involved!"

"Why?" cried Caitlyn, stung by his tone. "Because she's your sister? You were so quick to jump on my mother and tell me that she could be a murderer. You said: *just because someone is "family", it doesn't necessarily mean that they can't do evil*'—remember? Well, now that it's your own sister, you're singing a different tune!"

James glared at her, breathing heavily through his nose. Then he drew back, putting some distance between them.

"I think it might be best if we both retired for the evening," he said stiffly. "If you'll excuse me... Goodnight."

Without looking at her, he turned on his heel and stalked out of the study.

Chapter Thirty

Caitlyn had a terrible night, tossing and turning and constantly waking in fitful bursts. Even when she was asleep, she was plagued by nightmares in which she and James stood and shouted at each other, the ugly words playing over and over again like a loop in her head. When she opened her eyes and saw the faint light of dawn peeking through her curtains at last, she sighed deeply and rolled over. She felt absolutely exhausted, as if she hadn't slept a wink, but she knew that there was no chance she could go back to sleep again now.

Sitting up, she rubbed her gritty eyes, then headed into the ensuite bathroom, hoping that a hot shower would help her feel less groggy. As the steam and soothing flow of water cleared her mind, however, she felt a sudden jolt of conscience: *Nibs*. She had meant to ask James about the kitten last night— perhaps one of the staff might have seen him on the estate—but somehow, in the tense aftermath of their argument, it had completely slipped her mind.

Now she felt wracked with guilt. How could she have forgotten about Nibs? What if something had happened to him? The memory of Leandra's denial came back to her, and with it, that niggling unease again. Had she been telling the truth about not having Nibs? But then, why would she lie? *Especially if she is my mother*, thought Caitlyn. Surely Tara would have no reason to hide the kitten?

Feeling the sense of unease grow in

her chest, Caitlyn hastily dressed, then let herself out of her room and hurried down the corridor to Pomona's room. Rousing her cousin was difficult at the best of times, and early in the morning it was practically impossible. Still, with a mixture of threats and coaxing, she eventually managed to prise a grouchy Pomona from her bed and bundle her into the bathroom. Thankfully, the hot shower seemed to have the same revitalising effect, and by the time the two girls were hurrying down the main staircase, Pomona was almost cheerful, chattering away about the breakfast she planned to have once they'd found the kitten.

"*If* we find him," said Caitlyn worriedly. "I just don't understand why he wasn't in Leandra's barn. I mean, we saw her pick him up and take him in—"

"Maybe it happened exactly like she said," said Pomona with a shrug. "Maybe she really did put him out the front door, and then he ran off. Otherwise, it would mean that she's lying about the fact that she took Nibs—and why would she do that? It sounds nuts. I think you're reading too much into it," said Pomona. "I'm sure the little squirt is fine. He's probably just been enjoying a big night out. I mean, cats are nocturnal, right? So they love creeping around in the dark."

"Yes, but Nibs always comes home once it gets dark," Caitlyn protested. "He likes to curl up in bed with me—or with Bran when he's here at the Manor. He never stays out at night by himself."

"Well, he's growing up, isn't he? Kittens start getting more independent and exploring their territory as they get bigger, right? Okay, in Nibs's case, I know he's not actually getting any bigger physically, but he's still, like, growing up in his mind, isn't he?"

"I suppose so," said Caitlyn with a sigh. "It's true that he's been a lot more adventurous lately and venturing further and further away from the Widow Mags's cottage when he goes out exploring. But it's always in the daytime."

"Welcome to the teenage years," said Pomona, with a grin. "Next, he'll be growing his fur long and getting a kitty skateboard."

Caitlyn laughed in spite of herself and felt her worry ease slightly. Perhaps her cousin was right; perhaps she was overreacting. Still, she would feel better when they'd found the kitten. And with Pomona helping her, hopefully it wouldn't take long.

The house was quiet; it was so early that even the staff hadn't started their daily duties, and Mosley wasn't at his usual post, skulking about the hallways of the Manor. When they stepped outside, the air was fresh, with a stiff breeze that ruffled their hair and a sky that was still pale with the soft light of morning. Caitlyn glanced around, wondering if any of the Manor gardening team would be out already, going about their usual duties. She saw one figure in wellies and overalls moving about in the distance, but otherwise the gardens seemed empty.

"Hey, speaking of Leandra, what are you going to do about that?" asked Pomona as they made their way into the landscaped gardens.

Caitlyn glanced nervously at the other girl. "What do you mean?"

"Well, aren't you gonna, like, confront her? I mean, she's your *mom*, Caitlyn! Don't you want to ask her what she's doing and where she's been and stuff like that?"

Caitlyn shifted uncomfortably. "I don't know..."

Pomona looked at her in disbelief. "You don't know? How can you say that? You've only been searching for her for, like, forever! Now that you've found her and she's right there, in front of you, how can you not wanna talk to her?"

"Because she obviously doesn't want to talk to me!" burst out Caitlyn, unable to keep the hurt out of her voice. "She seems to be making a huge effort to hide her real identity, even from her own family. She doesn't trust me—her own daughter!—enough to tell me the truth and reveal herself."

"Well, maybe she's got a good reason," argued Pomona. "Maybe she's, like, got some master plan, which needs her to stay in disguise and put on that stuffy professor act. You won't know until you ask her." She cocked her head to one side, giving Caitlyn a knowing look. "You know what your problem is? You're too proud, just like the Widow Mags! You're feeling hurt 'cos your mom hasn't made the first move. I'm right, aren't I? Well, maybe *she's* waiting for *you* to make the first move... have you thought about that?"

"I'm not proud," protested Caitlyn weakly. But she had to admit that there was a certain truth in what Pomona was saying. She was silent for a minute, then she added in a grudging voice: "Maybe... maybe if I see Leandra later... I'll try to talk to her."

"Atta girl!" said Pomona, giving her a thumbs up. Then, in a different tone, she asked: "So did you and James have a romantic end to the evening?" She winked lasciviously. "I saw you guys heading off to his study."

Caitlyn groaned. "Pomona, you have no idea... no, no, don't get excited—it's not what you're thinking. We had a huge row."

Pomona frowned. "A row—you mean you had an argument? What about?"

"About Vanessa."

"Omigod, Caitlyn—you didn't tell him your suspicions, did you?" Pomona clapped a hand to her face as Caitlyn nodded. "I thought you weren't going to say anything until you had more proof?"

"Well, I just... what more proof do I need? There's enough stuff that if it was anyone else, we'd already be reporting her to the police," Caitlyn said defensively. "And I didn't *plan* to do it. I just... I don't know, somehow the conversation just seemed to go that way." She shook her head in frustration. "Anyway, it was James who was totally unreasonable! He immediately shut me down and wouldn't even consider the possibility—"

"Well, duh! You've seen the way he is with Vanessa. He, like, totally dotes on her and spoils her rotten. He's not gonna take kindly to you basically suggesting that his baby sister is a murderer."

"I didn't say it like that! Anyway, he had no problems suggesting that *my mother* is a murderer," retorted Caitlyn. "He was going on and on about Tara and how she must be responsible for Daniel

Tremaine's murder and probably Percy's death too. If James can vilify my mother, then I don't see why I can't denounce his sister!"

Pomona rolled her eyes. "Man, this is beginning to sound like a family feud. You're both, like, totally blinded by your personal loyalties. You guys should be on the same side, working together, instead of getting all defensive and attacking each other."

Caitlyn gave an irate shrug. "Tell that to James." She quickened her steps. "Anyway, I don't want to talk about it. Let's focus on finding Nibs."

Pomona looked as if she would protest, then she sighed and followed Caitlyn as they began a search of the grounds. They peered over hedges and under tall shrubs, checked shady alcoves and neat flowerbeds, and poked around various outbuildings and storage sheds, all while calling for the kitten.

They paused at last, feeling disheartened. They had scoured every inch of the gardens and hadn't seen any sign of Nibs. Now, they were standing in the rear courtyard area surrounded by the coach house restaurant and other outbuildings. Caitlyn glanced over at the converted barn in the distance. She couldn't help thinking that all their efforts were a waste of time and that the real place they should have been looking was in Leandra's residence. But with the woman flatly denying any knowledge of the kitten, the only way she could challenge that would be to break in again and really ransack the place from top to bottom.

"Hey! Check out that old well... what if Nibs fell in there?" said Pomona.

Caitlyn turned to see the American girl hurrying towards a round stone structure—an old stone well—half hidden behind some trees next to the coach house. She followed quickly and arrived to find Pomona peering through a circular wrought-iron grill which had been designed to cover the well opening.

"Do you see him?" she asked, suddenly having horrified visions of the kitten lying at the bottom of the well. *What if Nibs fell in and drowned? What if—*

"The well's been plugged," said Pomona, shifting sideways and craning her neck to see better. "I can see the base. It only goes down, like, five feet..."

Caitlyn leaned over the stone surround and peered through the gap in the grill cover herself. Since the well was plugged, the round cavity only went down about two metres, where it ended in a flat seal of stone and cement. She could see piles of dead leaves, stones, and other debris, but no kitten.

Caitlyn sagged, partly in relief and partly in disappointment. "He's not there," she said.

"N-noo... but there *is* something down there, under the leaves... Holy guacamole, it's Hosey Houdini!"

"What?" Caitlyn joined Pomona in peering down between the bars of the metal grill. She saw that there was indeed a pile of green hose coiled at the bottom of the shallow well cavity. It wriggled slightly, as if rousing itself, and then one end of the hose lifted and the brass connector "head" raised like a periscope.

"*Ss-ssss!*" it said, sounding for all the world as if it was delighted to see them.

"Well, whaddya know—we found it at last!" said Pomona gleefully. "C'mon! Let's grab him before he disappears again."

She reached for the centre of the metal grill, where a hinge running down the middle of the circle enabled one half of the grill to swing open like a trap door. It was a bit rusty, but after a moment, she managed to flip it up and back, revealing a gaping semicircular hole.

Caitlyn eyed the opening doubtfully. "Do you think we'll be able to get it out through there?"

"Well, it got in through there, didn't it? That must be what happened: someone left one of the grill flaps open, and Hosey Houdini decided to climb in and take a nap at the bottom of the well. And then, somehow, the flap was closed and he ended up trapped down there." She bent and reached her arm through the grill opening, groping for the end of the hose. "C'mon—help me lift him out…"

It took them several attempts, but they finally managed to haul the garden hose out of the well.

"I swear, this thing has gotten even heavier," Pomona complained as she heaved the last loop of rubber over the rim of the well.

"Maybe it was the rain last night..." panted Caitlyn. "It's almost like it's filled itself up."

Slowly, they began lugging the loops of hose down the path which ran through the gardens towards the front driveway, where Pomona's car was still parked. Caitlyn gripped the brass connector "head" whilst Pomona brought up the rear, staggering under the weight of the coiled rubber. They hobbled along, trying not to trip over the floppy loops or step in the puddles of water that pooled in their wake, whilst the hose sagged between them like some enormous, sluggish python, its rubber body dragging along the ground.

Caitlyn kept looking nervously around, but thankfully the early hour meant that there were still very few people about. She knew that wouldn't last long, though, and she tried to walk faster, heaving the garden hose higher over her shoulder to try to get a better grip. The hose seemed docile enough, twining around Caitlyn's arm and nuzzling its brass connector head into her armpit.

"*Sss-sss...*" it lisped sleepily, dribbling water down her arm.

"Aww, it likes you," teased Pomona, chuckling. "Maybe you should keep it as a pet."

"Shut up."

They continued struggling down the path, but as they rounded the side of the Manor, Pomona paused, gasping, and said:

"Stop... stop... I can't... I'm bushed..."

She dropped her end of the garden hose and sagged against the wall of the Manor house. Caitlyn looked sympathetically at her cousin. Pomona's face was flushed with exertion, her normally glossy mane of hair damp plastered to her forehead.

"Ugh! I'm covered in dirt and mud... and this top is dry-clean only," moaned Pomona, looking down at herself in dismay.

Caitlyn sighed and pushed a tangle of hair off her face. She had fared slightly better than Pomona, but her sleeves were wet as well, and the front of her jeans were unpleasantly damp. "Come on, Pomie—it's not that much further to your car. We've got to get it out of sight before too many people are up and about."

"I can't... I haven't got the strength to carry it anymore," groaned Pomona. "Besides, how do we know it'll be safe in my car? It got out of the trunk once—it could do it again."

"That's because you didn't lock it properly," said Caitlyn with asperity.

Pomona ignored her and said: "You know what we need? Some kind of magical bag that can hold anything and make it really small and easy to carry. You know, like Odin's saddlebag."

"Sorry?"

"Odin. King of the Norse gods," Pomona explained impatiently. "He had this magical sack that was, like, bottomless and could hold anything. He used it to carry treasures he gathered. Or another one would be Mary Poppins's carpetbag—"

"Pomie, Mary Poppins is a children's storybook character! And Odin is a character from myth! They're not real!"

"Witches and vampires aren't supposed to be real either," retorted Pomona, giving her a pointed look. "How do you know there aren't really magical containers out there that—*oh wait!*" She jerked upright. "There *are*! I can't believe I didn't think of it sooner! The Ælfpoca!"

"The what?"

"The Ælfpoca—the elf pouch!

Remember? We saw it in the Portrait Gallery on Friday evening. In the cabinet."

Caitlyn shook her head. She could remember Benedict and Pomona raving over so many things when they visited the Portrait Gallery that it was hard to recall any specific one.

"It was there," Pomona insisted. "And it could be the answer to our problem! The Ælfpoca is a magical container with the ability to hold objects of any size. We could stuff Hosey Houdini into it and carry him anywhere easily."

Caitlyn rolled her eyes. "Pomona, you know a lot of the things in the old Lord Fitzroy's occult collection might just be phony relics. I know they're supposed to be famous items from folktales and legends with magical properties, but they could just as likely be hoaxes that were sold and passed around until they gained some kind of fake 'authenticity'—"

"You don't know that," argued Pomona. "I mean, the hag stone that we took from the Gallery was genuine, wasn't it? It really had magical powers. So why not other things too? Anyway, how will we know until we try it?" She jabbed a finger at Caitlyn's chest. "You wait here. I'm gonna run up to the Portrait Gallery to get the Ælfpoca."

"Hang on, Pomie, we can't just take—"

It was too late. Pomona had already rushed off and disappeared around the side of the Manor house. Caitlyn sighed. She often envied her cousin's impulsive confidence, but sometimes it could be downright infuriating!

Glancing down at the garden hose still in her hands, she decided that she had better turn the connector head around so that it was pointing away from her. That way, if the hose decided to squirt water out again, she wouldn't get any wetter than she already was. She was just re-adjusting her grip around the first rubber coil, which squirmed in her hands, when she heard the sound of footsteps rapidly approaching.

Wow, that was fast, she thought, marvelling at the speed with which Pomona had managed to retrieve the Ælfpoca. Then, as a figure came around the corner of the Manor building, her heart gave a lurch.

It wasn't Pomona—it was Vanessa, and she was headed straight this way!

Chapter Thirty-One

Caitlyn looked wildly around but she knew that there wasn't really enough time to hide, especially if she had to drag the heavy garden hose with her. The only reason that Vanessa hadn't seen her yet was because the other girl had her head down, concentrating on something she was holding in one hand, but as she came around the corner, she looked up.

"Caitlyn!" she cried, faltering to a stop and hastily shoving one hand into her pocket.

"Uh... hi, Vanessa," said Caitlyn

weakly.

The other girl approached her, staring quizzically. "What are you doing?"

Belatedly, Caitlyn realised that she was still holding Hosey Houdini, with his brass connector head pointed straight at Vanessa, like the barrel of a gun.

"Oh! Er..." Caitlyn thought about dropping the garden hose, then she turned instead and waved it nonchalantly at the flowerbed next to the path. "I'm just... er... watering the flowerbed. You know... helping out... since the staff must be really busy with preparations for the Samhain Festival."

Vanessa looked even more bemused. "But... the hose isn't connected to anything."

"Oh!" Caitlyn made a show of looking at the other end of the garden hose and giving an exaggerated expression of surprise. "I didn't realise... silly me... it... um... must have come off the tap at the other end... Anyway, what are *you* doing out here so early?" she asked, hoping to distract the other girl from any more questions.

Vanessa gave her a sheepish grin and pulled the hand out of her pocket to show Caitlyn a cigarette and lighter in her palm.

"I came out for a sneaky ciggie," she confessed. "I can't smoke in my room; James would absolutely blow his top if he knew that I was smoking again, and I wouldn't put it past the staff to tell on me, especially that old stuffed suit Mosley." She looked earnestly at Caitlyn. "You won't tell James, will you?"

"No, of course not," murmured Caitlyn, although she couldn't help thinking again how very young Vanessa seemed. She sounded more like a teenager afraid of being grounded than a young woman of twenty-four who shouldn't have cared what her brother thought of her lifestyle habits.

It also made Caitlyn wonder if she had been completely wrong in her suspicions about Vanessa. The girl seemed way too naïve and childlike to be able to plan a murder—or even a spiteful poisoning! Suddenly, Caitlyn bitterly regretted her rash comments to James the night before. If she was completely wrong, she could have caused a rift between them for nothing.

Vanessa had put the cigarette between her lips and was now attempting to light it, but the blustery weather was making it difficult. She cupped her hand around the lighter and flicked it again and again, before finally giving a sound of satisfaction as a flame appeared, burning brightly.

"Ahh, about bloody time— *aaaaaiiiiihhh*!" she screamed as a blast of cold water suddenly hit her in the face.

Caitlyn gasped and looked down to see Hosey Houdini shooting streams of water at Vanessa like a giant water pistol. She grappled with the hose, trying to turn the brass connector head away. "Stop it! What are you doing?" she hissed through clenched teeth.

"*Ss-ssss!*" gurgled the hose happily, still squirting away. "*Ssss-ss! Ssss-ss!*""

Caitlyn realised suddenly that Hosey Houdini was trying to put out the flame from the lighter. As a stream of water hit Vanessa's hand and finally doused the flickering orange flame, the rubber coil in her hand stilled and subsided.

"*Aaagghhh!*" spluttered Vanessa, staggering back a few steps and looking down at herself disbelievingly. The front of her shirt was completely drenched in water; her face was shiny with moisture, and her hair hung down in dripping rattails. "What the he—"

"Oh my God, I'm so sorry... I'm so sorry, Vanessa," babbled Caitlyn, staring in horror at the other girl. "I... I don't know what happened... it must... there must have been some water left in the hose and maybe the pressure..." She trailed off weakly, unable to think of anything to explain what had just happened.

But to her surprise and relief, Vanessa began to giggle. Soon, she was joining in awkwardly as James's sister hooted and chortled with mirth.

"Darling..." Vanessa wiped tears from her eyes. "That was the most hilarious thing that's happened to me in ages!" She looked down at herself again, then regarded Caitlyn as well. "You're soaked too! Why don't we both go in and get into dry clothes?"

Caitlyn hesitated. The last thing she wanted to do was leave Hosey Houdini to his own devices, but given how wet she was, she couldn't think of any logical excuse to reject Vanessa's suggestion. She had no choice but to agree.

I'll just change as fast as I can and dash back out here, she thought as she placed the end of the bewitched garden hose down on the ground. She gave it a surreptitious pat and a silent plea to stay where it was, then turned and followed Vanessa into the Manor. Thankfully, they met no one else on their way back to the upstairs guest wing—Caitlyn had dreaded being dragged into a lengthy explanation and social chitchat—and Vanessa left her at her door with a smile before going to her own bedroom.

Caitlyn dashed into her room and slammed the door behind her, stripping her clothes off as she went. She grabbed a towel from a rail in the bathroom, gave herself a quick rubdown, then hurried into a fresh pair of jeans and a comfy, oversized sweater. She was back outside and running down the main stairs in less than ten minutes.

This time, she saw Mosley as she reached the bottom of the sweeping staircase, but she gave the butler a quick wave and ducked out the front door before he could say anything. Jogging swiftly, she headed down the path, around the corner of the Manor house building, back to their previous location.

Then she stopped short.

The path was empty; the place where she had left Hosey Houdini was bare.

"Nooo...." Caitlyn groaned. "Where's it gone now?"

She looked around, her heart sinking as she wondered where to start searching. Then she remembered Pomona. Her cousin might be back any minute. Should she wait for her?

No. God knows where Hosey Houdini might have slithered off to by then, thought Caitlyn grimly. Best to start searching for it herself first and hope that Pomona would join her soon.

She continued up the path until it

forked around a large stone birdbath on a pedestal. One branch of the path seemed to lead back towards the coach house restaurant, whilst the other continued in a wide loop around the Manor. Caitlyn chose the latter and soon found herself approaching the side where the Ballroom was situated. She was just wondering whether she should turn back and try the other branch when she spied a figure ahead of her.

Her eyes widened in surprise. It was Vanessa! The girl was still in her wet clothes and she had her head down, as if she was looking at something in her hands. It was exactly the same pose that she'd been in when Caitlyn had first seen her earlier, and suddenly all of Caitlyn's old suspicions came rushing back.

Vanessa had obviously lied about wanting to change her wet clothes—it looked like she had turned around and come straight back outside as soon as Caitlyn was safely out of the way. Why?

What was she doing?

Caitlyn leaned to the side, craning her neck and trying to catch a glimpse of Vanessa's hands, but with the girl walking directly in front, her body was shielding the view of her hands, and all Caitlyn could see was her hunched back.

Then, as the path curved ahead and Vanessa turned with it, her profile came into view. She was holding one hand out in front of her and something was dangling from the ends of her fingers. Something that caught the morning light with a golden glitter.

Caitlyn gasped softly as she recognised the chain with the cone-shaped pendant made of dull gold.

It was Percy's dowsing pendulum.

Chapter Thirty-Two

Caitlyn stared at the girl walking in front of her, her thoughts in a turmoil. A part of her was filled with dismay. The last thing she had wanted was to be proven right—she didn't *want* James's sister to be involved; she didn't want to have to confront the reality of Vanessa's duplicity. But at the same time, she also felt elated at having her suspicions confirmed. The only way Vanessa could be in possession of the dowsing pendulum was if she had been in the Library with Percy on the night of his murder. So she *had* been lying about her alibi... and about so many other things too. Even their encounter earlier was a clever act, with Vanessa producing that elaborate story about secretive smoking as a cover for what she had really been doing, which was using the dowsing pendulum.

And that must be what she was doing yesterday in James's study as well, Caitlyn realised as she recalled the golden glitter she had glimpsed in Vanessa's hands when the girl had whirled around. She had thought that it might be jewellery, but it had actually been the pendulum chain, which Vanessa had quickly hidden behind her back. And the girl had instantly produced a plausible excuse that time too, with her cute account of searching for James's "sweets stash". Caitlyn felt a grudging admiration. Even if Vanessa looked childlike and innocent, she was adept at thinking on her feet and coming up with clever cover stories.

Then she frowned. Despite the

jubilant satisfaction of exposing Vanessa's lies, she also felt more confused than ever. It was clear that Vanessa was searching for the *grimoire*; she was obviously hoping that the dowsing pendulum would lead her to the magical book, just as it had led Percy originally. But if Vanessa had been with Percy that night, then why was she still searching for the book now? Why didn't she have it? Wouldn't she have taken it from him?

And why would Vanessa want the *grimoire* in the first place? If it had been Leandra, it would have made sense. After all, she was really Tara, disguised by glamour magic, and her mother had always been obsessed with the *grimoire*. She would be doing everything she could to find it again. But Vanessa had never shown more than a passing interest in the occult. Why would she be so desperate to find the Widow Mags's book of spells, to the point that she would commit murder and lie to cover her actions? Was she doing it for someone else?

Up ahead, Vanessa had come to the end of the path which led to the long raised terrace that wrapped round the side of the Ballroom. There were several large half wine barrels on the terrace—Caitlyn knew that these were to be used in the "apple-ducking" that would be part of the Samhain Festival activities tomorrow, and she could see that they had already been filled with water.

Vanessa was mounting the steps to the terrace, her eyes still riveted on the dowsing pendulum swinging from the ends of her fingers. She turned as it directed her towards one of the half wine barrels that had been placed beside the balustrade at the top of the terrace steps.

As Caitlyn watched, Vanessa bent over the barrel and reached one hand into the water. She groped around, then yanked something out of the water, raising it, dripping, into the air. Caitlyn caught her breath. Vanessa was holding one end of Hosey Houdini!

She must have made some sound because Vanessa jerked her head up and their eyes met. There was a flicker of dismay and irritation in the other girl's eyes. But before either girl could speak, they heard the French windows at the other end of the terrace opening. There was the sound of male voices, and the next moment, James and Mosley stepped out of the Ballroom, deep in conversation.

"...like Lisa's idea of providing some refreshments in the Ballroom for people to enjoy after they've finished the games on the terrace. Can you speak to the catering staff about organising that?"

"Certainly, sir, and I believe we could use the..."

Vanessa glanced at Caitlyn and then

back at James with a calculated gleam in her eyes. She dropped the bewitched garden hose back into the water, straightened from the wine barrel, and began to call out:

"James..."

"No!" cried Caitlyn, rushing up the terrace steps. She wasn't going to let the girl hide behind yet another clever pretext. "I saw you, Vanessa! I know you've got the dowsing pendulum!"

She reached out to grab the other girl's hand—the one that had been holding the dowsing pendulum—but Vanessa screeched and jerked away, twisting her body so that she kept her clenched fist out of Caitlyn's reach.

"Let... go... of... me...!" she cried, squirming and panting. "James... HELP...!"

"No! You're not going to lie this time..." Caitlyn lunged angrily, trying to reach around the other girl. "I'm not going to let you—"

"Ness! Caitlyn! What the hell is going on?"

James's voice shouting... Footsteps rushing towards them...

The two girls struggled desperately for control.

And then Vanessa threw herself backwards, tugging hard—an action that wrenched her free of Caitlyn's grasp.

But the sudden move unbalanced her, and her triumphant cry turned into a scream of fear as she stumbled, then teetered at the top of the terrace steps.

The next moment, she fell, her body careering down the steps in a tangle of arms and legs, until she hit the bottom and lay still.

Caitlyn stood frozen at the top of the steps, looking down at the limp figure in horror.

"NESS!"

James ran across the terrace and rushed down the steps with Mosley clattering behind him. People were coming out of the Ballroom and appearing from the gardens in all directions, drawn by the sounds of the recent commotion. They all stopped and stared in consternation as James crouched next to Vanessa. There was a bloody gash on her forehead and her face was deathly pale.

"Ness?" James said hoarsely, running his hands over his sister's neck, searching for her pulse.

Caitlyn felt her heart hammering in her chest as she rushed down the steps as well and crouched beside James. She felt weak with relief when she saw Vanessa's chest rising and falling, although the girl didn't respond to any of James's attempts to revive her.

"Mosley—call an ambulance—*now!*" said James, his face white and set. Then his eyes met Caitlyn's and she flinched at the accusing look.

"I...I'm sorry..." she whispered. "It was an accident."

James said nothing, his expression hard, then he turned away and began barking out orders for staff to bring blankets, bandages, and other first aid items. Caitlyn backed away as people began rushing over, closing in around Vanessa's prone body.

"Omigod, Caitlyn—what happened?"

She turned to see Pomona standing beside her. Her cousin had a hand over her mouth, and her eyes were wide with concern as she stared at the scene in front of them.

"It was an accident, Pomie," Caitlyn said, her voice trembling. "I didn't mean to... Vanessa tripped and fell... but James thinks I pushed her!"

"Oh, honey," Pomona put an arm around Caitlyn's shoulders and gave her a squeeze, but for once, the American girl seemed at a loss for words.

They watched silently as the paramedics arrived and began the delicate task of lifting Vanessa onto a stretcher. James stood tensely beside them as they worked. He didn't even glance at Caitlyn as he followed the paramedics past her and Pomona, accompanying the stretcher out to the ambulance at the front of the Manor. Caitlyn hesitated, then rushed after them. She hovered uncertainly next to the ambulance as the paramedics loaded the stretcher in. When James began to climb in as well, though, she couldn't stop herself calling out:

"James!"

He paused and turned around.

"Should... should I come with you...?"

"No." His eyes were cold. "I think you've done enough for one day."

Then he disappeared into the ambulance and the doors slammed in her face. Caitlyn stepped back and watched miserably as the yellow-and-green vehicle sped away down the driveway, its sirens blaring.

Chapter Thirty-Three

"I'm sure James will understand once you explain what happened..." Pomona said. "And I'm sure Vanessa's gonna be fine. It's just, like, a small bump on her head. People get those all the time, right? She'll be back home before you know it."

Caitlyn gave Pomona a wan smile. She knew that her cousin was just trying to help, but she couldn't help wishing that Pomona would stop talking about the whole thing. It was agony sitting here, waiting for news from the hospital, and constantly going over what had happened just made everything worse.

Besides, it seemed as if everyone else was talking nonstop about it as well. She glanced surreptitiously around: Tori, Benedict, and Katya were sitting on the sofas nearby, their heads together as they discussed something in low tones; whilst, through the doorway, she could see Mosley and several other Manor staff in the hallway outside the room, huddled in small groups and talking in hushed voices. Every so often, someone would raise their head and glance in her direction, and Caitlyn squirmed as she imagined the accusation in their gazes.

She turned back to Pomona, who was still talking:

"...and it totally wasn't your fault. You just need to speak to James—"

Caitlyn sighed. "I've tried. He won't listen."

"Well, you need to make him listen! Why didn't you go with him in the ambulance?"

"He didn't want me there," said Caitlyn, trying to keep the hurt out of her voice.

"Aw, for Pete's sake, Caitlyn, men don't know what they want! Don't get all proud again, like that thing with Leandra—I mean, your mom. Look, you can still go now." Pomona pulled her car keys out of her pocket and dangled them in the air. "C'mon, I'll drive you—"

"No, Pomie. James said he doesn't want me there, and I... I don't want to force myself on him."

Pomona rolled her eyes. "You're not 'forcing yourself' on him! Man, you sound ridiculous. You're just, like, wallowing in self-pity now."

"No, I'm not!" cried Caitlyn, stung. "I just don't want to go where I'm not welcome, okay?" She stood up abruptly. "Sorry... I... I need to get some air."

"Oh, honey... want me to come with

you?"

Caitlyn shook her head. "No, it's okay. I just need a moment alone."

She hurried out before Pomona could protest, making sure that she didn't make eye contact with anyone as she left the room and hurried down the hallway. However, there were more members of staff congregated outside the front steps of the Manor, and as she stepped out of the front door, she couldn't help overhearing several voices saying:

"...I heard she hexed Miss Vanessa..."

"...yes, black magic! But what d'you expect? She's the granddaughter of that old witch in the village..."

"...it's the curse of that witch's recipe book striking again..."

"...no, she used a spell... that's why no one saw her push his Lordship's sister— she did it with magic, see?"

Caitlyn wanted to cover her ears and run from the horrible things she was hearing, but she forced herself to walk sedately away with her head held high. It wasn't until she was out of sight, deep within the gardens, that she allowed her shoulders to slump and the tears that she had been holding back to well up in her eyes.

I'm not going to cry, she thought fiercely, dashing a stray tear away. Then she stiffened as she heard a loud rustling behind her. She whirled and stared into the bushes.

"W-who's there?" she asked.

The next moment, a balding old man in an ancient black suit shuffled out from behind a large shrub, a cluster of bilberries clutched in one hand and an expression of self-satisfied contentment on his face.

"Oh, Viktor!" Caitlyn cried and impulsively threw her arms around the old vampire's neck, burying her face in his ruffled white shirt.

"Galloping garlic, what is the matter?" Viktor looked taken aback. "*Ahem*... yes, well... er..." He patted her back awkwardly as she sobbed into his chest. "Er... very windy weather we're having today, isn't it?" he said, sounding a bit panicked. He cleared his throat. "*Ahem*... would you like a cup of tea? Or a fruit pressé, perhaps? Marvellous things, you know, pressés—very good for emotional distress."

Caitlyn hiccupped and laughed in spite of herself, then she stepped back from Viktor, sniffing. The old vampire fished a yellowed lace handkerchief from his jacket pocket and handed it to her.

"Has someone mistreated you, my dear?" he asked. He puffed his bony chest out. "As your guardian uncle, I shall find them and challenge them to a duel. I shall avenge your—"

"No, no, Viktor—nothing like that," said Caitlyn, dabbing her eyes with his handkerchief. "It's just that something terrible has happened and... and I feel like it's all my fault!"

Gulping back fresh tears, she told him about the struggle with Vanessa on the terrace steps and how the other girl had fallen.

"Ahh... sounds like the time I was fighting a hobgoblin at the top of the castle steps in Scotland," said Viktor brightly. "Notoriously bad balance the hobgoblins have, you know. It's all the mushrooms they eat. Too much umami flavour. This little fellow took a step the wrong way and went tumbling to the bottom of the steps. His head cracked open like an egg. At least your young lady's head is still intact."

"Viktor!" Caitlyn stared at the old vampire in exasperated disbelief. "Is that supposed to make me feel better?"

"Eh?" Viktor scratched his head. "I thought you said it was the *other* young lady who fell down the stairs, not you. Do you require recuperation too?"

"No, no, I..." Caitlyn sighed with irritation, then paused as she realised with surprise that she *did* feel better. Somehow, Viktor's clumsy attempts at comfort had been more effective than Pomona's earnest consoling.

She took a deep breath, feeling calmer, and let it out slowly. "I just hope Vanessa is going to be okay, that it's just a light injury like Pomona said. I couldn't bear it if they find something really wrong with her."

"Hmm..." Viktor stroked his knobbly chin. "Reminds me of my last holiday in Transylvania, when I went to find my favourite *cârciumă* and it was gone. There was a new café or bistro or whatever they call it these days there instead, and it was in the same place and had the same view... and it *did* feel familiar somehow... and yet it was completely wrong!" He jutted his bottom lip out indignantly. "Dreadful palincă they served too. Nothing like the old *cârciumă*—nobody makes plum liqueurs like the ancient Transylvanian tavernas."

Caitlyn stared at the old vampire, completely bewildered. "Viktor, what on earth are you talking about? What café? What plum liqueur? What has all this got to do with Vanessa?"

"Same thing, isn't it?" said Viktor. "Something you remember, but nothing like you recall. Especially the scent—just like the plum liqueur. The nose never lies." He sniffed deeply as if to demonstrate.

Caitlyn shook her head in frustration and gave up trying to understand. "I need Vanessa to be okay, otherwise James will never forgive me," she said, in a small voice.

Viktor patted her hand. "My dear, let

me give you some words of wisdom which will help you immensely." He cleared his throat.

Caitlyn waited expectantly. Several seconds passed. She glanced at the old vampire, wondering if he had nodded off.

"Er... yes, Viktor?"

"Eh? Oh... yes... *ahem-ahem*..." Viktor cleared his throat again. "Yes, well, as I was saying: '*Errare humanum est, perseverare autem diabolicum, et tertia non datur.*'"

Caitlyn waited for more but nothing came. "Um... I don't get it," she said at last.

He looked at her peevishly. "Do they not teach Latin in school these days? Very well, I will translate. It means: '*To err is to eat hummus, to persist is diabolical, and the rest is just pitta bread.*'"

"What?"

Viktor gave a long-suffering sigh. "It means, my dear, that a man in love does not just toss you aside like last century's chamber pot for one mistake. He will forgive you, if you explain."

"I've tried!" cried Caitlyn angrily. "James just won't listen to me!"

"Well, then, it behoves you to try again. Remember, '*Superbia ante portas.*'"

Caitlyn groaned. "What does *that* mean?"

"*Pride is a peacock at the gate.*" Viktor wagged a finger in her face. "Don't let your pride block where you need to go. You might be Mags's granddaughter, but you don't have to walk in her footsteps." He smiled reminiscently. "Speaking of peacocks, they used to feed figs to the ones living in Kew Gardens. That was one of my favourite breakfast stops when I was living in London in the 1800s... ah, nothing like a fresh fig!" He smacked his sunken lips. "In fact, I might go and see if that old fuss-bag Mrs Pruett still has some dried figs in the pantry... mmm... would be perfect for my morning tea..."

Before Caitlyn could reply, Viktor turned and loped off in the direction of the Manor. She watched him go with that familiar mixture of exasperation and affection. Then she thought of what the old vampire had said: *"Don't let your pride block where you need to go. You might be Mags's granddaughter, but you don't have to walk in her footsteps."*

On an impulse, she whirled and rushed back into the Manor. Making her way back to where Pomona was still sitting, she dropped down next to her cousin and said:

"Pomie, does that offer of a lift still stand? I need to get to the hospital."

Pomona looked up in consternation. "Did something happen?"

"No, no, nothing bad. I've decided I'm not just going to sit here feeling sorry for myself—I'm going to speak to James."

Pomona beamed. "That's awesome. C'mon, let's go!" She sprang up from the sofa and led the way out of the Manor. As they got into the car, Pomona glanced at her curiously and asked: "What made you change your mind?"

Caitlyn smiled at her. "I had Latin lessons with Viktor."

Chapter Thirty-Four

At the hospital, Caitlyn hopped out of Pomona's car, waved her thanks and then swiftly made her way to the Accident & Emergency department. There was a large waiting area full of anxious relatives and friends, and she spotted James's tall figure almost immediately. Quietly, she went over and slipped into the seat next to him.

"Hi," she said softly.

He looked up and his expression was so forbidding that Caitlyn nearly jumped up and left again. But she forced herself to meet his gaze and ask: "Um... how's

Vanessa? Is there any news?"

For a moment, she thought James wasn't going to answer her. Then he sighed and ran a nervous hand through his hair. "The doctors are still assessing her at the moment."

He looked so worried, so scared and vulnerable, that Caitlyn's heart went out to him. She wanted to throw her arms around him and hug him close, but she didn't dare. Instead, she stretched a hand out hesitantly to touch his. But before she could make contact with his fingers, the double doors leading to the clinical area opened and a bearded man in green scrubs stepped out. He paused to speak to a nurse, who turned to point in their direction, and then the bearded man came over.

"Er... Mr Fitzroy?

James sprang to his feet, his face taut with apprehension. "Yes?"

"I'm Dr Gupta. Your sister has

regained consciousness but she's still very confused. She's having some scans done now to assess the extent of the head injury. I should be able to tell you more once we have the results." He gave them a nod, then retreated behind the double doors once more.

James sank back into his seat. His face was still strained but some of the tension had left his body. Caitlyn felt herself relax slightly as well. If Vanessa had regained consciousness, that was a good sign, wasn't it?

They sat quietly, neither of them talking, but it was a more companionable silence than earlier and Caitlyn felt her spirits rising. Maybe everything would be all right after all; maybe James would understand completely; and maybe she was even wrong about Vanessa, and the whole thing was a big misunderstanding...

Reminding herself of Viktor's wise words, she took a deep breath and said,

"James... I'm so sorry about what happened. It really *was* an accident. You have to believe me. I never meant to hurt Vanessa."

James rubbed his face tiredly, then finally raised his head and met her eyes. "What happened?" he asked.

"I... it's hard to explain. I think Vanessa was using Percy's dowsing pendulum to search for the *grimoire*. She had it in her hand. She'd lied about it earlier, you see, and... and about other things... and so when I saw her holding it, I wanted to force her to reveal it, so that she couldn't lie again." Caitlyn swallowed. "I was... I was trying to pull it out of her hands, and she was wriggling away from me, and then... I don't know... she just sort of jerked backwards and then lost her balance and fell down the steps. But I didn't push her—I swear!"

James looked at her for a long moment, his grey eyes searching, then finally his expression softened slightly. "I believe you."

Caitlyn felt her entire body go slack with relief. She gave him a tremulous smile and reached out hesitantly to touch his hand. Before she could say anything, though, the double doors opened once more and Dr Gupta came out again. He walked over to them, and the first thing Caitlyn noticed was that he was smiling.

"We've assessed your sister's scan results, and it looks like she might just have a mild concussion. She'll be kept overnight for observation, just in case, but otherwise she should be ready to go home tomorrow."

"Thank you, Doctor," James said, his voice thick with relief. "That's wonderful news. Can I see her?"

Dr Gupta nodded. "Just briefly. You might find that she's still very drowsy and confused. It's a bit unusual, given how light her concussion is..." He shrugged. "But everyone responds differently to injury. It's best to let her rest as much as possible. Sleep is the body's natural defence to allow your brain to heal itself."

He turned and gestured towards the double doors. "I'll take you to see her now."

James started to follow, then he glanced at Caitlyn and his face softened. "Doctor, can Miss Le Fey come too?"

Caitlyn felt a rush of love fill her heart as James reached for her hand, his strong, warm fingers interlacing with hers. He gave her hand a squeeze, saying more with that simple gesture than with any spoken words.

Dr Gupta gave an impatient nod. "Yes, that's fine. Now if you'll come with me..."

He turned and walked off. They started to follow but paused as James's phone rang. He let go of Caitlyn's hand

and pulled the phone out of his jacket pocket, glancing at the screen.

"It's Mosley," he muttered, ignoring the call.

The ringing wouldn't cease, though. The phone rang again. And then again, urgent and insistent. They were starting to draw irritated looks from people around the waiting room. James sighed and answered the call.

"Yes?" he said impatiently.

Mosley's voice came squawking out of the phone. He was so loud that Caitlyn could hear him clearly, even though James was holding the phone next to his ear. The butler sounded manic, his words so fast and garbled that he was almost unintelligible.

"Slow down, Mosley—I can't understand a word you're saying," said James. "What did you say? A phone call from London?"

Mosley's voice issued shrilly from the

phone: *"Yes, sir! I simply cannot believe it! If I had not heard it with my own ears... but it is no joke, I assure you. I recognise her voice. It is Miss Vanessa!"*

James frowned. "I beg your pardon? I think there's a problem with the reception, Mosley. For a moment there, I thought you said the call was from Vanessa—"

"That is what I said, sir! I know it seems impossible, but there is no mistake. Miss Vanessa was talking to me from London!"

"That's not possible, Mosley. Vanessa is here in hospital. I think you've been the victim of a practical joke—"

"No, no, sir—I assure you! I have verified her identity. Miss Vanessa's friends have all spoken to her, and they agree that it is she! It appears that she has been in some kind of strange sleep for the past few days. She has no recollection beyond the night before she

was supposed to leave London." Mosley's voice was breathless. *"I have contacted the Metropolitan police and asked them to attend to her immediately and also to provide any medical assistance necessary—although Miss Vanessa assures me that she is fine—but I felt that it was necessary to inform you, sir, as soon as possible, as I am unsure what else to do. Should I send for a car to bring her to Huntingdon Manor? Should I go down to London in person?"*

Caitlyn couldn't believe what she was hearing, and James seemed completely at a loss for words too. He stood frozen in place, his face blank with bewilderment.

"Sir?"

"Er... yes... thank you, Mosley. You've done very well. I'll... I'll get back to you," mumbled James before he hung up. Then he looked at Caitlyn. "Ness is in London," he said slowly.

"H-how?" she whispered. "I don't understand—how can that be?"

James turned to look at where Dr Gupta was waiting impatiently by the double doors. He didn't say anything, but Caitlyn could hear his thoughts as clearly as if he had voiced them: *If Vanessa is in London, then who the hell is the woman that the ambulance brought in?*

They didn't say a word as they followed the doctor through the doors and across the ward to a curtained cubicle near the nurse's station. But as Dr Gupta pulled back the curtains, Caitlyn let out a gasp.

Lying in the bed with her eyes shut was a beautiful young woman. The paleness of her face was a stark contrast to the vivid crimson of her hair, which spilled like liquid fire over her shoulders. It was almost the same shade of red as Caitlyn's own hair—but she didn't need that similarity to tell her what her heart already knew.

It was her mother, Tara.

TO BE CONTINUED IN:

A FONDANT FAREWELL:
Enchantments & Endings
(Bewitched by Chocolate Mysteries ~
Book 9)

About The Author

USA Today bestselling author H.Y. Hanna writes fun cozy mysteries filled with clever puzzles, lots of humor, quirky characters - and cats with big personalities! She is known for bringing wonderful settings to life, whether it's the historic city of Oxford, the beautiful English Cotswolds or the sunny beaches of coastal Florida.

After graduating from Oxford University, Hsin-Yi tried her hand at a variety of jobs, including advertising, modelling, teaching English, dog training and marketing... before returning to her first love: writing. She worked as a freelance writer for several years and has won awards for her novels, poetry, short stories and journalism.

A globe-trotter all her life, Hsin-Yi has

lived in a variety of cultures, from Dubai to Auckland, London to New Jersey, but is now happily settled in Perth, Western Australia, with her husband and a rescue kitty named Muesli. You can learn more about her and her books at: www.hyhanna.com.

Join her Readers' Club Newsletter to get updates on new releases, exclusive giveaways and other book news!

https://www.hyhanna.com/newsletter

www.ingramcontent.com/pod-product-compliance
Lightning Source LLC
Chambersburg PA
CBHW031729180726
48283CB00005B/1432